Praise for
Lion of Babylon and *Rare Earth*

"Description is so vivid you can smell the food and choke on the desert sand. . . . Bunn's fans will leap for this precise and intricate tale of cross-cultural friendship and loyalty in the heart of the Green Zone."

Publishers Weekly on Lion of Babylon

"Readers who were introduced to Royce in *Lion of Babylon* will be glad for this new adventure in which they will get to know him even better. Thorough characterizations, a fast pace, and attention to detail make this a sure bet for fans of Christian suspense stories. . . ."

Library Journal on Rare Earth

"This exciting, action-packed thriller features a strong sense of place in its depictions of the people and politics of the Middle East. It is sure to please [Bunn] fans and win him new ones."

Library Journal on Lion of Babylon
Selected by *Library Journal* for the 2011 Best Book Award

"A fast-paced, gripping thriller, *Lion of Babylon* is rich not only with adventure but also with visual details and dramatic, snapshot insights into the Middle East, its traditions, history, and people."

Phyllis Tickle
Former Sr. Consulting Editor at *Publishers Weekly*

"A phenomenal read. *Lion of Babylon* is far more than simply a great thriller. This book delves into a series of crucial issues, and does so with a sensitivity that left me literally stunned. Bunn tells a story that grips the reader and refuses to let go. . . . The descriptions are beautifully crafted, the characters vibrantly drawn."

Keith Hazard
Deputy Director (ret.), CIA

"*Lion of Babylon* is a terrific book, deeply moving with new insights into important connections between the world's faiths. . . . I have long admired and appreciated Davis's work and I will say I think this is his finest."

Jane Kirkpatrick
Novelist and Speaker

BOOKS BY DAVIS BUNN

Strait of Hormuz
Rare Earth
Lion of Babylon
Gold of Kings
The Black Madonna
All Through the Night
My Soul to Keep
The Great Divide
Winner Take All
Imposter
The Book of Hours
Tidings of Comfort and Joy
Book of Dreams
Hidden in Dreams
Unlimited

ACTS OF FAITH*

The Centurion's Wife
The Hidden Flame
The Damascus Way

SONG OF ACADIA*

The Meeting Place
The Birthright
The Sacred Shore
The Distant Beacon
The Beloved Land

* with Janette Oke

STRAIT OF HORMUZ

DAVIS BUNN

STRAIT OF HORMUZ

BETHANY HOUSE
a division of Baker Publishing Group
Minneapolis, Minnesota

Library of Congress Cataloging-in-Publication Data
Bunn, T. Davis.
    Strait of Hormuz / Davis Bunn.
       p.   cm.
    Summary: "Investigating the funding of Iran's nuclear program, Marc Royce must rely on an old ally to help him uncover the truth—before it's too late"— Provided by publisher.
    ISBN 978-0-7642-1145-4 (cloth : alk. paper)
    ISBN 978-0-7642-1138-6 (pbk)
    1. Intelligence service—United States—Fiction. 2. Nuclear weapons—Iran—Fiction. 3. Preemptive attack (Military science)—Israel—Fiction. 4. Hormuz, Strait of—Fiction. 5. Persian Gulf Region—Fiction. 6. Suspense fiction. I. Title.
PS3552.U4718S87 2013
813'.54—dc23   2013023254

Cover design by Kirk DouPonce, DogEared Design
Author photograph by Angel Grey

13 14 15 16 17 18 19   7 6 5 4 3 2 1

This book is dedicated to the next generation of readers.
With appreciation for the enthusiasm
of those who are especially close to me:

Guthrie and Jill
Riley and Diane
Macon

STRAIT OF HORMUZ

Chapter One

Marc Royce had never been to Switzerland before. He was there without backup. He was not prepped. He had come because the one person in the world he could not refuse had asked for his help. Urgently. Marc checked his watch, then pressed his phone's automatic dial. The ambassador answered instantly. Marc said, "I'm in place."

"Hold one." Ambassador Walton did not bother to muffle the phone as he asked an unseen associate for an update. He told Marc, "The target is inbound from his residence in Montreux."

"You have monitors in place?"

"We are tracking his cellphone. His GPS now belongs to us."

Which was interesting, given how Walton had refused to involve Swiss intelligence. There was a leak inside U.S. intelligence, of that Walton was absolutely certain. How or where their service had been breached, Walton had no idea. But Marc's target held such vital national importance that Walton had asked him to go in alone and unaided. He had come to Geneva without even alerting his embassy, which was a serious breach of protocol. But Marc was also no longer officially part of any intelligence agency. He had been fired and

11

dumped on the side of a Washington highway. By the same old man who now coughed into Marc's ear. Which meant his superiors could not be reprimanded, since he didn't have any.

Marc heard a new strain to the ambassador's voice, a hint that age was assaulting even this old warrior. "Are you feeling all right?"

"Focus on staying alive," Ambassador Walton replied. "You are good to go."

Marc left a ten-franc note anchored beneath his coffee saucer and headed across the street to the lakeside promenade. He said into his phone, "Don't you think now is a good time to tell me whose lead I'm following up here?"

Walton suppressed another cough. "An old friend reached out."

Which was all Marc had gotten the last time he had asked. "Must be a good friend for you to give it this much credence."

"He was and he is." The old man hesitated, long enough for Marc to assume he would not get anything more. But Ambassador Walton tended to relax his iron-clad grip on intel when his agents were walking into danger. "He's a British industrialist. A source I've known and trusted for twenty years. We've long suspected he also supplies intel to Mossad."

"Why isn't Mossad checking this out themselves?"

"A question I've been asking ever since he contacted me. Two possibilities come to mind. First, Mossad knows something we don't and want to rope us in. And second, they don't trust the source."

"Meaning he could be the leak?"

"Doubtful. But right now I am not ruling out anyone except us. And I only include you because you don't know enough to be a threat."

Marc did not take the bait. There was no need to look further than WikiLeaks to know how dangerous secrets could easily go public. He approached the gallery. "I'm in position."

"Target is twenty-four minutes out and closing."

Marc was hardly the only person walking along the lakefront with a phone attached to his ear. He was dressed in standard business garb, a dark gray suit and striped shirt and silk tie. He carried a slim leather briefcase slung over his left shoulder. He wished it contained a gun, but Swiss security made that impossible. The city served as a conduit for business from all over the globe. No one gave him a second glance as he walked along the line of tall, bulletproof windows. The interior looked dark, silent. "I see no guard."

"We've been over that. He relies on an electronic alarm system."

"I'm circling the perimeter."

"Roger that."

The side windows overlooked one of Geneva's many piazzas. Marc turned another corner and entered a rear alley. The tight lane was shadowed from the morning sun. A restaurant's trio of rubbish bins smelled of old food and disinfectant. Traffic echoed softly into his enclave.

Then he saw it. "We have trouble."

"What is it?"

"The perimeter has been breached."

"Show me."

Marc tabbed the app that turned his phone into a video camera with a live feed. He slowly panned the camera lens across the rear loading platform and the gallery's rear doors. The steel portals were no longer sealed. He stepped closer and listened carefully.

Marc said into the phone, "There is no alarm."

"Maybe it's a simple fault."

"Negative. This place is otherwise as tight as a vault. And it's wired. There are cameras in both corners."

"So security will have a record of your presence."

"The cameras have been on me since I crossed the street. That isn't the point. You send me over, and the morning I arrive there is a break-in. They knew I was coming. Your own intel is breached."

"Withdraw."

"No. I'm here, I'm seen. I'm going in."

"Marc, wait—"

He cut the connection, turned off his phone, and slipped it into his pocket. Any experienced operative knew the brass in their safe little bunkers responded to uncertainty by applying the brakes. Sometimes the guy in the field had to go with his gut. A successful operative was one whose hunches proved correct. They were the ones who made it home.

Kitra Korban had never felt so totally uncertain or out of place. Not even when she had been kidnapped and held in the poisoned plains of western Kenya while just up the road a volcano cleared its throat. She had secretly yearned for the chance, just once, to walk along a pristine lane in a beautiful European city, elegantly dressed and drawing stares from people who did not carry the weight of a thousand lives on their hearts and shoulders.

The air of Geneva was so different from the plains of Galilee. May was the first full month of the Israeli dry season. This year the rains had ended early. There was talk of a severe drought. Two of the kibbutz's wells had already gone dry.

Kitra's kibbutz was an island of green in a hot and dusty land. There were problems with the new factory's refining process. The shipments of rare earth arrived from Kenya faster than they could process them. Their potential customers were upset, the factory managers defensive and edgy. Everyone was exhausted, Kitra included. Other than the Sabbaths, she had not had a day off in seven months. They were working around the clock.

Adding further to the uncertainty and turmoil, Marc had broken off their long-distance relationship. She had sensed this was coming for months. Marc was a member of the American intelligence community. He was a patriot. He was, in fact, a hero. For most of the past year, Kitra had hoped he would become *her* hero. But his decision was hardly a surprise.

If only it did not hurt so much. Especially now.

Recently she had pinned a postcard from her parents to her office wall. After a mild heart attack, her father had decided to take his first holiday in nine years. Her brother was gradually becoming accustomed to his new position as acting head of the kibbutz. Kitra had always assumed she would run their community, and someday that might still happen. But just then, her days and nights were taken with bringing the factory up to speed. The postcard had been of a Paris café. Kitra often stared at it, yearning for the freedom to enjoy an idle hour. Europe might as well have been on the other side of the moon. Until, that is, she had been asked to make this trip.

The waters of Lake Leman sparkled across the way, blue as sapphires. In the far distance, the Alps gathered a morning crop of clouds. She passed a pair of lovers seated at a café. Being here in Geneva only amplified her longing for Marc.

15

The precise clocks of this pristine city chose that moment to chime the hour. Kitra increased her pace, excited over seeing Marc again and dreading the encounter in equal measure.

Marc tensed as the city's clocks began their hourly clamor. The Swiss attention to detail could be infuriating. Then he returned to his inspection of the gallery's rear doors. The steel had been punched by two blasts, probably from a shotgun holding solid rounds. Despite weighing over half a ton, the doors swung in with fluid ease. He stepped inside.

The gallery's chamber was a concrete cube, windowless and neat and precisely lit. Shelves held a wide variety of treasure and art. In the stockroom's center, three easels supported a massive canvas. Lights on tripods were positioned like a Hollywood film set readying for a close-up. An artist's table contained a variety of brushes and bottles. A magnifying glass was positioned above the center of the painting. The chamber smelled of cleaning fluid.

Marc clicked on his phone and hit the speed dial. When the ambassador answered, he asked quietly, "Where's the target?"

Walton's anger lowered his voice an octave. But the man was a pro. He had sent an operative into Indian country. Now was not the time for futile arguments. "Nine minutes out, maybe ten."

"Rate of speed?"

"Hold one." Walton returned swiftly with, "Holding steady at one-ten klicks."

A hundred and ten kilometers per hour was about seventy mph and ten klicks under the limit. "If the gallery's alarm had gone off, the company's owner would be pushing harder to arrive."

Walton hesitated, then said, "You have six minutes to complete your mission."

Kitra stood across the street from the gallery and searched the area for Marc. The morning rush-hour traffic competed with the continued ringing of all the city's clock towers. She felt both exposed and confused. Even so, she remained where she was. A man's life hung in the balance.

It had started with a phone call from her father thirty-one hours earlier. He had used the same voice as when he took on the Israeli government, keeping his community intact and alive. He had told his only daughter, a man is coming to see you. Do whatever he says.

Before Kitra could recover enough to ask what her father was talking about, he had hung up.

A few moments later, the man had knocked on her open office door. He had refused to give his name. Instead he simply told her that the next morning, at precisely three minutes past the hour, Marc Royce would enter Geneva's most exclusive art gallery, and die.

Just like that, her life had flown into an entirely different orbit. Bringing her to this point. Standing on Geneva's fashionable shopping street, desperate to save Marc Royce. The very same man she had recently told she never wanted to speak with again.

Marc slowly pushed through the leather swinging doors and entered the gallery.

The rooms were high-ceilinged and impossibly elegant. The art on the walls was powerful and distinctive and expensive. Three chambers opened into one another, each framed

17

by a mock passage and a single stair of polished granite. The middle room was dominated by a crystal dais, upon which was poised a bronze Rodin ballerina.

Marc gave the dancer a single glance before his attention was caught by the corpse.

The desk was positioned in the central room, so that the gallery owner could watch the doors and survey all three chambers. In the tight space between the filigreed legs and the window lay the body.

The man wore a pinstriped suit and highly polished shoes. His impeccable shirt and tie were stained by the blood that spilled from the wound to his chest.

Marc lifted his phone. "The target is not in the car."

"Repeat."

"Sylvan Gollet is here. And he's dead."

"Show me."

Marc hit the camera app and started around the desk. Then the light flashed, and he knew he was a breath away from a death all his own.

The light was a laser trigger, mounted to a compact charge. The package was fitted into the corner of the room and pointed straight down. Aimed precisely at where he now stood.

When the city's clocks finally went silent and Marc had not appeared, Kitra decided she had no choice. She crossed the street and pushed on the gallery door. To her astonishment, it was unlocked. She was surprised because the man who had come for her had described the situation in precise detail. The gallery would not open for another hour. Marc intended to break in and retrieve data from the gallery's computer. He was in Switzerland on false papers. He would not answer his phone or check his regular email account. He was operating outside normal intelligence channels. He would view anyone who approached him as an adversary. But the man asked her to travel so as to warn Marc that his enemies knew all this and were waiting for him. If Kitra did not reach him in person and in time, he would die.

Only there was no Marc. And the door opened easily.

Kitra remained where she was, halfway through the entrance, and called out, "Marc?"

He saw the front door swing open, and he heard the most beautiful voice in the world call, "Marc?"

He had already taken two steps before the trigger clicked. He then heard a further two clicks, meaning three charges were now primed.

He saw Kitra's lovely features grow tight with shock. It was impossible that Kitra was here, yet he knew also that he had no time for thought. Not if they had any chance of survival.

He gripped her by the waist and hefted her just as the first bomb blew. The compressed air hammered them through the front door. Marc allowed the second blast to shove them across the street, weaving through traffic that might as well have been frozen in space and time.

He then did the only thing that guaranteed Kitra's safety.

He dropped her into the lake.

And then he turned to face the danger he was certain lurked out there.

If only he had a gun.

Chapter Two

Rhana Mandana pulled up in front of her Lugano business and waited. The Bentley's clock showed precisely a quarter to ten. The city's central shopping street remained relatively quiet. The second hand clicked through twenty-nine seconds, then the night guard stepped out. Rhana rose from the car and said in Swiss German, "Good morning, Arnold."

"Madame Mandana."

"Everything satisfactory?"

"Perfectly, ma'am."

"You may go."

"Thank you." He waited as she passed through the bullet-proof doors. Then the guard locked the gallery's outer doors, slipped behind the Bentley's wheel, and drove her car to the underground parking garage.

Rhana let the gallery's inner doors click shut and surveyed her domain. Her establishment was one of the finest art galleries in the entire world. The item on the front room's central display stand was promised to the Getty Museum. Another had been reserved by husband-and-wife collectors who had a room named in their honor at New York's Museum of Modern Art.

She was halfway across the room when the phone on the

rosewood desk rang. Her assistant was not due in for another fifteen minutes. Rhana Mandana specifically ordered her staff not to arrive before ten. No doubt they were gathered in their customary café half a block up the Via Castiglione. She normally did not answer the phone. But she also knew one client who hated having the answering machine pick up. And this client never called once the shop had opened. She walked over and checked the readout. The caller ID had been blocked. Never a good sign.

She lifted the receiver and said, "Mandana."

"My people are out back."

"You are not expected until next . . ." But the client had already hung up.

Her shop was laid out like the formal rooms of a grand home. The front doors opened into a long gallery. The walls were pale teak, the floors granite and marble, the chandeliers Bohemian crystal. A room fashioned as a formal parlor opened to her left, and to her right was a mock study. Her assistant's desk was positioned just inside the parlor door so she could survey the chamber, the hall, and the entryway. Her own desk was located at the back of the study. The position meant that her aide could lead a recalcitrant buyer along walls holding almost a hundred million dollars' worth of art before finally arriving at Rhana's throne.

She coded in the security number that only she and her aide and the night guard knew, and entered the massive rear warehouse. The concrete and steel chamber covered almost a third of the shop's total floor space. Few people were aware that over a quarter of her treasures never saw the light of day. One of the few who shared this secret waited for her now.

Rhana waited for the gallery doors to click shut. She stood

just to the left of the doors, the one spot in the entire shop that was not swept by any camera. She had specifically designed the cameras to miss this point. On the wall beside her head was a fake light switch. Rhana placed her thumb on the fingerprint reader hidden behind the switch plate. There was a soft click, and all the security cameras shifted to a computerized loop, showing an empty chamber.

Rhana crossed the warehouse, punched in the security code, and the rear door drew up. Outside, a refrigerator truck rumbled softly. A swarthy man in blue coveralls jumped down from the truck's passenger door. The truck began reversing as the worker signaled, maneuvering the truck around until it was inches from the door.

Rhana complained, "I had nothing down for delivery today."

"We knew nothing until four hours ago." He handed her a clipboard bearing the correct code. When Rhana motioned him to continue, he opened the truck and flipped back the first set of covers. It was always this way. Same truck, same two men. "Thirty-seven items."

Normally this particular client brought her one or two items, three at the most. She resisted the desire to ask what was going on. If this man knew, he would not say. "Put them in the cage."

Rhana walked to a security box beside a door painted the same color as the concrete walls. The door cranked back on a pneumatic lift. Only when it was open could one see that the door's thickness was six inches of solid steel. She stood watching as the men carted one item after another into her treasure room.

As always, the driver handed Rhana his cellphone. She

turned from the two men and demanded softly, "Why a delivery today, and why so much?"

"Emergency," the man replied.

"I dislike being involved in—"

"I must receive one hundred million dollars."

She swallowed her protest. This client was not interested in histrionics. "Say again."

"One hundred million. Cash."

"When?"

"I will let you know. Two days."

"Impossible."

"Necessary. Have the money ready when I call."

"Even if I could get my hands on that much, you know perfectly well that large a sum would alert Interpol."

"You are buying an item. You know the drill."

"But a hundred million. I will need to notify the authorities—"

"That is out of the question. Do what is required. Be ready."

She expected him to hang up. He never spoke for very long. Rhana started to ask him what more he could require of her, what other impossible demands did he intend to foist upon her, when she saw the final item the workers carried inside. "I know that piece. Sylvan Gollet displayed it in his Geneva gallery."

"Officially, he still does. Parts of it, anyway."

"You are giving me a fake?"

"No. This item is the original."

Rhana raised a hand. The workers obligingly set down the sculpture. Rhana inspected it carefully. She had traveled to Geneva the day before Sylvan put it on display, to spend a few moments alone with this treasure. She knew it intimately.

She did not have her loupe. She did not need it. She knew she was inspecting Rodin's ballet dancer.

Rhana waved the men on, turned her back to them, and hissed, "It has been rumored that Sylvan started dealing in counterfeit items that he produced."

"The rumors were correct. The matter has been resolved. Permanently."

"What have you done?"

"Sylvan's gallery was destroyed this morning."

The only sound she could manage was a gasp.

The man went on, "His shop was demolished by a bomb."

Rhana understood then why the man had remained on the phone. His message was not how close she herself was to such destruction. She had known that since the first day the man had entered her world. No. The message for her was, the man took pleasure in such acts of annihilation. She forced herself to say, "I understand."

"I must have one hundred million in cash. You have forty-eight hours. Be ready for my call."

Chapter Three

Geneva's central police station stood near the industrial zone beyond the train station. The monolithic structure was functional, imposing, and stank of disinfectant. They escorted Marc through the central bullpen, down a narrow hallway, and locked him in an interview chamber. Kitra was nowhere to be seen.

The interview room had bland walls and plastic chairs and a battered central table. A narrow slit was set at eye level into the door. A side wall held a larger window of one-way glass. Marc grew very tired of seeing his reflection. He repeatedly asked for someone to call Ambassador Walton. He had alternated between giving them Walton's direct line and reading out the central system that plugged straight into the White House operators.

Two hours after his arrival, they brought him out into the bullpen proper and handcuffed him to a wooden bench. Marc assumed Walton had gotten hold of the embassy duty officer, strings had been pulled, and he was soon going to be released. But he sat there and watched the hands on the clock crawl. When Marc asked one passing officer what was happening, the woman offered to return Marc to the holding cell, otherwise he was to keep his mouth zipped shut. Her command of English surprised him.

The police inspector in charge of the bombing case returned to the bullpen. He looked like a middle-aged, midlevel bureaucrat. A green police jacket hung on his narrow frame like a cheerless costume. He was accompanied by a man in his late forties or early fifties, wearing a charcoal jacket and gray gabardine slacks. This second man might have been dressed as a civilian, and he might have been as sleek as a silver fox. But Marc knew a professional when he saw one.

The inspector looked immensely sour as he walked over. "You will please come with me now."

The entire bullpen watched as Marc's cuffs were unlocked from the bench and the two men walked back toward the holding cells. But as they arrived at the rear hall, Kitra appeared, led by the female officer who had ordered Marc to zip it. Kitra wore a set of gray police sweats. The sweatshirt was one size too large, the sleeves falling over her hands. Her makeup was gone, and her feet slapped the floor in cloth sandals. Her dark hair was uncombed and stuck out in a soft fluff. Marc thought she had never been more beautiful.

She was also very angry. "You ruined my suit!"

The outburst caught everyone by surprise, especially Marc. "I wanted to protect you from the blast."

"Oh, and the blast wasn't going to harm you? What are you, bulletproof?"

"Kitra, I just saved your life." Marc knew her anger was not over the suit. Or the lake. But she couldn't yell at him in public over the real source of her fury. "The police are waiting—"

"Let them wait. We're not talking about what I want to talk about."

"You're not talking, you're yelling." Mark knew she was really raging because he had refused to join her on the kibbutz and make a life together. The loss still hurt them both. Being right did not make it go away. It only made the pain easier to bear. For him. Kitra had no such consolation. And she did not beg. "I'm so sorry."

"You're *sorry*. Oh, and that's supposed to—"

"Enough." The inspector had a cop's ability to command softly. "Take her to room two. Mr. Royce, in here."

"Kitra, tell them the truth."

She struggled futilely against the female officer's grip on her arm. "*I* most *certainly* do *not* lie."

The police inspector tugged on his arm. "Now, Mr. Royce."

"Your passport states your full name as Kitra Korban."

"Yes."

The police inspector who had led Marc away was now seated across the interview table from her. The elegantly dressed gentleman was seated beside him. The policewoman who had remained her constant shadow stood in the corner, observing everything. The police inspector demanded, "How do you come to be in Geneva, Ms. Korban?"

"I was asked to come."

"By whom?"

"I don't know his name."

The two men who faced her across the interview table did not appear the least bit surprised by her answers. "And yet you came. Why is that?"

"My father told me I should trust this man."

"Your father, his name is . . ."

"Dr. Levi Korban."

29

"He is a medical doctor?"

"Engineering. Electrical."

"Dr. Korban accompanied you on this visit?"

"No. He is in France. Narbonne. With my mother." Saying those words should not have caused her to leak tears. "They are on vacation. Their first in years. My mother is French."

"Do you have a phone number where they can be contacted?"

"On my cellphone. Wait. It doesn't work anymore. Call my brother. Serge Korban." She gave the kibbutz's central line. "He will know how to reach them."

The policewoman, who had checked on her all day and brought her a sandwich and coffee, shifted off her position by the door and handed Kitra a tissue. The inspector was seated directly in front of her. The other man was dressed in a charcoal-gray jacket and chalk-blue shirt and striped tie. His hair was perfectly cut. His gray eyes were intelligent and featureless.

Kitra looked directly at him. "May I ask who you are?"

"No, Ms. Korban, you may not. I am asking the questions here." The policeman waited until she returned her gaze to him. "So a man who your father introduced, and whose name you do not recall, told you—"

"That is not what I said. My father called and said I would receive a visitor. He told me to trust this man. And do whatever he asked."

"Is this normal? Does your father often make such requests?"

"Never. This was the first time."

"Describe the man who asked you to come here."

"He was Israeli. Late sixties, perhaps older. But still very strong. He carried a cane. I think . . ."

"Yes?"

"I think he was Mossad. But he didn't say." Perhaps it was her banked-up fatigue, and the stress, and the impact of the explosion she still felt, but suddenly she was back there in the desert. "He looked like a bull. Muscular with huge hands. His hair was thinning but still dark. I don't think it was dyed, but I can't be certain."

The elegantly dressed older man spoke for the first time. "You recall him quite clearly."

"I've been working to complete a new factory our kibbutz is building. We are months behind schedule. There are problems everywhere. I didn't want to meet with him."

"You are saying that this gentleman impressed you."

"Very much. He was also a little frightening."

The elegant man sat in the plastic chair with the ease of someone who had spent years growing comfortable with himself and in whatever surroundings he found himself. "Please go on."

"He told me that Marc was coming to Geneva and was about to walk into a trap. They wanted me to go and warn him."

"You did not find this strange?"

"Of course I did. I refused. I told them to contact Marc's embassy. He replied that he couldn't because there was a mole."

The elegant man leaned forward. "Did the man tell you where the mole was based?"

"He didn't say anything more. He stayed ten minutes. Less."

"Then why did you agree—?"

"Because the last thing the man said was, then don't go,

and see what it feels like to live with the stain of a lost life on your soul. I . . ."

"Yes, Ms. Korban, you were going to say what?"

But there was no way she would tell them that she had already lost Marc once, and the pain was still almost unbearable. And, of course, there was the other secret, the one she did not even like to confess to herself. That despite every reason to the contrary, she had hungered for one more glimpse of him. Perhaps for the last time. Kitra dabbed her eyes with the tissue. "There's nothing else to tell you."

"How did you and Ms. Korban meet?" The police inspector sat across from Marc while the man in civilian clothes observed from the corner.

"We were in Africa," Marc answered. "Kenya."

"Where precisely?"

"A refugee camp west of the Rift Valley. Right after the volcano erupted. Maybe you heard about it."

The police inspector nodded, but whether because he had read about the eruption or because Marc confirmed what Kitra had already told them, Marc had no idea. Nor did he care. He had been left waiting in the holding cell for another hour. His left shoulder and ribs throbbed from the blast. "May I have something to eat?"

"Perhaps later, Mr. Royce. I want to know—"

"How about now. I have been here all day. No food, no water, no charges. Has my associate been treated in this manner? Is that standard Swiss protocol?"

The elegant man rose, knocked on the door, and spoke to someone in the hallway. The police inspector watched him with a sour expression, but did not protest. The police inspector did not speak again until the other gentleman had resumed his seat. "Tell us how you met Ms. Korban."

"I was sent by U.S. intelligence to infiltrate a security firm suspected of illegal activities in Kenya."

"All agents of foreign intelligence services are required by Swiss law to announce themselves to local authorities."

Marc knew this to be the most ignored law on the books of every developed nation. "I was previously a member of State Department Intelligence. But not now."

"You left?"

"I was fired."

"And yet they rehired you?"

"I freelance. I met Kitra because her brother was suspected of being kidnapped by the group I was investigating. She had gone to Kenya to find him."

"How does that connect you two here in Geneva?"

"I have no idea. I never expected to see her again."

"That makes no sense whatsoever, Mr. Royce. I must assume you are lying. Your attempts to cover up—"

"Two days ago my government asked me to come to Geneva. My objective was to copy files from the gallery's computer. My cover was the acquisition of a painting. They had been exchanging emails with Mr. Gollet in my name."

"Breaking into a Swiss firm to steal data from a Swiss computer." The policeman shook his head in practiced dismay. "Your crimes grow worse by the minute."

Marc took heart from how the gentleman to his left smiled at that. Marc pressed on. "They suspected Gollet of being a conduit for funds used to finance terrorism. They wanted to follow the trail of my cash and see where it led." Marc described his arrival at the gallery, finding the rear door open, seeing the bloodstained body, and hearing Kitra call his name.

"You did not expect her to come warn you, then."

"Not at all."

"And yet there she was. Right in the nick of time."

Marc described the explosive charges and the laser triggers. "They knew I was coming. They obviously planned for me to get blown up, make it look like I had come there to murder him and got caught in my own blast."

The man in the charcoal jacket asked, "Your associates in Washington were tracking the gallery owner's car?"

"Tracking his cellphone. The killer or one of his accomplices drove it to Geneva from Gollet's home as a decoy. Did you find the car?"

"Abandoned at the train station. Wiped clean. No prints."

The police inspector bitterly disliked this exchange. He reinserted himself with, "Here is what I think happened, Mr. Royce. You were sent by outside forces not to buy anything at all. You came to murder a Swiss citizen. Which you did. And Ms. Korban was sent to stop you. Why? Who knows. Perhaps the deceased was an ally of her own country's security. Perhaps something else entirely. But her arrival interrupted your destruction of the gallery, which meant you could not get away, not without killing the woman who came to warn you."

Marc was fairly certain the officer did not actually believe what he had suggested. But he was a cop, and he was a professional at placing blame. Marc replied, "Sorry, you got every bit of that wrong."

Marc assumed the well-dressed man was an agent with the Swiss FIS, the country's lone intelligence agency. Swiss intel was generally a closed door, as in nothing came in or out. Because of Switzerland's willingness to help tax dodgers and criminals hide away their money, and because they refused to accept court documents from other nations as legal requests, most nations refused to share any intelligence, under any circumstances, at any time.

Which made the elegant man's next move very interesting indeed.

He led Marc into the police inspector's office. A brass plaque on the door informed Marc that the chief inspector was named Remy Reynard. The elegant man did not introduce himself. He unlocked Marc's handcuffs, slipped them into his pocket, and pointed at a steaming plastic cup and wrapped sandwich on the edge of the desk. "These are for you."

"Thanks. Could you please make sure Kitra has been given something?"

"Already taken care of." The man picked up the phone on the desk and said, "He's here." He listened a moment, then handed the receiver to Marc, walked out and shut the door behind him.

Marc inspected the sandwich. It looked like it had spent so long in the wrapper the lettuce had molded to the plastic. He said into the phone, "This is Royce."

"Hold please for Ambassador Walton."

He took a sip from the plastic cup and grimaced. The coffee was vile. He dumped it and the limp-looking sandwich into the inspector's trash can.

"Marc?"

"Here, sir."

"Are you alone?"

"Roger that. But I can't say who might be listening in. I'm still inside—"

"I know where you are. I've been assured this call is confidential." Walton's voice had turned reedy, and his breath came in tight little puffs, like he had to battle for air. "On this side we are joined by an assistant director of Homeland Security and a rear admiral who heads a section of DOD intel. Everyone hear me?"

A man and a woman both responded with affirmatives. Walton said, "Tell us what happened."

Marc hesitated.

"We're waiting, Marc."

"Sir, permission to ask a question."

"Fire away."

"Do you intend for me to remain in-country?"

Walton hesitated, as though giving his associates a chance to reply. "Affirmative."

"Then I think we should have their intel operative join us for the discussion. Otherwise we run the risk of my being driven to the border and getting kicked out."

Walton gave that ten seconds. "I agree. Comments, anyone?"

The man's voice said, "It's a risk."

"It's trumped by what we currently face," replied the woman. "Invite him in."

Marc walked over and opened the door. The agent stood across the bullpen, arms crossed, listening to the inspector. The policeman looked irate, probably because Marc had been released from the cuffs and granted use of the inspector's office. Kitra sat on the hard wooden bench by the side wall. She looked tired and worried and very small. All three faces turned his direction when Marc stepped out.

Marc signaled to the agent. "Can you join me for a moment?"

"What is this, a private gathering in my office?" The inspector's voice rose to where the entire bullpen observed the exchange. "You want me to cater in something, perhaps? A nice *fois gras*, a carafe of wine?"

The agent shut the door behind them, and Marc hit the speaker button. "We've been joined by—sorry, I don't know your name."

"Bernard Behlet."

Walton demanded, "You're Swiss intel?"

"FIS. That is correct."

"My name is Walton. I am special adviser to the White House on matters pertaining to international—"

"I know who you are, Mr. Ambassador."

The phone went silent, then Walton said, "Explain."

"You were formerly director of State Department Intelligence, the smallest of the American agencies. We met once, actually."

"Sorry, your name doesn't ring a bell."

"There is no reason it should, sir." The man's voice held the calm strength of someone long used to dealing with power and egos. "I was on temporary duty at our Washington embassy and accompanied our ambassador to a reception in the State Department's formal chambers."

"Right. Very well. Let us proceed. With me are two senior directors involved in the current situation. We want to begin by asking Marc to tell us—"

"If you will excuse me, sir, I think we should invite the police inspector to sit in as well."

The DOD officer growled, "Oh, good grief."

"Chief Inspector Reynard has a murder on his hands,"

Behlet went on. "One of the country's premier art galleries has been blown up. The main avenues fronting the lake were closed for six hours. The blast zone covered almost a square kilometer and included Geneva's most exclusive shopping street. The city is in chaos. Reynard is already being pressured by the city council for answers. He has every reason to be your man's enemy. If the problem you face is more than simply the theft of art and treasures—"

"It is," the woman said. "Much more."

"Oh, come on, Sarah. Do we even know who this man is?"

"What I *know* is the clock is ticking, and we are *desperate*. Agent Behlet, bring in the inspector."

When the policeman was brought in and introductions made, Reynard barked at the Swiss agent in French. Behlet replied in English, "I know this is true because I have met Ambassador Walton and I recognize his voice. I also know because the number I was told to dial is the central line for the White House." He handed over a slip of paper. "You can check online to confirm."

The inspector had the ability to frown from his receding hairline to his shirt collar. He did not like it, but he stifled further objections. Behlet said, "You may proceed, Mr. Ambassador."

"Marc, brief us on what happened."

He laid out the events in the clipped manner Walton preferred. Starting with his arrival at the airport, the taxi ride, circling the gallery, seeing the rear door was ajar, entering, spotting the body, noticing the infrared trigger, seeing Kitra. The race for the door, the blast, and here.

Walton said, "Kitra Korban, the nurse you worked with in Kenya?"

"Roger that, sir."

The woman said, "Who?"

"Royce's last assignment was in Kenya," Walton explained. "He investigated a security corporation by the name of Lodestone."

"I remember this," the woman replied. "The attempted theft of rare earth. That was Royce?"

"It was. Marc, what's your assessment?"

"I was set up." He fought fatigue, hunger, a pounding head, and aching ribs as he said, "Even though we circumvented all regular channels, there was still a leak."

The admiral demanded, "How did this Korban woman find you?"

Agent Behlet replied, "Ms. Korban states she was visited by a man her father said she must trust. He did not identify himself, but we must assume it was Mossad."

Marc said, "Mossad must also know about the leak, so they refused to send their warning through the same channels you distrust. Maybe they have some idea of who our target is."

There was a moment's silence, then Walton said, "Which means Mossad knows what we face."

"Of course they know," the woman responded. "The threat originates in Israel's backyard. They have to know, and they are obviously as concerned as we are, both about the leaks and the threat."

Bernard Behlet cleared his throat. "Might I inquire what it is that has you so alarmed?"

"I for one would like to know the very same thing," the police inspector agreed.

"Tell them," Walton said.

"Are you both out of your minds?" The admiral's voice

carried the strength of pounded steel. "We already have a serious leak, we have a ticking clock, and you want to share this intel with strangers?"

The woman's voice was softer, but equally firm. "We face serious time constraints. And you heard our agent—"

"Correction. Royce is no longer a member of the service. He was *canned*."

Walton corrected, "I dismissed him because I had no choice. He was facing a personal crisis—"

"This is nuts."

"Correction. This is crucial," the woman snapped back.

"I do not concur. There is no hard evidence to connect any of this to Switzerland. Your *ex*-agent is operating in the *wrong* country."

Chief Inspector Reynard leaned forward and opened his mouth. But before he could speak, Bernard lifted one hand. Wait. Marc liked the man for his smooth control.

Walton replied, "Marc Royce is trying to follow the money trail. The destruction of this gallery—"

"Means nothing."

"With respect, I disagree," Walton replied. "Regardless, we are proceeding."

"I object in the strongest possible terms."

"Duly noted." Walton rarely barked, but he did so now. "Proceed."

The woman said, "Eleven days ago, nine containers left a missile factory in North Korea. The containers traveled by rail to Pyong Yang, where they were placed on a Liberian freighter. The manifest claimed it was bound for Karachi, Pakistan. Five days later, the ship radioed that it was experiencing engine troubles and put in at Singapore. Satellite photos indicate that all nine containers are now missing. We have not been able to locate them."

Walton added, "The factory makes motors and guidance systems for long-range missiles. Iran wouldn't dare try and transship the whole rocket. It would be like painting a giant bull's-eye on the side of the vessel. These motors are two generations further along than anything the Iranians have built. An Iranian missile equipped with this propulsion system has the capability of striking American soil."

The woman continued, "Just prior to this event, we received credible reports of a pending attack on a U.S. port. Atlantic seaboard. All indications point toward this incident being large enough to take out the entire city. We are talking about an unprecedented loss of American lives."

Behlet asked, "Where does the Geneva connection fit into this?"

The admiral snarled, "It doesn't. At all."

Walton replied, "There was fragmentary evidence of the gallery being a conduit for illicit funds used to circumvent the Iranian sanctions."

The admiral snapped, "I've seen your so-called evidence. There is *nothing* that makes a direct link between the gallery bombing and the missing shipment."

Marc countered, "But it does make for a perfect motive. They must be planning a major incident to set me up and blow up this gallery."

"The timing," Behlet quietly agreed, "could be significant."

"We have three options that are now on the president's table," Walton said. "The Israelis have warned us that if we do not stop this shipment, they will bomb the Iranian nuclear facilities. All of them. Do I need to tell you what that means?"

Behlet glanced at his associate, who had gone very still, and replied, "No, Mr. Ambassador. You do not."

"Option two. We stop every ship coming through the Strait of Hormuz, including those bearing the Iranian flag. Do you understand what that means?"

"It is an act of war," Behlet said, his eyes still on the inspector.

The Strait of Hormuz formed the only sea passage between the Persian Gulf and the open ocean. Almost a quarter of the entire world's oil was shipped through those narrow waters, making it the most strategically vital passage on earth. At its narrowest, the Strait was less than twenty miles wide. To the south, it was bordered by the United Arab Emirates, Oman, and islands belonging to Saudi Arabia. To its north ran the shoreline of Iran.

Ambassador Walton confirmed, "The instant we board that first vessel, we will be officially at war with Iran."

"And option three?"

"We determine where those containers are. We stop them."

"Walton, you're wasting my time," the admiral snapped. "I am out of here."

When the admiral clicked off, Walton sighed. "As you have probably detected, the military feels we should support an attack by Israel, and back them with a blockade of the Strait."

The woman from Homeland said, "Our last best hope of an alternative to all-out war is to track the money."

Walton said, "As of this morning we have put through official requests to the Swiss government for their assistance. We need the gallery's funds and accounts to be frozen, and all recent transactions traced."

"I will see what I can do to speed things along," Bernard

said. "I will inform you through Agent Royce if anything turns up."

"That would be much appreciated," Walton said.

Marc asked, "How much time do we have?"

The woman replied, "Tracking out the shipping time from Singapore, the earliest the vessel could possibly arrive at the Strait is seven days."

"One week, gentleman," Walton rasped. "You heard the admiral. After that, the gloves come off."

Chapter Four

The policewoman drove Kitra to the train station to retrieve her suitcase, then took her to a modest but very pleasant hotel between the station and the lake. Kitra twice started to ask where Marc was, but both times decided she was better off not knowing. Her hotel room had a narrow balcony overlooking a small plaza. She slept beneath a duvet as soft as a cloud.

She awoke at eight forty-five the next morning, two hours later than normal, and that without an alarm or banging kibbutz bell or frantic knock on her door. She took a long bath in a huge tub and used every amenity the hotel had to offer—shampoo and conditioner and perfumed lotion and a fluffy white robe. She then dressed in fresh clothing from her suitcase.

A room-service breakfast was served on her balcony. Below the wrought-iron railing, traffic swirled and people scurried. Between two high-rise office buildings she could glimpse the sparkling waters of Lake Geneva. It was her first free morning in nine months. The air was sweet, the day both warm and cold as only an Alpine spring could be. Kitra used the linen napkin to dab at the corners of her eyes, and told herself she had every right to be happy.

When the knock came on her door, she assumed it was Marc. Her heart thumped as she crossed the room, which was simply ridiculous. She paused to check her reflection. What was sillier still was the fact that she had spent so much time on her makeup and clothing because of this moment. She wore her second-best outfit, a tan linen skirt and silk blouse and matching hose. If only there was something she could do about the hollowness in her eyes.

She took a long breath, then told her reflection, "Don't let him hurt you again."

But when she opened the door, she was startled to find it was the Swiss agent. "Good morning, Ms. Korban. Your associate has been called to his embassy. He asked me to speak with you."

"Marc is in Bern?"

"Yes. Mr. Royce left by train two hours ago. He hopes to be back by lunch. May we speak privately?"

Bernard Behlet might be a government official, but Kitra did not feel comfortable inviting him into her room. "Let's go downstairs."

"Of course." He swept his arm down the empty hall. "Please."

But as she gathered up her purse and room key, the phone rang. She motioned for Bernard Behlet to wait. "Hello?"

"Ms. Korban, we met four days ago." The voice was deep and spoke Hebrew with the guttural ease of a native Israeli. "At the kibbutz."

"I remember."

"Are you alone?"

"No. How did you find me?"

"That's not the question you need to be asking. Did Marc tell you what we're facing?"

"He started to." She glanced at her watch. It was midday in Tel Aviv. "Are you calling from Israel?"

"That's not important either. Listen carefully to what Royce tells you, Ms. Korban. Then you have to decide. Are you with us or are you part of the scenery? We need to know this, and we need to know now."

"I . . . I don't understand."

"Marc claims you are perhaps the most intelligent and perceptive young woman he has ever met. Ambassador Walton's secondhand impression is precisely the same. Our reports from allies in Kenya mirror these assessments. Your kibbutz has riled a number of powerful people. I like that. It means you're fighters. You stick up for your principles. That's what we need."

"What is it you want?"

"For you to pass on a message. Do you have a pen and paper handy?"

"Wait . . . All right, go ahead."

He rattled off a number. "And tell Marc Royce *yes.*"

"That's it? Yes?"

"That's enough, if he asks the right question. And I hope you tell him the same thing, Ms. Korban. Your friend is heading into serious danger. He needs someone he can trust to watch his back. It might just keep him alive."

Marc's meeting with the U.S. Embassy officials in Bern proved utterly futile. The CIA station agent and the ambassador had obviously been briefed by Washington, which meant they were not free to voice the rage they both felt over being kept out of the loop. The fact that Marc could tell them nothing, and Washington had obviously ordered them not to ask, only made things worse.

Marc took the next train back to Geneva and walked to the hotel where he and Kitra were booked. He had never felt so conflicted in his life. He could not wait to see Kitra again, and yet he dreaded it in equal measure. He half hoped she had already decided to return to Israel—for both of their sakes, even though it would break his heart once more.

He was about to enter the hotel when he spotted her. Kitra was seated in a café fronting the plaza and the traffic. She was turned so that her face was directed toward the sun, her chin tilted upward. She wore dark sunglasses, but Marc thought her eyes might be closed. He stepped back down to the street and recalled the first time he had ever seen her. She had been serving as a nurse in a Kenyan refugee camp, in the shadow of an erupting volcano. Her brother had been kidnapped while tracking the theft of rare earths. She had been frantic, and utterly alone. Then, when all had seemed darkest, Marc had arrived and brought her brother out safely and helped her establish a new commercial lifeline for her kibbutz. Now, as he studied her profile, he understood why his heart felt so heavy. He knew she was sad, that he was the reason for her sorrow. It was all his fault. And he could do nothing about it except send her away.

But he could not do that again. He did not have the strength.

She must have sensed him, for she jerked slightly as though coming awake, and turned toward him. There was no greeting in her features. If anything, the sad lines around her mouth deepened.

Marc entered the café's veranda. "May I join you?"

She gave a nod. Marc took that as the only invitation he was going to receive, and seated himself. When the waiter appeared, he ordered an omelet with herbs and salad. He asked, "Did Agent Behlet speak with you?"

"For almost two hours."

"May I ask what he said?"

Her voice took on a hollow singsong. "As of last year, the nation's intelligence agencies have been merged into one new organization called the Federal Intelligence Service, or FIS. In French, *Service de Renseignement de la Confederation Suisse.*" Her accent was impeccable. "I don't remember the German and couldn't pronounce it if I did."

"I was talking," Marc said quietly, "of the threat."

She waited while the waiter set down his meal. "Is it real, Marc?"

"Very." He forced himself to take a few bites. "The final components required for Iran to deliver a nuclear threat to U.S. soil are now on the high seas. If our military takes over, the result will be global destabilization. Possibly a regional war."

"The authorities in Singapore can't help?"

That was the only bit of useful intel that had come from his morning at the embassy. "It appears we missed them by a day. Two hundred and eleven vessels came and went in that time, everything from fishing dhows to the largest container ship in the world. We think they off-loaded to a small private vessel, then halted again in Malaysia and changed vessels a third time." Marc nodded his thanks as the waiter refreshed his water glass, but made no move to eat more. "Which is both good and bad. Bad, because we can't track the ship. Good, because it adds a couple of days. Maybe."

"How long do we have?"

Marc described the discussion in the police inspector's

office. "If we haven't ID'd the vessel, in six days the U.S. Navy will close the Strait."

She inspected him for a long moment. "Eat your meal."

"I'm not hungry."

"You look half starved. And exhausted. Did you sleep at all last night?"

Marc stared out over the piazza.

Kitra slid the plate and the salad bowl closer to him. "Eat."

He did as he was told. "The ambassador met me at the service entrance with a Marine guard and took me straight to the comm room. I spent over an hour on the secure phone. Walton claims nobody in Washington believes the Swiss investigation will lead anywhere. The one connection they had to the money trail has been blown to smithereens. Even with Agent Behlet's help it would take weeks to unlock the Swiss system and give us access to the gallery owner's financial transactions."

"Bernard says he has already looked at them."

Marc stopped with his fork in midair. "What did he find?"

"Eat and I will tell you."

"You sound like my mother."

That was enough to draw a slight smile. Then her lips crimped into a tight line. "Behlet assures me the money trail goes nowhere. All he has is a list of attorneys and shell corporations. He says they broke a dozen laws accessing this information." She opened her handbag and set a sheaf of papers on the table. "This did not come from him."

"Don't worry." Marc made the pages disappear. "Can I ask you something?"

"All right, yes."

"Why are you here?"

She was silent for so long Marc feared she might be deciding how to tell him that she was leaving, that she never wanted to see him again. And he would tell her that she was right, that she should go, and that it was over. All the words formed in his brain and cascaded across his heart like lead rain.

But when she spoke, it was to describe the phone call. Marc had difficulty focusing on what he was hearing. "A man we assume was from Mossad gave you a phone number and told you to tell me the one word *yes?*"

"That is correct. He also said you were headed into danger. He said . . ."

"Kitra, it's important I know everything."

"He said you needed me to watch your back."

"And you're sure this man was the same one who came to see you in Israel?"

"Positive."

Marc tried to tell himself there was no reason for him to feel so elated by her staying. They were, after all, not a couple. They never would be. But the words did not stop his heart from soaring. "Describe him, please."

"I already did. Once for you, and about a dozen times for the police."

"Once more, please."

She did so. "I had the feeling he wanted to be my friend. And yours. He didn't come to the kibbutz just to deliver this message and ask me to make the trip."

"He wanted to get your measure," Marc suggested. "He wanted to scope you out, see how you'd handle yourself in the field."

He could see the information impacted her deeply. "They know, don't they? The Israelis."

"Probably for a lot longer than the Americans. This is their backyard, and they've been warning about Iran and nukes for years. Sure they know."

"So why are they leaving you here alone?"

"Same as the Americans. They don't think this is going to lead anywhere. But they have to be certain."

"What are we going to do?"

It was a hard question to hear. He was trained to assess, measure, decide, and act. But there was no direct way forward. No clear avenue to take. Neither about the threat nor about them. To speak was to admit defeat. He sighed, "I have no idea."

Chapter Five

Rhana Mandana left her home in the burning chill of predawn. The stars were out and the roads empty. She entered Lugano and drove to the back of her gallery, where she opened the car's trunk and then coded her entry into the warehouse doors. She had called ahead, so the guard merely stepped into the warehouse, offered her an alert greeting, then departed. He was well used to such visits and knew her desire for privacy. She cut off the security cameras, entered the cage, wrapped the selected artwork in a packing blanket, and carried it out to the car. The item was quite heavy, and she was out of breath by the time she shut the trunk lid. Rhana reentered the shop, closed the cage, restarted the cameras, and resealed the rear entry. Then she left the city and joined the highway headed south. It was her favorite time of day for a drive.

She obeyed the speed limit to the border with Italy, was waved through customs, then pulled over and dropped the Bentley's convertible roof. It was still quite cool, but she was dressed in a leather driving jacket, with a cashmere scarf knotted tightly over her hair. She turned up the heater, slipped back onto the highway, and unchained the beast under the hood. The Bentley's turbocharged W12 roared with delight and accelerated the four tons of metal and luxury to a hundred miles per hour in less than ten seconds.

Her father had always claimed that danger was the most intense of all spices. Her mother had hated such comments, especially when he enlisted his only daughter in his games. Her brother had been much more like their mother, conservative and hesitant and carefully measuring every step. Little good it did them. No, their father had been right all along. Risk could be an exquisite pleasure, so long as it was taken on her terms, and done with an elegant flair.

Her name was a private joke. *Rhana Mandana*. In Farsi, her mother tongue, it meant "the sublime princess." The few Persian customers who had the funds to be her clients loved the lyrical play on words. Farsi was a tongue made for poetry. Rhana Mandana was her legal name now—she had changed it the year she had arrived in Switzerland. Her birth name was *Maliheh Masoumeh*, which translated as "beauty in sinless innocence." The name had become a bitter lie. Rhana was well rid of it.

She joined the highway heading west from Milan and pressed the accelerator further toward the floor, lifting her speed to over two hundred kilometers an hour. Almost fast enough to flee the memories.

When she approached the outskirts of Genoa, she turned into a nameless rest stop and reached into her purse for the phone. It was a risk to contact these people, especially now, when death was close enough to breathe down her neck. But she had outrun all the other early morning traffic. And she was using a cheap phone she would immediately destroy. She dialed the number from memory.

She had not heard the voice in eight months. But she recognized it instantly. He answered sleepily, "Yes?"

"This is Rhana."

"Good morning. You are well?"

"The moment we have expected and feared is arriving."

The man was silent for a fraction of a second. In that instant, all drowsiness vanished from his voice. "You are certain?"

"I am."

"Tell me why."

She described the Geneva gallery's destruction and the man who had phoned her.

"I saw the newscast," he said to her. "I was concerned they might have taken you as well."

"I am well. For now."

"Where are you?"

"Genoa. Turning north on the highway to France."

"How can we contact you?"

"Best if you do not."

"Understood. What do you need?"

"A team in place to assist me if this is indeed the moment we have planned for. Close enough to move fast."

"I will attend to this matter myself."

"You will be ready when I call?"

"My dear Rhana, I doubt seriously that I shall sleep between now and the end."

She cut the connection, and discovered that her hands trembled on the wheel. She rose from the car and paced a slow circle around the parking area. Only when her tremors had passed did she return to the Bentley and the autostrada. The man's final word resonated through the dawn-streaked sky. More than likely her phone call did indeed mark the beginning of the end for them both.

There was nothing for her to do but take what small pleasure she could from this life's final danger.

Rhana entered France and took the hairpin descent from the main highway into Monte Carlo. Beyond the sunlit roofs sprawled the lazy blue Mediterranean.

The berth holding Sir Geoffrey Treadwick's yacht stood alongside the Riviera's most famous beach and cost more than a Manhattan apartment. The vessel measured two hundred and seventeen feet, and was sculpted from steel and carbon fiber and teak and chrome and money. A sailor in pressed whites was scurrying down the gangplank before Rhana cut the engine. She opened the trunk and asked his help carrying the blanket-wrapped item onboard. The sailor radioed for another mate to come take her car, then led her up the gangplank.

Sir Geoffrey was there to greet her. "My dear Rhana, what a delight. Have you eaten?"

"Not since last night."

"Then we must do something about that. How do poached eggs with truffles and caviar sound?"

"Perfect." She allowed the portly gentleman to peck both her cheeks. "You are looking splendid, Geoffrey."

"I'm not. I'm too pale and I haven't exercised in weeks. But your presence will prove a tonic." He gestured to the sailor still holding the parcel. "What have we here?"

"Something for your eyes only."

"Take it into the stateroom." To Rhana, "Shall we leave it until after breakfast?"

"Business first, truffles later."

"This way, then." He led her through the main living area and along a hall as broad as a manor's. The walls displayed a king's ransom in art. It was a testimony to Sir Geoffrey's wealth and obsession that he would display such artwork on a boat he used only four or five times a year.

The stateroom dominated the stern's main deck, with a sweeping view over the harbor and the city and the hills. Rhana directed Sir Geoffrey to shift a table over so that it was centered directly below the crystal chandelier. She waited until the sailor departed before unfastening the wrapping and letting it drop to the floor.

"Oh, I say." Sir Geoffrey circled the sculpture. The bronze glimmered in the lights like the jewel it was. "Is this genuine?"

"I am assured it is."

The polishing had never been completed. Some critics claimed it was because Rodin had been overtaken by illness, and released the ballerina only when he feared he would not survive. But Rhana thought otherwise. The rough texture in certain places only added to the piece's distinctly human nature. The fragile figurine remained poised in that singular moment between rest and flight. Rhana shivered with the joy she knew only in the presence of such sublime art. Rodin had not created a sculpture. He had captured life itself. She could almost hear the music that would bring the dancer into motion.

Sir Geoffrey cleared his throat and wiped his eyes. Rhana liked him the more for his unabashed emotions. "This is magnificent."

"It is. Yes."

"Rhana, you must be aware, at auction this one piece could fetch your entire asking price."

"Not without provenance. Which it does not have. And then there is the matter of confidentiality."

"Of course." He continued to stare at the sculpture. "This came from Sylvan's gallery in Geneva?"

"It did. Yes."

"Did you . . . ?"

She appreciated how he did not allow himself to complete the question. "Sylvan might have had some very serious weaknesses, but he remained a dear friend. I had nothing to do with the blast. And don't bother asking how I came to possess these items. The answer is, I don't know. And even if I did, to tell you would be to sign my own death warrant."

"Yes. Of course." He spoke to the bronze dancer and not to her. "You are offering me everything from Sylvan's gallery?"

"As far as I know. Every item in his collection at the time of the blast."

"Then what are the police pawing through?"

"I assume they are fakes. From what I have heard on the news, there is nothing left of the establishment except charcoal and puddles of molten bronze."

"Am I in danger, Rhana?"

"No one knows you are taking possession."

"No one can *ever* know."

"Precisely. For both our sakes."

"How do you propose to pass them to me undetected?"

Midway through her explanation he managed to drag his gaze from the bronze. "That is an excellent plan."

"Thank you. I thought so."

"I accept your offer. Where do I send the funds? Your usual accounts?"

"Not this time. I have a shell company in the Caymans." She slipped the paper from her pocket. "As far as I know, there is no connection between me and those accounts."

"I will have the funds transferred by close of business today."

She thanked him and allowed him to lead her back to the main deck, but only after she had bade the dancer a fond farewell. She ate a meal she did not taste and then allowed Sir Geoffrey to usher her personally back to her car. She did not breathe easy until she was back through the Swiss border crossing and on her way home.

She was taking a huge risk, and it had nothing to do with Sir Geoffrey keeping the art a secret.

In fact, her only hope of survival lay in his doing the exact opposite.

Chapter Six

M arc went for a run along the lake's perimeter. He was in the shower when his phone rang. Walton said, "I may have a lead."

"Why does that leave you sounding so worried?"

"You mean, other than facing a possible nuclear threat and all-out war with Iran?" Walton wheezed noisily. "I have received a call from the contact who directed me to the Geneva gallery. The man's name is Sir Geoffrey Treadwick. He has a possible lead. Emphasis on the word *possible*."

"Do you want me to follow up?"

"I have convinced him that you are both legitimate and highly discreet. He has agreed to a meeting."

"So what is the problem?"

"He has agreed on one condition," Walton replied. "That you bring Ms. Korban."

Marc was silent. Thinking.

"I told him nothing about the lady," Walton went on. "He already knew."

"Which confirms your suspicion that Mossad shares your confidential source," Marc said. "And he doesn't care if you know. Or maybe even, he *wants* you to know. Which means Mossad does as well."

"I agree on all counts."

"How did you two link up?"

"Sir Geoffrey approached me directly during the last spate of security breaches, back in the late eighties. It was as bad as the WikiLeaks scandal, only far more personal. His father was American, his mother linked to one of London's oldest Jewish families. At that time, the British secret service leaked worse than our own services. Sir Geoffrey asked that I never officially place him on our books. He operates at the level of prime ministers and presidents. Extremely rich."

"Where's the meeting to take place?"

"He is sending his private jet to collect you. It is landing in, ah, twenty-two minutes. He would not say where exactly the meeting is taking place, which means you are going in cold."

A man who sends a private jet to carry them to an undisclosed location suggested someone who knew the value of secrets. Marc started to point this out, but was interrupted by Walton's cough. "Are you ill, sir?"

"I can't seem to shake this cold." The old man wheezed hard. "And I don't have time to do what the doctor wants, which is to lie down."

"Maybe you should."

"First we must save the world. Good hunting."

The jet was a new Gulfstream IV, one of the world's largest private jets. The tables were burl veneer, the cup holders sterling silver, the seats ivory doeskin. Once they were airborne, the copilot offered them champagne, coffee, meals, then slipped back inside the cockpit and left them alone.

Kitra took in the luxurious cabin and said, "I really don't have the clothes for this."

"I doubt seriously," Marc replied, "that how you're dressed will make any difference."

"I don't mean with me. I mean, at all."

"I understand."

"I've never considered clothes very important. I know a lot of girls did. It was something I saw in the movies and on the television. I always thought of it as another of the odd things about life beyond the kibbutz. How women could spend hours at the mall, buying things they didn't need." She was seated directly across from him at the jet's front table. She avoided meeting his gaze by watching clouds beyond her window. "The Valentino you ruined was the first designer outfit I'd ever owned. I enjoyed picking it out. I didn't expect that, how much pleasure could come from shopping."

"I'm sorry about your suit. I really am."

"Why did you throw me into the lake?"

"Revenge."

Her lips compressed, hiding the smile that dimpled her cheeks. "You are so dead. Give me your gun."

"I pushed you in the lake to protect you from the blast. I stayed on the sidewalk to shield you from incoming danger. I didn't think it through. It just happened."

"You did what you did because it's who you are." Her face went solemn. "I shouldn't have yelled at you in the police station, in front of all those people."

"You had every right."

"It wasn't because of the outfit."

"I know."

She studied him for a long moment. Sunlight through the window turned her gaze impossibly clear. "I was wrong to expect you to join me on the kibbutz."

He did not know what to say.

Kitra went on, "You are who you are. An agent for the United States government. A man who is loyal to his cause and his nation. You would perish in the Judean plains."

He tasted words, but could not bring himself to speak.

"I will do this with you," Kitra continued, "because I am loyal as well, to my country and my cause. Because this is bigger than us, or our needs, or our pain, I will help you. And then I will go home."

"I understand," he managed.

"Do you believe me?"

"Yes. I wish I didn't. But I do."

"Will you be strong for both of us?"

"Kitra . . . I don't . . . I can't be certain."

She nodded slowly. "Will you at least try?"

They were escorted from the jet and bundled into a waiting Mercedes S-500. A customs official waited until they were inside the air-conditioned limo to request their passports. Marc saw their driver cast a condescending glance over Kitra's cotton shirt and drawstring pants and sandals, and hoped she hadn't noticed.

The drive from the Nice airport took just under an hour. Marc spent the time passing on Walton's intel regarding the man they traveled to meet. Sir Geoffrey Treadwick was chairman of a company founded by his maternal grandfather. He had taken over after the sudden death of his father when Geoffrey was only twenty-nine, and built it from a supplier of automotive and truck components into one of the world's largest conglomerates. He oversaw more than a hundred companies in virtually every country in the world. His passion was art. He had begun collecting as a teenager, when he had spent a small inheritance on the only artwork he could afford—drawings from second-rate impressionists and oils by a few modern artists that caught his eye. He proved to be as astute in his tastes as in his business, for by his twenty-second birthday his collection was estimated to be worth five million dollars, more than ten times what he had spent.

His most recent acquisition had been Edvard Munch's famous pastel entitled *The Scream*. The dramatic twelve-minute bidding at Sotheby's had set a new world record for art sold at auction, and the buyer's identity remained a closely guarded secret. Unlike most serious collectors, Sir Geoffrey had no interest in sharing his acquisitions with the general public. He was patron to no museums. He loaned out none of his works. Very few people were ever invited even to view his collection. Those few who did spoke of his treasures in hushed tones.

Sir Geoffrey's yacht was moored at the point where the longest harbor pier joined with the road lining the quayside. Across the quayside's avenue sprawled cafés and hotels and piazzas and fancy shops and the kind of people who never bothered to check prices. Passersby pretended not to stare as two uniformed sailors saluted Marc and Kitra and ushered them across the sidewalk, lifted the embossed rope guardrail, and led them onboard. Only tourists gawked in Monte Carlo.

The boat was a floating palace. Sir Geoffrey was a professional at putting people at their ease. He settled them on the foredeck and had his staff extend a broad canopy, which blocked the seafront avenue and the glitz from view, and granted them an uninterrupted panorama of the harbor, the lazy sailboats, and the Med. A cold lunch was swiftly set in place, smoked and poached salmon, tongue in aspic, salads, fruit, and the largest cheese board Marc had ever seen.

Geoffrey shooed away the staff and served them himself. He moved with the ease of a man long accustomed to playing host to the world. Kitra gradually relaxed, and even smiled a time or two. Marc was content to sit and wait for this man to make the opening move.

Kitra, however, did not share his patience. When the industrialist finally filled his own plate, she said, "Don't you think it's time we stopped this waltz?"

His smile seemed genuine. "I always did appreciate the direct manner of your people."

"Some would call us brusque."

"And there is nothing the matter with that. Far from it. The older I grow, the more impatient I become to fill my remaining hours with words and deeds that carry meaning."

"Will you tell us why we are here?"

"Because I may have something of value. But your respective governments do not agree. And because I know of the current rash of leaks, I insisted that any contact lay outside the purview of your intelligence agencies."

Kitra persisted, "But you specifically named me, Sir Geoffrey. How is that possible?"

"We share a common ally. As I do with your silent young man."

"If you are referring to the man who ordered me to Switzerland, I do not even know his name."

"You will. In time. If it is necessary." His gold cuff links sparkled as he dabbed his lips with the napkin. "It took me almost six years."

"What is your connection to Israel?"

"Officially, I have none. Unofficially, my mother's family was Jewish. Sephardic. They converted in the late middle ages, when the British crown offered the Jewish community three choices. Convert to Christianity, leave, or die. Most Jews returned to their faith and their synagogues once the ban was lifted. My own forebears decided it was better to let their roots remain hidden."

Marc knew his silence was making their host uncomfortable. But for the moment, it seemed useful to let Kitra play lead. She asked, "Do you know who blew up the gallery in Geneva?"

"Not for certain. But I can guess."

"Will you tell us?"

"Of course." His tone hardened. "Our enemies."

Kitra nodded slowly, as though he had given the answer she had expected. "Is that why we are here?"

"Indeed so." He set down his linen napkin and rose to his feet. "I suppose now is as good a time as any. Would you come with me, please?"

The Rodin was not a large piece, scarcely three feet tall. The dancer was frail and young and delicate. She waited for the chance to grow wings once more and fly to music Marc could almost hear. There was no reason for the art to make him sad, or wish for a chance to hold the woman next to him.

Sir Geoffrey said, "I understand you entered the Geneva gallery."

Marc cleared his throat. "I did, yes."

"Can you identify this item?"

"I saw a bronze statue of this dancer. But only for an instant.

I don't know anything about art. I can't say if it was this specific item or a duplicate."

"You know nothing about sculpture and yet you are moved by this, yes? Don't deny it, Mr. Royce."

"I'm denying nothing. It doesn't take an expert to appreciate beauty."

"Indeed not."

Kitra said, "I saw it too. From the doorway. I think this was it."

"I am assured it is. I was merely seeking confirmation that such an item did indeed reside inside the gallery just prior to the blast."

Marc asked, "How did it get here?"

"There is a woman I have known for years. A Persian. Her name is Rhana Mandana. It is a distinctly Persian mockery, to change one's name to something that rhymes. It means the queen of style, or something similar. Rhana is a leader in the international arts community, one of perhaps two dozen gallery owners who could approach me day or night and I would take their call. She is based in Lugano. Her clientele is legendary. Saudi princes, Nigerian oil kings, Chinese billionaires—her list contains many of the world's richest and most powerful names."

They were both watching him now. Marc said, "Persian."

"She does her best to hide her past, but I made it my business to check it out. I could not be seen to do business with a source of potential scandal. She was born with the name Maliheh. Members of her family were very high up in the revolution that overthrew the shah. She broke with them and fled the country. She married into money, a Swiss baron. He died quite young, and she opened the gallery. That was twenty-three years ago. Since then she has gone from strength to strength."

"Any indication she does business with the dark side?"

"None whatsoever. And I have checked, believe you me. As have others. There has never been a whiff of anything approaching impropriety."

"Until now," Marc said.

"Yes, well, precisely." Sir Geoffrey revealed his first moment of uncertainty. It did not suit him. He was bluff and hearty and robust, with a full head of grayish-blond hair and the ruddy cheeks and the heavy limbs of a man who lived a full life and loved every minute of it. Worry rested upon him like a borrowed cloak. "It leads one to wonder."

"Whether she perhaps sought you out specifically," Marc said, filling in the blanks. "Whether she knows about your contacts. Whether she is more than she seems, and on many levels."

Sir Geoffrey showed Marc tight approval. "I'm ever so glad you appear to be as sharp as Ambassador Walton described. Shall we return to the foredeck?"

When they were seated and coffee was served, Sir Geoffrey said, "The art world has suffered like everything else from the economic downturn, all but the very highest tier. This one level has become completely unhinged from reality. There are a growing number of new buyers, mostly Russian and Chinese, but the Arabs are back and the South Americans are showing some new financial muscle. They are desperate for safe places to park their money, and eager to show class by owning such items. For them, these works are not art. They represent two things: financial security and social leverage.

"Prices are rising so fast, no one can tell how much anything is worth. It's more a question of who is in the market and how much will they pay. And because so many of these acquisitions are secret, where the buyer and the seller are represented by attorneys and payments made through numbered accounts, there is always the risk that the deals are, in fact, illicit."

Marc had not been aware of the passage of time while they had been in the stateroom. But from the sun's position he had to assume they had lingered downstairs for over an hour. It surprised him. Viewing the dancer in that very private space, situated on a coffee table beneath the chandelier, had made for a very intense experience. He stared over the bow, out to where the waters sparkled golden in the late afternoon light, and wished he could return downstairs. Nothing about this spectacular setting compared to that little bit of bronze.

Sir Geoffrey went on, "Several months ago, I began hearing rumors. Not even that. Fragments of sentences. But when put together, they suggested something quite disturbing. Items were being put up for sale, but it was all a myth. They did not change hands at all. Instead, funds were transferred from one place to another. Everything aboveboard. Taxes paid, commissions, the works. But in truth all that happened was, money was being funneled past the barriers intended to isolate Iran. We're talking a few hundred million dollars, which is quite a lot, but not enough, say, to rebuild their oil industry or establish a new refinery."

"And then you heard about the development of long-range missiles," Marc said.

"At first I thought it was preposterous. But the intelligence community has wondered for years how North Korea man-

aged to scrape up the technology and the money to manufacture such long-range missile engines."

Kitra said, "So Iran has been using North Korea as a test
site."

"Perhaps," Marc corrected. "We're still lacking hard evidence."

"I must say, the very thought of those two pariahs col-
laborating on a missile fills me with dread."

"What do we do now?"

"That depends on whether Rhana has anything to offer,
and if so, whether she will help us. Do either of you know
anything about the art market?"

"Nothing whatsoever," Marc replied.

"I know enough to appreciate it, and nothing about buying it," Kitra said.

"But you need to play the lead on this," Marc decided. "In
case I was tracked to the gallery."

"I'm not doing this without you," Kitra declared.

"I've been told I make a fairly good bodyguard."

"You are that." Kitra turned to Sir Geoffrey. "You want
me to adopt a new identity?"

"If it can happen swiftly. And you'll most definitely need to
look the part—someone able to acquire high-end artwork."
He gave Kitra a careful inspection. "I suggest you return to
Geneva wearing the height of fashion."

"I am a product of the kibbutz," Kitra said. "I have made
a profession of being broke."

Sir Geoffrey managed to bow from a seated position. "Perhaps you will allow me to assist you in that regard."

"Excuse me, I need to check in." Marc rose and walked to
the stern railing, back where his voice could be swallowed by

the late afternoon traffic. He phoned Walton, summarized swiftly, then waited.

"I cannot get you and Ms. Korban papers in a matter of hours," Walton stated flatly. "Once, perhaps. But not now. The trails are too complex. It would require at least a week, and that is only after I have received approval."

Marc related what Kitra had told him about the mysterious caller, then said, "I'm thinking it may be time to phone that number."

Walton mulled that over, then said, "Do it."

Marc cut the connection, fished the paper from his pocket, and dialed. A man answered with one word: "Speak."

"This is Royce."

"What do you require?"

"A non-Israeli ID for Kitra Korban. She should come from old money. I'm her security."

"Where are you now?"

"On a boat docked in the Monte Carlo harbor."

"In that case, her return to Switzerland should be under the new alias. Give me four hours." Instead of hanging up as Marc expected, the man said, "We have friends in common, Mr. Royce. And I've checked out your file. Your extraction in Baghdad was most impressive work."

"Thanks. Where do we hook up?"

"Planeside at Nice Airport. I'll be in touch." The man clicked off.

Chapter Seven

Marc escorted Kitra to the Lanvin shop down the quayside from Sir Geoffrey's yacht. The industrialist had insisted upon this designer because their clothes suited the conservative perspective of old money, elegant and refined. He obviously did considerable business there, for they were met at the door by the shop owner. The cultured older woman took Kitra under her wing and shooed Marc away.

He walked to a stylish café down the boulevard. Dusk arrived in the languid manner of the Riviera. Most of the people strolling along the quayside were decked out like walking flowers, in pastels and sandals and jewelry. Their footsteps formed a leather-clad rainfall upon the cobblestones and the sidewalk fronting the harbor. Their talk was beautiful, though he did not understand a word. French spoken in the fragrant Mediterranean air was like a soft aria. Even the laughter was different here, coming more easily than anywhere else on earth.

He had never felt more isolated, more cut off from what other people called life.

He had always run toward danger. Risk was a part of life, something to assess and measure and analyze and overcome. He knew his strengths and he worked to overcome his weaknesses. In his own eyes, he managed to succeed where most failed. He survived.

And yet Kitra had managed to defeat him.

Only it was not Kitra. Nor was it their relationship. It was his fault. He could not control his feelings. He could not balance things out. He could not . . .

He lifted his espresso, then set it down untouched. There was only one answer. One solution.

Solitude had called to him for years. His wife had temporarily managed to keep him from turning that way, but she was gone. Stolen from him by a fate as cruel as what he now faced. He was never to love. He was a loner. Why fight it? Why allow himself to be hurt? His emotions were *his*. He was *not* powerless.

All he had to do was stop caring. Cut himself off from what made others weak and vulnerable.

Even as he formed the thought, he sensed the change. The strength he had taken for granted, the agility and the fierce power and the distilled rage all coming together. The force had been waiting for just such a chance. He clenched his hands in a reflexive response, as though his external body needed to reveal some tiny shred of what was happening inside. His heart did not freeze so much as gradually turn to steel.

He remained like that, locked in the act of shutting down his emotions, until his phone rang. He forced himself to breathe a long sigh and respond, "Royce."

"This is Kitra's contact in Tel Aviv. I thought now was a good time to introduce myself."

Marc started to ask how the man had gotten his number, then decided it would not do any good. "Yes, thanks."

"How were you planning to return to Geneva?"

"Sir Geoffrey has offered us his jet."

"Inform your ally that you have made other plans. Then proceed to the airport. Your papers and your jet both are waiting."

Most of Kitra's younger years had been spent worrying that the kibbutz would not survive. Her parents had done their best to shield their two children from the pressures they faced. But the realities surrounded them—in the air, in the superheated summers, in the dry arid soil. They were seeking to do the impossible, to build a community for Messianic believers. And the government as well as most of Israeli society wanted them to fail. Judeans who had acknowledged Jesus Christ as their Messiah and Savior were shunned by the greater community. Some Israeli families disowned anyone who openly followed Jesus. Other families said the *kaddish*, the prayer for the recently deceased. Their sacrifice for their faith was total. Their need for a haven was equally great.

Now that the rare-earth operation in partnership with the Kenyan cooperative was coming online, the kibbutz's future looked far more secure. And yet all the earnings would go to the community, not to the members. Kitra had no problem with this. She had always assumed that the world's hunger for possessions had passed her by.

But now, as she tried on one astonishing outfit after another, she was no longer so sure.

The store manager treated Kitra as she would a teenager in to buy her first adult outfit. Which, in some respects, was very true. The manager steered Kitra away from anything loud and cutting edge, which was a relief. Together they picked out two classical designs, a linen day dress in ivory and a professional suit in a rough silk weave that was colored like polished gray pearls. The collar and the cuffs were of silk velvet, as were the buttons down the jacket's front and the skirt's left side. The hem was just below her knees, but opened up the side with the buttons. The result was an outfit that looked both alluring and youthful. Kitra managed to avoid even glancing at the price tags. Then there were stockings and two blouses and a pair of slacks and three pairs of Ferragamo pumps. Nothing, not even genuine claims of exhaustion, was permitted to halt the process.

Kitra was then led next door, where a hair stylist and cosmetician awaited her arrival. She was shampooed and cut and given a facial. A manicure and a pedicure followed. She had never experienced either.

She returned to the shop dressed in café au lait slacks and matching blouse, with the signature looped gold Lanvin belt and purse and shoes. Marc took one look and froze. "Whoa."

She had never thought one word could cause so much pain.

Kitra noticed the change in Marc as soon as he recovered enough to announce, "We need to be leaving. Our plane's ready."

He hefted a number of Kitra's bags and led her out to a waiting taxi. The store manager personally escorted them, carrying the rest of her purchases. All Kitra held was the slender purse, fashioned from the skin of some reptile and dyed the color of face powder, with a gold clasp and a shoulder strap of woven leather and gold. It sparkled as she crossed the walk and slipped into the taxi. Marc did not slide in beside her, as expected. Instead he shut her door and stepped around to the front passenger door. The driver started to protest in French, for he had a newspaper and a book and a bagged meal spread out over the seat. But one look at Marc's stonelike expression was enough for him to shift the items into his lap.

Once they were under way, Marc said, "You understand why I'm up here?"

"Yes, Marc."

He spoke swiftly, his voice low, in case the driver understood some English. "From now on, this is what the world needs to see."

"Is something wrong?"

Marc hesitated. She had the impression he was sorting through various responses. "Our friend in Tel Aviv told me to cancel Sir Geoffrey's jet."

The taxi's rear seat smelled slightly of suntan oil and stale perfume. "Why is that important?"

"Any change at this point is a possible concern. We'll soon see."

The taxi wound its way up the Corniche and joined the autoroute. The rear seat felt empty to Kitra. The blue sky and the sparkling waters and the palms and the lovely houses all lost a touch of their allure. She knew she should not care that he had drawn away from her. They were headed into danger. People's lives were held in the balance.

These were the important things. This was why she stayed. So that they could help save lives.

Without turning, Marc said, "You look nice."

"Thank you, Marc." There was no reason why his words or the flat way he spoke them should hurt like they did. None at all.

As they approached the Nice Airport, Marc said, "Tell the driver we're going to the private jet terminal." She translated into French, and the man turned toward a small building on the north perimeter. Marc went on, "Someone should meet us at the gate."

The driver proceeded down the long palm-lined lane and halted by a uniformed official and another man in a short-sleeved white shirt bearing pilot's wings. The pilot grinned and offered them a two-fingered salute. Marc rose from the car and told her, "Please wait here."

She watched through her open window as Marc approached the pair. The pilot was lean and taut and probably in his fifties. Something about him left Kitra certain he did far more than fly jets. He shook Marc's hand and said something that Kitra could not hear. Marc responded, and the man's features turned feral. The pilot had sunglasses dangling from his shirt pocket. His eyes were gray and blank.

He walked back over and held her door. "The pilot's name is Carter Dawes. I've worked with him before."

She accepted his hand and rose from the car. "When was that?"

"A while ago, back in Iraq. Carter flies for a government contractor. Having him meet us is your Israeli's way of saying that he is in the loop. Right to the top."

When Kitra walked over, Carter saluted and handed the customs officer a French passport. The documents were neither old nor new. The officer checked her against the photograph, inspected Marc's documents, handed them back and wished them a pleasant flight. Marc told Carter to give him a hand, and together they returned to the taxi for her purchases. Carter then led her across the tarmac while Marc followed. Both men kept their gun hands free. She had no idea why that should frighten her so.

The plane was a Lear, smaller and tighter inside than Sir Geoffrey's Gulfstream, and the interior showed signs of wear. Kitra settled into a middle seat and felt an unexpected wave of longing. For what, she could not say. Marc slipped into the opposite seat and handed her the false passport. "Memorize the name."

She opened the cover and read, "Dominique Deschamps."

"The family name is real. Your details have been inserted into the federal system. You are from Nantes. It's a safe sort of city. Very conservative, very rich. And it's too far off the beaten track for anyone to check you out on the ground. A stranger asking questions about a wealthy family in Nantes will be noticed."

"How were they able to do this?"

He glanced out the window as the jet taxied toward the runway and took off. When the engines' noise became muted, he replied, "Governments call these a cover. They are developed over time. It takes a lot of resources. The wealthier the identity, the tougher it is to pull off. My guess is, either Mossad or CIA have allies within the family. If this is the case, Dominique is real, and she's agreed to go off grid until we're done."

She watched Carter Dawes step through the cockpit doorway and move down the aisle. He slipped into the seat beside Marc and asked, "Where are we at?"

"She was asking about her cover."

"To have the French offer you a clean cover means there are a lot of people who are taking this threat very seriously," Carter told her. "You do speak their lingo, right?"

"Yes. My mother is French." She asked Marc, "What about you?"

"I'm Marc Royce, fired from State Department Intel, hired as an operative by Lodestone Security, contracted out as your bodyguard." His smile held no humor at all. "Nice to meet you."

Carter asked Marc, "Can you tell me what this is about?"

"It's a fishing expedition. You didn't know?"

"Only that I'm on standby for the duration." He handed Kitra a sealed envelope. "This contains your brief."

She opened the flap and slid out a one-page overview, detailing family background and company holdings and addresses. There was also a pair of diamond-level credit cards and a French driver's license. "She's very rich."

"*You* certainly are," Marc corrected. He said to Carter, "We need a booking at some lakefront hotel."

"You're set for the de la Pais. I hear it's nice. They don't let help like me through the door."

"We also need a ride. Something flashy."

"Already taken care of."

Marc studied him. "You know the guy who calls Tel Aviv home?"

"We've met. Briefly. Once."

"You think maybe you could tell me who he is?"

Carter grinned. "I sort of figured having the dude draw me in was all you'd ever need in the way of establishing his creds."

Marc nodded. "Just asking."

"I expect the man will decide when you need to know something more. Right now, what you haven't heard can't be told to somebody else." Carter cocked his head. "Something else bugging you?"

"No."

"It's just . . . you strike me as a man headed into a free-fire zone. I always thought of Geneva as a place to get away from all that. You know something I don't?"

"We're five by five."

Kitra understood the flat tone behind Marc's words. He had gone cold. Carter thought it was because they faced an unseen threat. She knew better. It was not some immediate danger. It was *her*.

Carter rose to his feet, studied Marc a moment longer, then said, "Just so you remember, when things get noisy, I'm your man."

The flight to Geneva was so brief, the need for altitude over the Alps so great, as soon as they finished ascending they began their descent. The Lear dropped like a bird of prey. Kitra gripped her armrests against the sudden loss of weight. They landed so smoothly it was almost like kissing the earth. The plane taxied over, the stairs descended, and Marc gestured for her to remain where she was as he scoped the terrain. Then, "All right, we're ready."

Carter Dawes took a double handful of her shopping bags before stepping out. He followed them across the tarmac and waited while the customs officer checked their papers. The officer showed no surprise at a young woman accompanied by a pilot and a guard and no luggage other than multiple shopping bags. Carter followed them through the private-jet terminal and out into the evening. The day's final light was a faint glimmer that turned the western hills into purple silhouettes. Marc asked, "Any idea which ride is ours?"

"All I was told, the ride is red and the keys are in the ignition."

Marc pointed. "I see only one red car."

Carter Dawes laughed out loud. "That's not a car. That's a rocket."

The Ferrari was long and liquid and very low to the ground. Marc tried a door, and looked inside. "This must be it."

Carter laughed a second time. "Someone sure is trusting, leaving the keys inside a half-million-dollar ride."

Kitra gaped at the vehicle. "That car cost five hundred thousand dollars?"

"Don't get too comfortable," Marc warned. "This is only a loaner."

"What *is* it?"

"Ferrari F12 Berlinetta," Carter told her. "They call it a tourer, which means it won't rattle your bones as hard as the rear-engine models."

Marc found the lever beside the driver's seat and opened the trunk. "You know this how?"

"What can I say? I've been a petrol head since before I could walk."

Marc finished stowing the shopping bags and then shut the trunk. When he started for the driver's door, Kitra said, "Stop right there."

"What's the matter?"

"You think I'm going to let you drive this?"

"I'm your security, remember?"

"A lady doesn't have a car like this so she can be *chauffered.* Get real."

"Kitra, I think . . ."

He stopped because she showed him the flat of her hand. "First of all, it's Dominique you're addressing. Second, *I* am the decision maker. *Me.* And I say, I drive."

Carter watched this exchange with a smile that almost

split his face. "Now I see why the man was so tense. You folks play nice now, you hear?"

Kitra slipped behind the wheel, shut her door, and halted any further discussion by hitting the ignition button and letting the engine scream for her. He climbed into the rear seat.

The car was so much fun to drive, she waited through half an hour of heart-stopping speed to ask, "Where are we going?"

"Geneva. Back that way." Marc waited until she had turned the car around to ask, "Think maybe you could slow it down?"

"Most certainly," she replied. "But why?"

She waited for Marc to answer with some lip. But he merely glanced over his shoulder, back through the narrow rear window, and said, "At least we don't have to worry about anybody following us."

When Kitra pulled into the forecourt of Geneva's most exclusive hotel, the bellhops sprang into action. They pulled away a cone blocking an empty spot directly in front of the hotel restaurant's flower-lined balcony. Diners craned and ogled as she pulled into the spot, punched the gas one more time, then powered down.

Marc opened his door and said, "Wait for me to come around."

She could feel eyes on her as he shooed away the bellhop and opened her door, blocking her from the street with his body. She turned away from him, as though she had been doing it all her life, nodded to the bellhop, and started up the front steps. The majordomo was there to bow and push the revolving doors and welcome her in both French and English. She swept into the palatial lobby, stopped for one brief gawk, and decided that a girl could definitely get used to this.

She sat on a gilded settee while Marc signed them both in. He waited as she took her time deciding whether to accept the hotel manager's offer of coffee or champagne. Kitra declined both, then started toward another bellhop holding the elevator doors open. Two more attendants followed with her shopping bags. Marc trailed behind as the manager escorted her into the lift and spoke about the weather. On the way up she decided the last thing she wanted was to sit across from this stone-faced man over dinner. "I'm tired."

The manager spoke to her in French, "Mademoiselle can order anything she wishes from the restaurant and dine in her suite."

"Splendid," she replied. A suite, no less. "Thank you."

Their destination was a pair of double doors that opened at the end of the corridor. She had to remind herself not to gape, for when the manager unlocked the doors and bowed her through, the first thing she saw was the harbor fountain, burnished by massive lakefront spotlights, rising directly in front of her balconies.

Balconies. Plural. Two off the living room, another off her bedroom. Which was *five times* the size of her apartment on the kibbutz.

The living room of her suite was so large, and held so many flowers, she almost missed the baby grand piano in the corner.

Marc tipped the various attendees, checked every room and closet, then said, "I'm next door in six-fifteen."

"Fine."

"Do I need to tell you to contact me if you want—"

"No, Marc."

"Right." He walked to the door. "Double lock the door after I leave. Ditto for the balconies."

"Wait." She watched him turn around, searched his face for any scrap of emotion, saw none. "What time do we need to start?"

"We're waiting for a green light from someone in the know. And a direction we should take in the hunt. I'll call you as soon as I hear anything."

She nodded, accepting the unspoken. Wishing it did not hurt. Willing herself to be as impersonal and distant as he. "Good night."

Her suite came with its own personal butler, a fact she discovered when she tried to order dinner and the operator told her to press the button beside the phone. She ate on the balcony and watched the stars and the lake and the people below. Music drifted up from the restaurant. Lovers strolled and the wind sang.

She discovered a painful sort of pleasure in accepting Marc's coldness. In a sense it was right, very logical, and correct from every angle except the heart. Which could not be helped. By the time she finished dinner, she had decided there was nothing she could do except throw herself into the moment. She undressed and slipped into the hotel robe and slept and did not dream.

Chapter Eight

R hana left her home before dawn. She had not slept well, as the previous day's events had caused her past to rear its vile head and shatter her sleep. She could hear the fatigue in her voice as she phoned ahead and alerted the gallery's night guard of her arrival. There was nothing she could do about either her weariness or her dreams. If she was right, the past was about to become her future.

Westerners dismissed revenge with a few short quips, as though they could ignore the need to settle ancient wrongs. And perhaps they could. Americans in particular seemed to give little importance to the past. But Persians of Rhana's generation held a very different perspective. The past and the present were one. The future was often viewed as dark and burdensome, because so many of their actions and emotions were fated by what had already come before. Just like now, when she had very little chance of surviving, and knew there was no other way forward but to finish what she had started, all those long years ago. When she had sworn revenge on those who had destroyed everything and everyone she had once held dear.

She climbed from her Bentley and told the guard he was done for the night. She locked herself in the gallery and went to the storage unit. She turned off the cameras and opened the rear doors. The bonded transporters were there waiting, the truck pulled up to the loading platform. She opened the cage and instructed them to wrap each item, no need to box anything. She had worked with this particular group for years. They did their work swiftly and silently. She stood at the cage's outer door, where she could observe both the packing and the loading. When they were done, she signed the documents and saw them off. She waited for her staff to arrive, gathered them in her office, explained that she was working on a big new project and her movements might be unpredictable over the coming days. They accepted this in silence. It had happened before. She assigned them their duties and departed the way she had arrived.

She had scarcely begun her journey when her cell rang. She answered, and the deadly familiar voice said, "I await your news."

She felt the same adrenaline dread she always did upon hearing the man's unique blend of ice and silk. "I have your money."

"Of course you do. Have you not always performed as required?"

"Where shall I send it?"

"The same Geneva bank as before. How much did you make off this particular transaction?"

It was an improper question. But this man could demand anything of her, and he knew it. "Fifty million dollars, less expenses."

"Not bad for a week's work. What will you do with all that cash?"

"The same as always. Spend most of it on art."

"I never have understood your fascination for daubs of paint."

He then surprised her by asking, "Who made the purchase?"

She started to refuse, but a faint warning bell sounded deep within her. "His name is Sir Geoffrey Treadwick. He has been a client for many years. He is chairman—"

"I know all about Treadwick. Where is he now, still on his little toy boat?"

She glanced in her rearview mirror, terrified he might be tracking her, but saw only lines of trucks and cars. "We are meeting in Geneva in . . . in a few hours."

"I am glad you decided to trust me, Rhana. I would hate to lose you as well as our master forger, Sylvan. What a disappointment he proved to be. What a loss to us all."

She gripped the steering wheel more fiercely and waited for the tremors to pass. "Is that all?"

"No, Rhana. It is not. Where will the transfer of goods take place?"

"Why do you ask?"

"That should be clear enough. The Englishman is a loose end. We cannot permit that."

Rhana swallowed hard. Death followed very close indeed. "We are meeting at the Freeport Vaults."

He paused a moment, then decided, "That location won't do for closure. They are too well protected. You must draw Sir Geoffrey away. Someplace relatively isolated."

"He won't . . ." She was sure her pounding heart was audible.

"Yes, Rhana? What will your client not do?"

"I just thought of a place." She described what she had in mind. The act of speaking filled her mouth with ashes.

Which was hardly a surprise. Unless she was very careful, and they were all very fortunate, she had just consigned a trusted friend to the grave.

"This is a good idea, Rhana. You are certain he will come?"

"No. But I can try."

"Very well. Make it happen."

"He will be guarded. He always travels with security."

"Leave his bodyguards to me. Oh, and Rhana?"

"Yes?"

"Half of that commission you made—it is mine. For my troubles, and expenses. It is very costly to blow up a Geneva art gallery and demolish people's lives."

"Of course." She had feared he might even take it all. The fact that he had not done so implied the man was not done with her yet.

Rhana waited until he cut the connection to breathe out her fear. There was still a chance she could save Sir Geoffrey. Slim. But a chance.

Yet there was the risk that by saving Sir Geoffrey, she might well find herself claiming the crypt as her own.

Switzerland's methods for hiding illicit wealth did not end with numbered bank accounts. The government had mastered the art of selling secrecy. The entire legal system was built on the premise that no outsider, no government agency, nor any official body could breach their walls. They hid money for the vilest of people, through the darkest moments of recent history. And their efforts did not stop with cash.

Rhana took the turnoff for the Geneva Airport and drove past the terminals. She turned into a parking area and instantly found herself encircled once more by Swiss efficiency.

The lot was surrounded by a towering security fence topped with razor wire and lights. Her documents were carefully inspected by a vigilant guard, her name checked against a computerized list. Finally she was cleared to go inside.

Within the gates there was no indication as to why security was so tight. The windowless structure was squat and built of gray concrete and exposed steel. The reinforced portals were also gray. There was no sign indicating what lay within. For those fortunate few who had business here, none was required.

The Geneva Freeport Vaults was to art what a numbered Swiss account was to money. As long as goods were stored here, their owners paid no import tax or duties. All transactions were registered in Switzerland only, and the records were sealed by Swiss federal law. The names of buyer and seller were strictly confidential. No sales tax was charged. If the owner chose to take an item with them, that was their business. So long as the Swiss records were correct, the government felt no need to inform any other country as to what had happened, or where the item was going, or who was taking it. This one location was responsible for more illicit art transactions than everywhere else in the world combined.

Rent at the Freeport Vaults was astronomical. Their security was the best in the world. No break-in had ever occurred. Only the Swiss knew precisely how much treasure was held here. And they were not telling anyone.

Entering the vaults followed the same pattern as accessing a Swiss bank's safety deposit chamber. Rhana handed her passport to the guard at the front desk. Her fingerprints were checked. She informed the guard that a guest would be arriving. She was then passed through a second set of bulletproof doors and was escorted down a hallway.

When they arrived at Rhana's vault, the security passed his ID over one electronic reader while Rhana did the same at a second. The readers were positioned to either side of the steel doors, which meant that in the unlikely event of a security guard being overcome, no individual could access the two readers alone. And each additional visitor was matched by an additional guard. The Swiss were obsessive when it came to precautionary measures.

By the time Sir Geoffrey arrived, Rhana had stripped away the packing material from over half the items. Her visitor showed his avid love of art in the way he inspected each item. He did not observe. He *absorbed*. Rhana studied the treasures with him, and the man himself. She hoped desperately that he might manage to survive the coming assault.

He sighed his satisfaction, "There are more?"

"All the items are gathered here. I did not have the time—"

"No need. I will unveil the remaining pieces at my leisure. What you have here is more than enough to justify the purchase price."

"There is no provenance," Rhana reminded him. "Nor can you risk bringing in any expert."

He waved that aside. "You have made it perfectly clear. These are for my personal enjoyment only."

"Did you do as I suggested and contract for a vault yourself?"

"It's all been arranged. They were kind enough to give me one just down the hall." He even managed to wince with grace. "I don't mind telling you the cost is staggering."

"But worth it." She reached for the phone connected to the side wall. The internal phone system was essential, for the building was designed to blanket all incoming signals.

Rhana requested the assistance of five movers. They came within minutes. All the security guards carried white cloth gloves for just such occasions. The packing and moving of treasures was all part of their training.

When the transfer was made, Sir Geoffrey asked, "Do you have time for a late lunch?"

It was the opening Rhana had been looking for. "Nothing would please me more. But I have booked myself into the Rhone Spa. Why don't you join me?"

"I believe I've heard of it somewhere."

Rhana pretended to be astonished. "My dear, it is the most exquisite place on earth. You *must* come. We can lunch there, and then you will take a course of treatments and emerge transformed."

He smiled thinly. "I am a bit old for such transformations, I fear."

"What nonsense. The waters are rejuvenating; they've been in use since the Romans. And the place itself is divine."

"And equally expensive."

"Well, of course it is, darling. But never mind that. You will be my guest."

"Stuff and nonsense."

"I insist. Actually, it's the only way you can come on short notice. They require references. It is that sort of place." She smiled. "Who knows, you might even meet your fourth wife."

"Fifth, my dear. Fifth."

"Oh my, you are a rogue."

"I had hoped to introduce you to a friend's daughter," he said. "The Deschampses of Nantes. Perhaps you have heard of them?"

She caught the ever so slight false note to Sir Geoffrey's enthusiasm. The air seemed to evaporate from her vault. "The name, perhaps."

"New money. Industry and communications, mostly. We do business together. Their daughter, Dominique, is a charming young lady." With every word, Sir Geoffrey's casual gusto became more clearly artificial. "The family knows nothing about art, but Dominique appears very open to instruction. She's recently acquired a lovely apartment in the eighth *arrondissement* and is eager to start a collection of her own. Naturally I thought of you."

Rhana wondered if he might possibly hear the thunder of her heart. "By all means, you must bring her along."

Rhana left Geneva on the main lakeside highway. She waited until she had rounded the lake's far end, some fifty miles away from the city center. She pulled into a highway rest stop and walked over to stand between two idling trucks. She used a brand-new cellphone to make the call.

Her secret ally answered on the first ring. "Yes?"

"I have news. Perhaps."

"What is that noise?"

Rhana told him where she was. "For this, I need to be certain we cannot be overheard."

"You are right to be cautious. Proceed."

Rhana related the morning's phone call, the way the money was to be handled, the discussion regarding Sir Geoffrey, everything. As she finished, one of the trucks revved its engine and drew away. She walked around the remaining truck, staying as much as possible in the shadows.

Her ally's name was Amin Hedayat. In Farsi the words

94

meant *honest guide*, which he most definitely was. Especially now. Amin said, "I grow increasingly certain that this could be the moment we have long awaited."

Having her most dreadful hopes expressed by a man she trusted with her life only heightened her apprehension. "What should I do?"

"No, no, Rhana. You are the one who has been living this. You are on the front line. First you tell me."

She had to stop and take several tight breaths, as though each word had to be forced out through her fear. "Let them make the attack. See if this Dominique Deschamps is who they say she is. Or something more. And if more, how good they are. Because if we are to survive . . ."

"They must be very good indeed," he finished for her. "Very well. I agree. Only one thing, Rhana."

"Yes?"

"If you can, do your best to stay alive. We need you still."

Chapter Nine

Sir Geoffrey demanded, "Is this a safe line?"

"My cellphone is brand-new," Marc replied. "The only people who possibly could be listening in are doing so because we want them to. What about at your end?"

"I don't . . . I did as I was instructed. I bought a new phone from a kiosk I selected at random."

"Then we're good. Where are you?"

"The back room of an utterly dreadful café. The area surrounding the Freeport Vaults houses mostly an immigrant population. The next table is smoking a hookah."

"I imagine you're safe. What's up?"

Sir Geoffrey described what had happened. "Can you make any sense of this?"

"It's one of two things," Marc decided. "Either your friend, this Miss Rhana, wants to thank you for a sizable cash deal, or she is setting you up. Unless . . ."

"Yes? Do go on."

"Unless she has made these arrangements precisely because she wants to meet with us. Somewhere safe and remote."

"Which this most certainly is. The Rhone Spa is out beyond Chamonix."

"Where is that exactly?"

"Clear on the other end of the lake, right down the Rhone Valley. The spa itself is quite lovely, from what I've heard. Frightfully expensive."

"Do you have the time to do this?"

"My helicopter is standing by, and I left my day free."

Marc felt he had to point out, "You can't keep the art-work."

"My dear boy, I'm well aware of the price of honesty. What shall we do?"

"The only thing we can," Marc replied. "Go and meet her. But first I'm going to make a few calls."

Kitra was seated on the hotel restaurant's veranda when Marc appeared. Marc wore his dark suit and a dark gray shirt and matching tie. He also wore his mask. "We have to go."

Kitra was already rising. She said to the waiter, "Would you please put this on my room?"

The bellhop took unique pleasure in pulling the Ferrari around the hotel's front loop. Kitra slipped in behind the wheel, revved the engine, and asked, "Where are we going?"

Marc unfolded a map and pointed at a location far down the length of the lake and beyond. "We need to hurry."

The gearshift was a small lever positioned just below the starter button. There were two selections for drive. One put the car in fully automatic mode. Kitra chose the other, which activated the paddle shifters on the steering wheel. "Good."

Marc spent the entire journey on the phone. For a time, Kitra listened with one ear. She knew he was making these calls in her presence so she would understand where they were going and why, and what the risks might be. He did not speak directly to her except to give directions.

Eighty kilometers after leaving Geneva, the lake ended at the nondescript industrial city of Aigle, where the road turned north and west. They stopped for gas and headed into the Rhone Valley. The Alps rose in ponderous majesty to either side, great green slopes topped with ice that gleamed fiercely. Kitra knew all about the region's history. When she had been young, she read every book on geography the kibbutz's meager library contained. They had provided her escape from the Judean plains that both protected and imprisoned her.

The Rhone valley had been formed by one of the largest glaciers that had ever ground its way through Europe. A deep layer of sediment had been its departing gift to a newly formed valley. The road wound through verdant fields, sparkling and fresh with the greens of a growing season. The lower slopes on either side were traced like corduroy with vineyards. Higher up clung the glacier's final remnants.

The road began climbing, and the Ferrari responded with the tightly controlled ferocity of a car that had been born for such moments. The hairpin curves rose and swooped and twisted in waves as beautiful as poetry.

The Rhone Spa was a medieval castle poised upon its very own mountain. Kitra turned off the main road leading up to Chamonix, navigated down a narrow defile, then roared up a hill shaped like a perfect cone. Every inch of the slopes was given over to vineyards. She powered down her window and the fragrances of fresh earth filled the vehicle. There was no reason why the perfume of a new season should make her sad. None at all.

They pulled through ancient battle ramparts and parked in the forecourt. The rear bastions had been torn down, granting the castle an uninterrupted view of the mountains and the valley. To her left was a small grassy landing strip holding a helicopter. To her right sprawled an array of luxurious vehicles. She pulled the Ferrari between a Maybach and a pearl-gray Bentley and cut the engine. The silence was deafening.

Marc said, "You drive beautifully."

"Thank you, Marc. My brother, Serge, is the car fiend. He will turn absolutely green when he hears what I have been doing."

He studied the castle up ahead. "You will be meeting with a Persian art dealer who has sold an entire gallery of stolen goods to our ally. Washington is split down the middle about this Rhana Mandana. Half think she is actively supporting terrorism. The other half thinks she's just another parasite who couldn't care less what side of the law she stands on, so long as she gets paid."

"What do you think?"

He settled back in his seat. "Either could be right. But of all the clients she could have approached with this deal, she went to the one man who's connected to U.S. intelligence. And possibly to Mossad."

"Aren't those connections secret?"

"Yes. Just like my mission to Geneva." He looked at her. "Ready?"

Chapter Ten

Rhana's first thought upon meeting Sir Geoffrey's young friend was, she is as lovely as she is sad, and she is very sad indeed. Sir Geoffrey played the doting patron well, but Rhana was not convinced. "Rhana, may I have the pleasure of introducing Dominique Deschamps. My dear, this is the lady I mentioned, Rhana Mandana."

The beautiful young woman spoke in French, "A distinct honor, madame."

Rhana detected a slight accent, the heady flavor of desert spices. "What a delightful flower you are. I am certain we will soon be the very best of friends." She turned to the hovering attendants and announced, "Sir Geoffrey will have the treatments we discussed."

"Of course, madame."

She pretended not to notice the man's worried frown. "Have a good time, Geoffrey."

"But . . . I had hoped to join you."

"Don't be absurd. Why on earth would you want to enter the women's section?"

"I'm responsible for the young lady's safety."

"The spa is as private here as a harem, and just as safe. You should feel completely reborn by the time we meet you again in three hours for a meal." She beckoned Kitra forward. "Come along, my dear."

The dressing cubicles were lined in fragrant sandalwood. Rhana slipped into a spa robe and sandals and was waiting when the young lady emerged. She made the fluffy robe appear as elegant as an evening gown. Rhana said, "With your youth and natural beauty, you need very little pampering. But my bones ache, and a sauna and a whirlpool will do me a world of good. Would you indulge an old woman?"

"I am in your hands, madame."

"I insist you call me Rhana." She led Kitra down the winding stone stairs, into what once had been the castle crypts. The ancient stone had been polished, careful lighting warmed the place, and the chambers were opulent. Rhana waited until they were inside the sauna to ask, "And what should I call you?"

"My name—"

"Please wait a moment. We are thirty feet below the surface, surrounded by solid granite. No one can hear us. It may be our only chance for utter confidentiality. So I want you to think carefully. Do you truly want to waste this time on a lie? Because we both know that you are not born to wealth. You might have the clothes and the car and the bodyguard. But frankly, you wear them like someone else's fur stole."

The young woman hesitated briefly, then replied, "If people have gone to all this trouble to create a fiction—and I am not saying that it is—why should I trust you?"

"An excellent question. You have requested that I grant you trust in return. Very well. I agree. Do you know my true name?"

The young woman did not hesitate. "You were formerly known as Maliheh Masoumeh."

"Correct. So here is my most precious secret." Even though she had come knowing such a moment would probably arise, even though she had invested much into making it happen, still she felt her throat constrict with the effort of revealing secrets she'd held close for decades. "My father, blessed be his memory, was one of the largest purveyors of carpets in all Iran. But my father also had a secret. One that only a handful of people knew. He was a pastor."

The news rocked the young woman. "What are you saying?"

"In the final years before the imams took power, missionaries roamed far and wide throughout Persia. They came in as teachers and businessmen. But they brought with them Bibles, and they stayed to teach. Many of my people became followers of Jesus. But all in secret. Such secrecy you cannot imagine. They hid from the shah's secret police, from the imams, from their own families.

"The best carpets are woven by women in small villages, who learn the art of weaving from their mothers and grandmothers. All winter they weave, and perhaps they finish one carpet. One carpet per family per winter. So my father traveled, and he became the, how you say . . . ?"

"Conduit," she replied softly. "The go-between."

"Thank you. My father was the one safe channel between these small gatherings. Home churches, they are called in the West. In Iran, they were havens. The only place of safety many of these believers ever knew. And then, well, you know what happened."

"The shah fell." The younger woman almost chanted the words. The singsong way she expressed her sympathy made Rhana sure she carried Middle Eastern blood.

"The shah fell and chaos resulted," Rhana agreed. "But

my father continued to travel. He had to. Families depended upon him. Even though we knew we were being watched, he went. Everyone who had money was under surveillance." Rhana became silent, remembering the long, dark hours of worry. The concerns, the fears that grew and grew until they finally blossomed with the inevitability of death. "Seventeen months after the shah fell, my father went on another journey. He never returned."

"I'm very sorry, Rhana."

She inspected the lovely face and thought she saw tears. Remarkable, coming from a stranger. "The Revolutionary Guard claimed bandits killed him for the money he carried. We accepted this, and we mourned our loss. We escaped, my mother and I. We came to Switzerland, where my father had established a carpet business as a haven, in case of just such an event. It took four years for me to learn what truly happened. By that time, my mother, thankfully, had passed on. My father was betrayed by someone in one of the home churches. He was taken. He was questioned. He did not give up any other church. But he paid for his silence. Oh, how he paid."

Rhana stopped, forcing herself to find a way to breathe. How could it happen, that grief could emerge so fresh and raw after all these years? Why was there no healing?

Kitra finished for her, "All the other churches managed to escape because of your father's sacrifice."

Rhana rose to her feet. "Come. We have been in here too long. The heat has gotten to my head."

"My name is Kitra Korban."

"You are indeed French?"

"Through my mother. And Jewish American through my father. I was born and raised in Israel."

"What are you doing here in Switzerland?"

"I have wondered that," Kitra finally said, "from the moment I arrived."

They were seated in the walled garden connected to the women's changing rooms. One other table was occupied by a young woman and a crone in a wheelchair. Rhana had seen them here before. The old woman was the matriarch to one of Switzerland's oldest banking families. She and her live-in caregiver came to the spa once each week because the waters rising from the springs helped the woman's rheumatism.

Rhana asked, "Your father has connections to Mossad?"

"Apparently so. I never knew of such a thing until he called and said I should trust a man who never told me his name. It's all very confusing."

"Of course it is. What does your father do?"

"He runs a kibbutz."

"I know the word, but I do not understand. This is a communal farm, no?"

"We have a farm. But we also run high-tech industries. My father founded the kibbutz to make a home for followers of Jesus who have been shunned by Israeli society."

It was hard to say what shocked Rhana the most, the news of their shared faith, or the matter-of-fact way Kitra spoke the words. "Shunned?"

"Banished, fired, disowned. There are several kibbutzim that serve as such havens. My father wanted more. He sought to give believers a place where they could grow and prosper, where their talents could be fully utilized."

105

"And the man who waits by your lovely car, he is connected how?"

"Marc Royce is a former intelligence officer with the U.S. State Department. He was fired four years ago because he took leave to care for his wife, who was dying. She did eventually die."

Rhana heard the affection in Kitra's voice, though the young woman did her best to retain the neutral tone. But the love and the anguish were there, for someone who had a lifetime's training at perceiving secrets. Rhana said, "And now he protects you."

"Actually, in the beginning it was the other way around." Kitra described how she had been sent to warn him of the attack, and how he had barely managed to survive the blast. Then she asked, "Did you cause the bomb?"

"No, my dear, I did not."

Kitra nodded, a simple gesture that carried a world of meaning. As did her words, "I believe you."

"And for that, I am sincerely grateful."

"Who was behind the attack?"

"That answer requires my receiving permission from others. You understand, yes? My allies must decide for themselves to offer you the hand of trust."

"Marc will also want to ask you questions before he accepts you as an ally. There are many in Washington who wonder if you are the enemy."

Rhana shivered at the words. "Though that news is hardly unexpected, it fills me with fear."

Kitra nodded solemnly. "It should."

Chapter Eleven

The castle's circular drive ran between the main building and the front gates. Remnants of a moat formed a narrow channel between the rear gardens from the green landing strip and was crossed by a carved stone bridge. One of the gatehouses was used by the bodyguards. Its coffee table held a variety of magazines, and a flat-screen television aired a soccer match. Broad windows overlooked both the castle's front drive and the road leading back to Chamonix. Marc poured himself a cup of coffee, checked in with Walton, and waited. Ten minutes later, a Citroen sporting the flat blue color used only by police parked next to Kitra's Ferrari. Marc approached as Agent Behlet rose from the passenger side and Chief Inspector Reynard opened the driver's door.

Behlet smirked as he said, "You of course remember Inspector Reynard."

"Inspector."

"If it isn't the American secret agent."

"Remy, please. There is no need—"

"I completely agree. There is no need for this secret agent to remain on Swiss soil. Have you blown up any businesses lately, Agent Royce?"

Behlet sighed.

"You were right to bring him. And I'd appreciate it if you both please call me Marc."

"Remy, you see? This gentleman is being as nice as he possibly—"

"This is not a discussion about manners. This is about murder. This is about bombings on Swiss soil."

"And we are all looking for the killers. Are we not, Marc?"

"That's why we're here," Marc replied. "Before we go any further, I need your agreement that nothing will be passed on to anyone, at any level, without my express permission."

Inspector Reynard colored, but before he could erupt, Agent Behlet said, "I agree for the both of us."

The Geneva police officer rounded on him. "How *dare* you say such a thing. You are no longer even a true *agent*."

"Our federal government disagrees." Bernard remained unruffled by the policeman's ire.

Marc asked, "You are seconded to the insurance industry?"

"Very good, Marc. I am impressed. Actually, in this country we make a clear differentiation between insurance and reinsurance. You understand the term?"

"You insure the insurers."

"Correct. The Swiss reinsurance industry is third in size only to banking and tourism."

"And your investors have a great deal at risk with this recent bombing."

"Over half a billion dollars." Bernard smiled thinly. "Needless to say, we are eager to get our hands on any information that might assist us."

Marc said, "We have evidence that the original artwork was replaced with forgeries before the blast."

Bernard's eyes widened. "You are certain of this?"

"I have no knowledge of art. But since the bombing I have seen a bronze statue of Rodin's dancer that looked genuine to me."

Bernard returned to the car, pulled a file from his briefcase, and extracted a photograph. "Does this look familiar?"

Marc inspected it carefully. "It appears to be exactly the same. But so did the one I saw inside the gallery."

"To create a copy of that quality means this has been planned for some time."

"It would be hard to find a forger?"

"Very difficult indeed. There are two, perhaps three people in the world who could duplicate a Rodin bronze."

Marc said, "What if . . . ?"

"Yes? Do please continue."

"What if they used the gallery owner to obtain the forgeries?"

Bernard showed no surprise whatsoever. "There is a vicious irony to the thought, no? But to reply, we have been hearing rumors. Which my superiors tend to disregard. But I heard that our dearly departed gallery owner was feeding a gambling addiction through illicit activities."

"Which would explain why Sylvan was murdered," Marc said. "If his cohorts discovered his gambling was out of control, putting their plans at risk."

"Sylvan Gollet had business in Hong Kong. He always stayed in hotels with large casinos. Where he gambled. Nightly. And lost. His losses are hidden by the casinos, who are almost as secretive as our native banks. But yesterday a source confirmed that Sylvan has managed to lose several fortunes."

"So the bad guys learned of his habit," Marc said. "And how he was making extra money by selling well-executed forgeries. And started drawing the attention of federal authorities."

"So they decided to use his errors against him," Behlet continued. "They made him forge duplicates of everything in his shop."

"And then they replaced the originals with the forgeries. And then killed him. And set me up."

The inspector's gaze shot back and forth between them. "All right, that is enough. Who is 'they'?"

Behlet gave him mock surprise. "Why, that should be self-evident, Inspector. The killers."

"And who are these killers?"

"That's why we're here," Marc said. "To find out."

"And the original artwork?"

"Most of it is in a Geneva Freeport vault, waiting for you to collect it," Marc replied. "The gentleman who helped us is very certain he has been given the originals. I am proceeding on his word."

"You say, *most* of the items."

"The Rodin bronze is elsewhere. I would like to ask that you lease this item to the man who has helped you retrieve the others."

"*Lease* this to him."

"That's correct. For a dollar."

"For how long?"

"The remainder of his life."

Behlet pretended to give this careful thought. "Does he know of this request?"

"No. I thought of it myself. If you can't do it, he will never know."

"He is important to you?"

"Very. Oh, and you'll need to repay him for the cost of acquiring your articles."

"How much?"

"A hundred and fifty million dollars."

Bernard Behlet stifled the inspector's protest with an up-raised hand. "I will need to pass the lease arrangement by my superiors, but I see no problem with either—"

"I need something else."

The Swiss agent had a truly pleasant smile. "I thought there might be more."

"Several things, actually. One now, the others later. I want your government's permission to fly a drone over this region." Marc relayed the activities that had drawn them to the spa. "We are hoping to be used as bait."

The inspector wheeled about. "We are trapped?"

"Don't stare, Remy. Of course we're not trapped. Marc has no intention of dying. Isn't that right, Marc?"

"Hopefully not today."

"Where is the drone now?"

"Hovering above the NATO base in Strasbourg, waiting for your green light."

Behlet fished the phone from his pocket. "One moment."

The two spent the next hour together in adjoining cubicles, worked over by women who were trained to take every muscle in the body apart, then put them back together, doing so with a minimum of discomfort. Rhana could sense Kitra's presence through the shoji-screen wall, and knew the young woman would not speak unless Rhana did first. Kitra was a product of many cultures but had learned respect for her elders and was polite by nature. And honest. Behind her closed eyes,

Rhana saw again how Kitra released a great burden simply by telling the truth. Which was so alien to Rhana's world that she felt threatened.

Kitra's character formed a mirror, in which Rhana saw clearly the truth about herself. She had sensed it for years in odd, quiet moments. It was one reason why she gave herself so fully to whatever indulgence was closest, and why danger had always held such a heady allure. Everything about Rhana's life had been structured so as to push away the truth.

Spending time with Kitra had heightened Rhana's awareness of how the corruption had eaten away at her soul. She was tainted. She was lost. She had created such a distance that she could condemn good people, even lay here in coddled opulence while they faced death.

Her face was cradled in a pillow that looped around her forehead and cheeks, with a central opening through which she could breathe. Rhana shifted her face from side to side, wiping away the tears.

The masseuse asked, "Is madame comfortable?"

"The session must end early," Rhana replied. She raised her voice. "Kitra?"

"Yes, madame?"

"Please send away the attendant."

A few seconds' pause, then, "What is it?"

Rhana asked her attendant to leave and then slid open the woven screen. "I must ask you a question, and in return you must give me the truth."

"I have given you nothing else."

"I believe you," Rhana said, and felt the burning remorse of having lost the comfort of such candor. "Tell me this. Did you and your people have anything to do with the attack on the Geneva gallery?"

"We did not."

"I accept your statement. Others doubt you. I need proof that you are on our side. That is why we are here today."

Kitra nodded acceptance. "Whose side is that?"

"Proof," Rhana replied, shaking her head. "Give me this, and I will answer all your questions. For now, all I can tell you is, by speaking to you as I do now, I put my life and all I possess in your hands."

"I thank you for the gift of trust, madame," Kitra said quietly.

"The young man in the forecourt, you must warn him."

Kitra gripped the towel more tightly. "What do you mean?"

"There is going to be an attack. How it will be fashioned, I do not know. They are going to come after Sir Geoffrey, and they will slaughter everyone who stands in their way."

Kitra gave no time for further questions. She slipped on her robe and bolted, only to stop just beyond the portal and return long enough to hug Rhana with a fierceness that she felt in her bones. Kitra whispered, "Thank you," and vanished.

When Rhana finally moved, it was with the slow motions of a very old woman. As usual, she avoided glancing at her reflection as she passed through the foyer. But as she climbed the stairs up to the changing rooms, Rhana found herself wondering if there was indeed the chance, however slim, that one day mirrors would no longer be her enemy.

Chapter Twelve

Walton told Marc, "We have no sign of infiltrators."

"Hold one." Marc hit the speaker button on his phone. "Sir, I am joined by FIS Special Agent Behlet and Geneva Police Inspector Remy Reynard."

"Gentlemen."

Marc explained to the two Swiss officers, "This is my superior in Washington. We spoke with him in the chief inspector's office."

For once Remy Reynard was willing to follow the agent's lead. Behlet said simply, "Understood."

"Go ahead, sir."

"The drone has done two full circuits of your environ. We have tracked both visually and with infrared scanners. The road beyond the Chamonix turning is empty. The only movement within five klicks comes from a pair of deer."

"Thank you, sir."

"Keep me in the loop."

"Roger that. Royce out."

Remy said, "So we made this trip for nothing?"

Bernard Behlet pointed out, "We have recovered the stolen artwork."

"So *he* says."

Marc shook his head. "They're out there. The danger is real and inbound."

"But your superior just told you—"

"What he said was, they could not be seen. Which means only one thing. They are already here."

The police inspector started to scoff, but was halted by his associate's reply, "I agree with your assessment."

"What do you—?" Marc's phone rang. He checked the readout. "I need to take this."

Kitra's voice held the steely tone Marc had last heard in Kenya. "The attack is real."

"Rhana told you that?"

"She did, yes. Marc, she says by giving us this information we place her life in our hands."

"Understood. Did she say who is the target?"

"Sir Geoffrey."

"Any details?"

"She doesn't know any. Only that it is happening. Here. Today."

"All right. I want you to get the lady and Sir Geoffrey and meet me in the lobby ASAP."

"Two minutes."

"Make it less." He cut the connection and relayed what he had just heard.

Bernard Behlet demanded, "Can we trust her?"

"My Washington people would say no. My gut says yes."

The chief inspector scowled. "I am thinking we should arrest—"

"Remy, you need to learn to trust this man," Bernard said. "Lives may be at stake. He is a specialist at such events. If anyone can keep us all safe, it is Marc Royce."

"You know this how?"

"I have accessed his records. He is precisely who he says he is. He has given us nothing but the truth from the very outset. The time for doubt and argument is over. He says we must protect this Rhana, this source, and I accept this, and so should you."

"We have to move," Marc pressed.

Bernard gave the inspector a long look, then asked Marc, "What do you want us to do?"

"How long would it take to get reinforcements up here?"

"Half an hour," Remy replied. "They would need to drive up from Aigle."

"Too long. I need a gun."

The police inspector sternly replied, "No gun. Guns are forbidden to foreign operatives on Swiss soil. We do not protect Swiss law by breaking it."

Marc had expected the response. "Please tell me you're carrying."

"The ban on weapons is directed at you, monsieur. Not an officer of the Swiss police. Of course I'm armed."

"As am I," Bernard confirmed.

"Okay, the inspector comes with me. Bernard, you watch the entry. No one comes through those gates."

Marc and the inspector climbed the stairs and entered the spa's foyer, where he found Kitra standing between a striking older woman and Sir Geoffrey, who demanded nervously, "What on earth is the matter?"

"We have an indication that the spa might be coming under attack."

The woman at the front desk reached down, and Marc snapped, "Don't touch the alarm."

"Monsieur, I have specific instructions—"

"Do as he says," Remy barked, and showed her his badge. "Chief Inspector, Geneva Police. You are duty manager?"

"Yes, Inspector."

"How many staff are on duty?"

"Including the chef and masseuses and cosmeticians, eleven. Plus the duty guard at the front gates."

"Are there any guards inside the building?"

"No, monsieur. They are strictly forbidden to go beyond this front foyer."

Marc asked, "Besides these three, how many other guests are there?"

She checked her book. "Sixteen."

"Are any besides Sir Geoffrey here for the first time?"

One glance at the police inspector was enough for her to reply, "One other. A woman from Finland. Referred by a client we have known for many years."

"Ask her to join us. Immediately," Marc said. "Don't tell her anything."

The duty manager nodded at a hovering attendant, who vanished.

Marc asked, "Is this the only way in or out?"

"There is a rear entry leading to the kitchen. For supplies."

Remy asked, "Can it be sealed?"

"Certainly, monsieur." She turned to the computer connected to the security system. "It is done."

Marc gestured to the three who watched with wide-eyed alarm. "We need to get the two women and the gentleman safe. If there's an attack, these three are the target."

"We have a security room in the cellar." The duty manager lifted her phone. "May I call for an assistant?"

"Do it." Marc turned to Sir Geoffrey. "Did you come with bodyguards?"

"Two gentlemen I've known for years."

"Can you phone and tell them to do whatever I ask?"

As he made the call, another attendant arrived and was directed to lead Kitra, Rhana, and Sir Geoffrey downstairs. As they departed, a woman in her fifties entered from the women's wing. Her English was crisply irritated. "What's the meaning of this?"

Remy showed his badge. "I beg your pardon, madame. Would you happen to have your passport with you?"

The attendant said, "I took the liberty of bringing up your purse, madame."

"What on earth for?" But she did not wait for a response. She fished through her purse, handed over her document, waited while it was inspected, then said, "Now will someone tell me what is going on?"

Marc had seen enough. The woman was pudgy and flaccid and carried herself with the lax attitude of someone not at all familiar with exercise. He gave Remy a slight shake of his head. Not an assassin.

"I beg your pardon, madame. We had word of a possible thief intending to rob patrons. Your name was one of three guests who are here for the first time."

"Well, I suppose I should be angry over the interruption, but it is nice to know we are granted such protection."

Remy sketched a salute. "I do so hope you enjoy your stay."

When the attendant had led the woman back into the rear chambers, the duty manager asked, "What now?"

"If there's indeed a threat, there can be only one other place for them to hide," Marc said.

The duty manager's name was Helene. In her early forties, tall and pale blond, her skin almost translucent, she
led them across the forecourt carrying a tray of fresh sandwiches. Marc held a coffee urn while Remy carried a dozen
clean mugs. One of the security detail held the guardroom
door and smiled at their arrival. Helene did a quick swing
around the room, speaking with each guard in turn. There
were nineteen in all, eleven men and eight women. Some of
their female clients insisted on being guarded only by men;
others refused to have a man anywhere near them. Helene
asked the gathering which of them accompanied Sir Geoffrey and said she had a message. The two men followed
her outside.

They crossed the forecourt and climbed the front steps,
where Helene announced, "This is as far as I can allow them
to come."

"Understood." Marc turned to the security detail. "You
received a call from Sir Geoffrey."

"Affirmative."

"My name is Marc Royce. We suspect that a killer is among
the guards. His target is your man."

To their credit, neither showed any reaction. The taller of
the pair said, "Any idea who?"

"None."

The shorter man was built like a fireplug, with a shaved
head and a jaw that would have done credit to a Brahma bull.
"You certain there's a definite hit?"

"No. But the source is credible. We are assuming the risk
is real."

"The bloke with the smart clothes, the one standing by
the guard-station door, he's with you?"

"He is FIS. Swiss intel. And this is Inspector Remy Reynard with the Geneva Police."

"So how do you want this to go down?"

Marc asked the duty manager, "Did you notice anyone suspicious among the guards?"

"Not really." Her hands started to flutter. "But I seldom have any contact with them. They do not come inside. I normally send a maid out if anything is required."

"How do you alert a guard when the guest is to depart?"

"I ring the guard station. In Sir Geoffrey's case, it would be a few minutes early because they have to start the helicopter and request clearance for takeoff."

"Who flies Sir Geoffrey's chopper?"

The fireplug raised his hand. "That would be me."

"Okay, here's how we'll play it. You go start the chopper. Helene, when you hear the motor revving, bring Sir Geoffrey to the lobby. Remy and I will go watch the duty room." Marc nodded to the tall man. "You hustle Sir Geoffrey across the lawn and into the chopper."

"I can do that," the tall man said. "That is, assuming the baddies don't pull out a weapon and blast away."

The duty manager clenched her arms so tightly her hands went chalk white. "That can*not* happen."

The chopper pilot asked, "Any chance of a bit of firepower?"

"No guns," the inspector said firmly.

Marc stifled further protest with, "Okay. We've finished our chat. Everybody smile and shake hands in case we're being watched."

Chapter Thirteen

Marc lounged by the guardhouse door, just another mildly bored security specialist. He inspected the empty road through the room's rear window. He glanced across the silent forecourt to where Remy Reynard leaned against the stone wall bordering the spa's front stairs. For all his grumpiness and suspicion, the inspector knew how to follow orders. Remy wore an extremely bored expression as he surveyed the surrounding Alps.

Helene ignored Remy as she descended the steps and crossed the forecourt, carrying another tray of sandwiches. She did a quick turn of the guardroom, then motioned for Marc to pick up the empty coffee urn. Behlet sat on a sofa, leafing through a magazine. Together Marc and Helene started back across the forecourt. Marc waited until their footsteps on the raked gravel drive would mask their quiet conversation. "Did you see anything out of the ordinary back there?"

"Nothing." Now that Helene was out of the room, her nerves emerged in the form of a breathless and shaky voice. "But as I said, I rarely have any contact with our clients' security."

Sir Geoffrey's two guards were over by the chopper. Marc liked how they also held to an easy boredom, one of them playing with his keys while the pilot went through his pre-flight check. There was nothing to alert an attacker that anything was out of the ordinary. No sign that he had in fact now had the castle's front perimeter ringed by allies. "All right. We are going to go inside and get ready to move Sir Geoffrey."

The industrialist waited for them in the front lobby, his urbane demeanor in tatters. Sir Geoffrey was a man afraid for his life. "Are you sure we must proceed with this?"

"I can't tell you what to do. But there's no other way to determine if we face a real threat." Marc turned to the hovering duty manager and attendant and said, "Give us a moment." When they were alone, Marc added, "This isn't just about seeing whether Rhana is trustworthy. This is about flushing out a global threat. You understand?"

"Well, yes, I suppose so." He swallowed audibly. "That is—"

"Before you put your life on the line," Marc finished for him.

"It all seemed so simple until about ten minutes ago. Rather a lark, really. Use my position for the greater good." His hands trembled as he patted down his still-damp hair. "I'm too old for this."

"Say the word and we'll stop."

"No, no." He did his best to dredge up a smile. "I had always thought the danger element was rather fun."

"You'll do fine." Marc called to the duty manager, and when she reappeared, he said, "Walk with me and play along."

He opened the front door, stepped through, waved his arms angrily, then said through the front door, "This is the third time she's changed her mind!"

Helene showed a professional's ability to ad lib. She retorted, "The mademoiselle is your patron!"

Marc stomped down the stone stairs. "I'm a professional and deserve to be treated like one!"

A pair of heads appeared in the guardroom's doorway as Helene snapped, "You are an employee and should show your betters some respect!" She then turned to the lounging inspector and added loudly, "And you will be so good as to find somewhere else to lean!"

Marc kicked at the groomed gravel and fumed his way over to the line of parked cars. Remy made a show of rising from the steps and sauntering across the forecourt. The other guards showed them cynical humor and retreated. All, that is, except for Behlet. He now leaned against the open doorway, offered his trademark slit of a smile, and partially blocked the guardroom's only entry.

Marc watched as the helicopter's turbine gave a whining noise that rose in pitch and volume. The tall security man walked from the chopper toward the spa. Marc felt his adrenaline surge in time to the snap of blades. He pushed his sunglasses up onto his forehead and pretended to rub weary eyes, scouting in every direction, wishing for a gun.

When Sir Geoffrey appeared in the front doorway, Marc stretched and yawned and blinked at the sun, then bent over and gathered a double handful of gravel. He tossed a rock at the valley beyond the groomed perimeter, and allowed his throw to spin him partly around, taking in the keep and the guardhouse and the forecourt and the parked cars. Out of the corner of his eye he watched the guard lead Sir Geoffrey in discreet haste. The bodyguard was a pro and shielded the industrialist with his own body. Marc kept the pair in the perimeter of his vision as he tossed another rock. Waiting.

The attack came from the direction he had both expected and feared. The one area where they were most vulnerable.

Two of the vehicles parked between the Ferrari and the front entrance were new Rolls-Royce Silver Ghosts. They were the world's largest mass-produced cars, as heavy as an empty bus, with trunks large enough to house a family of four.

The vehicles had smoked security glass that shut off the rear cabin from view. Anything and anyone could hide inside. It was far from unusual for bored guards and drivers both to sneak into the back and catch a quick twenty winks. And no way for Marc to check without showing his hand.

Over the thrusting noise, Marc heard the click because he was waiting for it. The instant the first one appeared, he knew they were in trouble. The assailant rose from the rear seat of the car furthest from Marc and threw something across the forecourt.

Marc yelled, "Grenade! Down, down, everybody down!"

And for once, everybody *went* down. Remy dropped into the garden behind the stair's wall. The tall security agent tossed Sir Geoffrey onto the grass and landed atop him. The swift reaction saved three lives, because the first attacker was joined by another rising from the car's other side. The two men were dressed in black—shirts, ties, slacks, belt, shoes, shades. Their hair was black, their skin olive; the only thing bright about them was their teeth.

The grenade blasted gravel in every direction, taking out two windshields and pelting the spa's façade. The attackers lifted Heckler & Koch (HK) machine pistols and released a double spray of bullets. The German-designed submachine guns were favorites for mayhem-makers around the world. They were lightweight and intended to be held at waist level and fired from a crouch. Their stubby snout and truncated grip meant they could be almost as easily concealed as a .38. Their elongated clips held an astonishing thirty bullets, which was necessary because the HK sprayed like a hydrant.

It was also impossible to aim. The guns tended to ride up even when gripped by pros, which these two men clearly were. At a distance of more than twenty feet, the attackers would have had a better chance of hitting their targets if they threw the guns.

But at this stage the attackers were not after a strike. They were after mayhem.

A second grenade rattled across the top step, then took out the front door with an earsplitting blast. The HKs kicked up their own fuss, hammering the air with a ripping, shredding sound. Before the gunners could level down their fire, the tall bodyguard had crawled behind an ornamental stone fountain, dragging a terror-stricken Sir Geoffrey along with him.

Remy Reynard showed amazing speed for a man moving like a crab, rising and shooting and then ducking down just as the left-hand gunner chewed the wall beside Remy's head.

The Rolls trunk lid popped open, and another pair of attackers scrambled out. They too were dressed in black— slacks and sneakers and tight black T-shirts. Though they wore sunglasses on their sweat-streaked faces, they squinted in the sudden light. Marc saw this because he had been waiting for their appearance. He was already moving around the Ferrari, not quite on his knees, but close.

He had to assume the inspector and Bernard Behlet would be targeting the attackers already firing. So Marc headed for the second squad. The ones who would be the least prepared for what he intended to unleash.

The man closest to him showed immense surprise when Marc popped up beside him. He lifted his HK, but too slowly, and Marc was ready.

The attacker snarled something Marc didn't need to understand, tried to hammer his nose with the gun. Marc responded with more force than the man expected, and powered the gun back into his forehead. The attacker shouted for help and fired off a long round, which was what Marc had been after.

The HK had another troublesome feature. The stubby barrel tended to overheat, hardly a surprise given the speed of fire. So long as the shooter kept his hands on the trigger and the forward grip, there was no problem. But as the superheated gasses expelled with the bullets, the barrel turned into a branding iron.

Marc forced the gun back, until the barrel touched the attacker's neck. The man screamed in agony and tried to scramble away.

Marc let him turn, and spun along too. He flipped the man over his shoulder, flinging him high up and then down hard, straight onto the trunk lid of the neighboring Rolls. The man arched his back in agony and released his weapon. Marc saw the man fumble at his waist. He was going for his backup piece.

A voice to his right shouted, "Down, get down!"

Marc hammered the attacker's forehead, then leaped over the trunk, pulling the inert attacker with him. Behind and above, a metal rain struck the Rolls, the bullets hitting so fast they sounded like a giant metal zipper.

From the array of cars came a response of pistol shots from

the other side. They sounded impossibly slow after the HKs, but they were enough to cause the second man by the trunk to spin away. Marc watched from beneath the car as the other attackers dropped empty clips to the ground, slapped fresh ammo into place, and fired at the front keep.

Marc had no idea whether the attacker he held was fully unconscious, nor could he take any chances. He slammed the man's head into the gravel, punched him in the temple, then scuttled behind a tire as another gunner pelted the Rolls with fresh fire. He dragged the inert man over close enough to search his pockets and found two clips for the HK and an oversized .45 Colt in a shoulder holster. Marc shoved the Colt into his belt, slapped a loaded clip into the HK, and came up firing.

At nothing.

The three attackers were gone.

He yelled, "Where, where?"

Behind him, Bernard replied, "Circling behind the spa!"

They were running around the building, using it as a shield, still intent upon their target. Marc yelled for the inspector, "Remy!"

"Here!"

"Go left!"

"On it."

"Bernard, go right!"

Marc headed for the fountain while shouting, "Friendly inbound! Say again, friendly! Move Sir Geoffrey back inside!"

The guard was moving before Marc finished the words. He gripped Sir Geoffrey's jacket by the collar and literally plucked the man from the ground. Sir Geoffrey's air was partly cut off, and he struck ineffectively at the man's grasp as he tried his best to race backward across the lawn with his employer.

129

Sir Geoffrey's position was impossible to maintain, especially when his limbs were turned liquid by fear. Marc managed to get there just as the industrialist tripped. He hefted Sir Geoffrey onto his shoulder and slapped the HK into the guard's hands just as gunfire erupted from the rear of the building.

Marc said, "Man in tan jacket, he's on our side. Ditto for agent in white shirt. Anyone in black, you blast."

"Done!" The guard turned and lowered himself into a crouch.

For someone carrying one and a half times his own weight, Marc made good time. The only external sign of his effort was the grunt he gave with each step. The tall guard swept the grounds in constant tight arcs, covering their backs.

Which proved to be a very good thing. The three attackers came around the building's rear at full roar. From their speed, Marc had to assume the police inspector was down.

The guard managed to get off three bursts. Marc saw one of them stumble. But the lead attacker flipped over, went prone, and shot back. The guard yelped and went down. "I'm hit!"

Marc did not climb the final stairs so much as take a single great leap, bringing him close enough to flinging Sir Geoffrey through the ruined doorway. The older man cried out when his ribs made contact with the doorframe. Marc said, "Get inside!"

The industrialist grabbed his chest with one arm and scrambled into the building.

Chapter Fourteen

The sound of gunfire resonated through the cellar chamber where Kitra sat. They were twenty-nine in total, all females except for the chef, who was more frightened than any of them. He had the olive skin and broad features of a North African, and when the first blast struck, he gibbered with such terror Kitra knew he had hidden before from men with guns.

"My friend is outside," she said calmly. "His name is Marc. He is trained for such times. He will protect us."

One of the younger attendants shredded the words with her fear. "How can you be so certain?"

"Because," Kitra replied, "he has saved me before."

Rhana was settled into the nicest of the chairs, backed in the furthest corner from the doorway. "Saved you from what?"

"I was working at a refugee camp in eastern Kenya. Perhaps you heard of the volcano's eruption? I was there . . . on another project. My brother was kidnapped. I had stayed to search for him. Marc was sent in to help. He was investigating—"

The sound of shots came fast and furious, a vicious hail that left several women weeping openly. Rhana's gaze did not waver. When the shots faded, Rhana said in the same calm voice she had used in the rear garden, "Yes? Your Marc was in Kenya investigating?"

"He was searching out corrupt officials. Then I was kidnapped. He rescued me as well."

Rhana's next words were cut off by more gunfire and shouts. One of the attendants wailed, "They sound so *close*."

"I expect," Rhana said mildly, "it means they have blown open the entrance."

"What do they want?"

"That's simple enough," Rhana said. "They are targeting one of us."

"Are they coming for us?"

"No," Kitra replied. "Marc won't let them."

Once Marc was certain Sir Geoffrey was safe inside the spa's foyer, he dropped to the steps, shielded partly now by the knee-high stone wall that climbed alongside the steps. He slipped the pistol from his belt, cocked it, and rolled down the stairs. He did not come up where he would have been expected, which was on top of the wall. Instead, his gun hand pushed through the flowering shrubs at the stairs' base. And caught the gunman completely by surprise.

Marc gave him a double tap to the chest. Or tried. His limbs were trembling now from the effort required to get Sir Geoffrey to safety. He knew the first shot went wild. But the second connected and spun the man about, sending his HK flying.

But the attacker was not done. He tried to pull his pistol free from its holster. Marc raced over and kicked the gun away, then kicked the man again at the point where his jawline met his chin.

Marc spotted one of the other gunners swing his way, and yelled, "Hand! Hand!"

The injured guard caught the message and was reaching out when Marc scrambled past. He snagged the hand and dragged the man behind the wall as the gunner took aim. They were showered with stone dust and clumps of earth. Marc yelled, "Bernard!"

In reply, the agent appeared around the palace's side wall, firing and running hard. Marc scrambled back into view, his body a target, forcing the two remaining gunners to split their aims. Marc ran sideways, curving out and around the ornamental fountain. The cherubs were chipped, and the spray was a sheet rising from half a dozen new holes. Marc fired back and saw one gunner go down. Then the second dropped, and Bernard shouted, "Clear!"

"Where's Remy?"

"One in the leg. You?"

"Fine. We have another injured. What—?"

Marc's words were chopped off by the sound of more gunfire and a revving engine. Two of the guards were firing back through the doorway. One had red fingers to his neck as he fired. Behind them, the second Rolls roared and spewed gravel in a wide arc as it raced from its parking space. Marc got off his remaining three shots, as did another guard through the keep's blasted window. Bernard remained where he was, his pistol directed at the downed gunners. The Rolls bounded over the central lawn, plowed a ragged furrow through the carefully tended flowers, clipped the front keep's side wall, and was gone.

Marc raced for the Ferrari, yelling, "Gun, gun!"

One of the security men by the guardhouse doorway

slapped in a fresh clip and flipped his pistol like a Frisbee. The gun sailed over the Maybach and into Marc's hand. He pried open the Ferrari door, slipped inside, and mashed the starter button so hard he felt the engine's ignition at the base of his skull.

The passenger door flew open and Bernard tumbled in. "Go!"

"Who's securing the gunners?"

"Everybody else! Drive!"

Marc dropped the pistol, a black Beretta .45, into the side well and slapped the miniature shifter into drive. He jammed the gas pedal to the floor. The Ferrari did not so much depart as launch.

Marc overcorrected and made a spinning exit, plowing the rear tires all the way across the central postage stamp of lawn. He caught sight in his rearview mirror of rose bushes and ornamental shrubs spewing out from behind. Then the tires found traction and he flew through the front gates.

Bernard said, "You are bleeding?"

Only then did he notice the red stain on his gun hand. "Not mine, the guard's."

Bernard lifted the pistol, wiped the grip on his pants, made certain the safety was on, and set it back down. "Stop fighting the car."

"I'm not—"

"You are fighting it." The agent sounded impossibly calm. "You've never driven a sprint machine, yes? This is how they are known in Italy. An entirely different category from normal sports cars. Sprint machines cannot be fought, because they will win. They cannot be pushed to the limit, because their limits are beyond yours. They must be *managed*."

Marc caught the steady drone of a professional instructor, and forced himself to ease back. "So how do I manage?"

"The paddle on your left. Hit it now. Curve coming up. Downshift. Don't oversteer. Good. Hit the paddle on your right. Accelerate out of the curve. Straight ahead. Right paddle, upshift, left paddle, downshift, prepare for the curve, brake, brake, turn, not too much, accelerate out of the curve."

"You should be driving."

"Perhaps you will let me do so on the return, yes?" He pointed through the windshield. "There is your target. Two kilometers, three o'clock."

"I see them."

"Watch this curve, it's a hairpin, downshift, downshift again, don't worry about redlining this engine. It's only happy above seven thousand rpm. Good. Now push it hard, gear up, again, accelerate harder, now gear up, curve coming, forget your speed and watch the road. Distance to target is down to fifteen hundred meters and closing."

The Rolls was close enough for Marc to see it tilt sharply at the next curve. The massive limo was not made for a high-speed Alpine descent, and it left four black burn marks in the road. The driver overcorrected out of the turn and hammered the guardrail before accelerating away.

Marc forgot about the Rolls. He forgot about the distance. He ignored the approaching truck and the blaring horn. He stopped worrying about the next curve, the next rise or blind spot, the paddles and the shifter. He had worked with spotters before. A good agent learned to trust his spotters with his life. The spotter was responsible for everything beyond the life-or-death instant. Bernard was the best spotter Marc had ever worked with. He never raised his voice. He showed no fear. He spoke in a flat drone, giving terse instructions, relaying intel on the target ahead, freeing up Marc to do his assigned duty. Which was to manage this amazing vehicle and close the distance between them and the escaping killers. And keep them both alive.

Bernard interrupted twice to lift his phone and make terse phone calls. Both were in French. Marc did not need to understand the language to know he was ordering backup. The second call was made the instant the Rolls took the downward turning at the Chamonix crossing. Bernard spoke in clipped sentences, cut the connection, and said, "Roadblock is being set up this side of Aigle."

"How far out?"

"Eight kilometers." Bernard permitted himself a smile. "At your current flight speed, about forty seconds."

The road descended to the valley floor. The Rolls hit the straightaway and started pulling away. Marc pushed the Ferrari up to 140, 150 mph.

"Don't worry about catching them. Let the roadblock do that for us."

The Rolls continually had to brake before racing around slower vehicles. The two-lane road was not full but well traveled, and all the horns blended into one angry blare of protest by the time the oncoming vehicles reached Marc.

"Roadblock dead ahead, nine hundred meters."

Marc saw the flashing lights and the burning flares. The Rolls saw them too, for its brake lights came on. But only for a second. And then the vehicle started accelerating.

Bernard yelled his protest in a rising wail, "No, no, no!"

The Rolls struck the barrier going well over 130 mph. The

car smashed through, only to ram into the line of police vehicles beyond. Policemen sped away as if fleeing a bomb, which they were, as a myriad of gas tanks exploded in one unified blast of heat and sound, enough to cause the slowing Ferrari to shudder and almost leave the road.

Chapter Fifteen

The next morning, Marc was seated at Chief Inspector Remy Reynard's bedside. Bernard leaned against the window, through which Marc watched a sailboat plow a lazy furrow through the lake's sunlit waters.

"Let us be precisely clear on where we stand," Bernard Behlet told Marc. "For you, this is about an international terrorist threat. This is about protecting your national interests. For us, this is about an attack on our homeland."

Sir Geoffrey's helicopter had flown Remy and the two injured bodyguards to the nearest trauma unit in Lausanne. The attackers were driven by ambulance to the secure unit at the Geneva hospital. Because Switzerland handled so many diverse people groups, with the possibility of their importing both danger and infectious diseases, the hospital's wing was very secure indeed. Marc had driven the Ferrari down with Bernard, but only after they had finished speaking with the local police, which had taken hours. Kitra had left earlier in Rhana's Bentley. The older woman had assured Marc that she could protect them both, and Marc had believed her.

"This is domestic terrorism," Bernard went on. "This is the Swiss government's nightmare come to life. Just like what happened in the Second World War, we have become pawns in someone else's conflict."

After his surgery the previous evening, Remy had woken up twice, just long enough to open his eyes and glance over. The first time he had asked Bernard about his family but fell asleep before hearing the reply. The second time he awoke, his wife was seated next to his bed. Remy took her hand, smiled at Marc through the observation window, and was out again.

Remy's wife was an attractive woman with an athlete's frame and a leathery Alpine tan. She carried herself with the no-nonsense air of many police spouses. She shed a few tears over her husband's state and the might-have-beens, but only when Remy was asleep. Marc and Bernard had relieved her a half hour earlier and sent her home to rest.

Marc asked Bernard, "Why are you telling me this?"

"Because I am now authorized to give you whatever you want. Unofficially, of course. Completely off the record. But the normal Swiss reserve and obsession with laws and protocol, none of it applies any longer. My superiors are asking that you please pass this on."

"Superiors in the reinsurance group, or FIS?"

"My friend, I am referring to people so high up the ladder, such designations no longer matter." He shifted from his place by the wall. "I believe the good inspector has decided to rejoin us."

Marc sat and waited while the inspector and the federal agent exchanged pleasantries in French. When the inspector gummed his dry lips and nodded toward the side table, Marc held the cup of cold water while Remy drank, then refilled it and held it again.

Remy asked hoarsely, "The two Rolls?"

Bernard showed his customary humor. "I would tell the good inspector to let us worry about such matters and rest, but he is a policeman, and he will heal more swiftly if he is involved." He then spoke in English to the inspector, "The cars were reported stolen two days ago in Paris. They bore limo tags stolen from a business in Zurich."

"And the gunners?"

"Nothing so far. No names, no records. But Interpol is involved, and we have widened the search."

Bernard left to find a nurse, and Remy gave the silence a long and grateful moment before saying, "I disliked you the first moment I saw you."

"I know."

"I saw a warrior. A *foreign* warrior. On Swiss soil."

Marc nodded. "It didn't matter whether I was involved in the blast or not. I was a threat to your peace."

Remy studied him. "I was wrong."

"No," Marc said. "Actually, you weren't."

Their conversation was cut off by the doctor's arrival. In the middle of his examination, Marc's phone rang. He expected it to be Kitra, but did not recognize the number. "This is Royce."

"Agent Royce," a male voice said, "I am the friend of Rhana. Perhaps she mentioned me."

"Just a moment." Marc stepped through the doorway. As he did, he murmured to Bernard, "It's him."

The agent followed him from the room. Marc said, "Rhana told us you might make contact."

"And here I am."

He held the phone so Bernard could listen in. "Tell me you didn't have anything to do with the attack."

"We did nothing. We played no role, except as observers. We are after the same thing as you, Agent Royce. We hear the ticking clock. We need answers."

"Who are you?"

"You may call me Amin Hedayat." His tone showed mild humor. "In Farsi, it means 'honest guide.' Which I hope you will find me to be."

"Who attacked us?"

"Their leader is known as Hesam al-Farouz. It means 'Sword of Triumph.' He is rumored to be a member of the Revolutionary Guard's high council. He trained as a physicist and has been spotted at several international conferences on nuclear science. But we have no background on him whatsoever. We do not know where he came from or where he trained. Nothing. We are operating on rumors, and this worries us."

"His men were very professional."

"You will please inform us if they reveal anything, yes?"

Marc replied, "That depends."

"Trust for trust, yes, I quite agree. In Iran we have a saying: When you most need a friend, it is too late to find one. Meaning we must prepare now. The clock is ticking, Agent Royce. Please join me outside. Alone."

"How will I . . . ?"

But the man was already gone.

Bernard accompanied him down the stairs. "They are going to make Remy into the nation's hero. Our minister of the interior is on his way down as we speak. The evening news will announce that Remy will soon receive the nation's highest civilian medal for valor. I assume you have no interest in receiving a medal of your own."

"Absolutely not," Marc said. "I wasn't there. How could I be rewarded for something I didn't do?"

"But you did, and everyone knows it. The minister will want to have a word."

"Tell him to call Washington. I plan to be otherwise occupied." He stopped by the front doors. "The man said I needed to do this alone."

"As I said, this is a national terrorism issue. I must insist."

"Not this time." Marc lifted his phone, hit the code for Bernard's cell. When it rang, Marc slipped the phone back into his shirt pocket. "He didn't say anything about you listening in."

He walked outside where he had time for one breath and one blink at the late afternoon sunlight before a dark Mercedes SL500 swooped in on silent wings. Marc opened the front passenger door and noticed the thick dimension, the heaviness, the precise balance of the hinges. He slipped inside. "Nice ride."

"Thank you, Agent Royce. It is yours for the duration. Midrange bulletproofing." He pulled away, slipped out of the hospital drive, and joined the city's fray. "Ms. Korban may find the Ferrari a bit too vulnerable, after yesterday's mayhem."

"You operate a limo company?"

"Limos, taxis, corporate buses," he said while expertly navigating through the traffic. "We have allies and partners in Germany and Holland and California and Minneapolis and Michigan and Washington and Canada. We are the Persian diaspora. We fled in the chaos between two oppressive regimes. Where we landed, we sought to hide in plain sight. From the moment we planted new roots, we shared one dream: to bring down the fanatics and build a democracy in our homeland."

"Rhana told Kitra about her father, the pastor. You are part of the Christian immigration?"

"We are, and it amazes us that Rhana would share her most carefully guarded secret with a complete stranger." Amin Hedayat was in his late fifties or early sixties, and spoke with the ease of a man who had made himself comfortable in many tongues. He wore a black double-breasted jacket and woven gray tie and carried himself with the air of one who was at ease with wealth and power. Amin was far more than a limo driver. "Those Christians who did not escape before the imams took over are lost to us. We will greet them with gladness and tears on the last day. Until then, we seek to reclaim our beautiful land from the fanatics who would like to pretend we do not exist."

Marc disliked the isolation created by the bulletproof glass. "Why am I here?"

"We have questions, Agent Royce. Things that do not add up."

"I'm listening."

"And so are others, I suspect."

In response, Marc pulled out the cellphone and set it on the padded armrest between their seats. "I ask again, why am I here?"

Amin Hedayat eyed the cellphone as he would a roach that had dared enter his pristine vehicle. But he did not protest. "Questions, Agent Royce. Many questions, few answers. What do you know about the Revolutionary Guard?"

"Almost nothing."

"Their full name is *Sepah-e Pasdaran-e Enqelab-e Elami*,

which translates as the Army of the Guardians of the Islamic Revolution. Whatever ragtag rabble they might have been when they stormed the U.S. Embassy and held your people captive, now they are transformed beyond recognition. They number over one hundred and fifty thousand active personnel, and also control the Basij militia, similar to your National Guard, which gives them access to another half-million men."

Amin drove slowly past a lakefront park. Beyond the thick windows stretched an emerald lawn and groomed shrubbery and laughing children and sparkling waters. Everything neat and orderly and utterly removed from their discussion. "The Guards have taken an increasingly assertive role in every aspect of Iranian society. They have forced successive governments to grant them even more power, especially since the riots of four years ago, because they are all that stand between the regime and defeat. Since the 2009 election, they have become so powerful we believe they actually surpass the clerics in Qom. They operate a multi-billion-dollar business empire, second in wealth only to the national oil company."

"I am still waiting," Marc said, "for the questions."

"Let us assume for the moment that the rumors are correct, that Hesam al-Farouz is indeed a leader of the Sepah. That is how opponents of the regime refer to the Guard, by the way. Using that name is a declaration of where one stands. Regime backers call them the Pasdaran." He held up one manicured hand to halt Marc's comment. "Yes, yes. Questions. The Sepah is split into three distinct groups. The main group contains the Guard's land, naval, and air wings. A much smaller unit is called Quds, or Special Forces. The third is the smallest of all, and is known as the Missile Forces. When Iran began its nuclear-enrichment program, the missile group was granted special status. They are an elite, secretive force that answers directly to the ayatollah and no one else. Their connection to the Sepah, the rest of the Guards, is marginal. They are universally loathed." Amin turned on his left-turn signal and took the United Nations exit. "You can guess what I am about to disclose."

"You have a spy inside the missile group."

"No, Agent Royce. We have several. And none of them report to us any unexpected activity. Do you understand what I am saying?"

"If they were planning to set off a bomb, there would be movement."

"There would be ferment. There would be exhilaration. They would say nothing, and few would know anything. But the tension would be felt, be tangible."

"You're certain what your people are telling you is correct? They haven't simply been identified and forced to lie?"

"They are at different levels in different compounds. Scientists and military officers both. I tell you this without doubt. *Nothing is happening.*"

"Then why am I here?"

"Because we can confirm something you may already suspect. Nine containers of dubious nature were shipped from North Korea and lost in Singapore. A gallery in Geneva that was used as a financial conduit has been destroyed. And then our dear friend Rhana, an art dealer in Lugano, has been handed an entire gallery of stolen merchandise and told to turn over to our foes a hundred million dollars. And they say it is extremely urgent. Words they have never used with her before."

"I'm sorry. I don't mean to play the cynic. But there are

people in Washington who think we're chasing our tails. For all we know, it could be nothing more than an international art theft."

Amin pulled to the curb across the street from the American legation to the UN. "And they could be right, except for the missing containers."

"And the timing."

"Yes, I agree. That they would demand payment so quickly just as the containers go missing is a concern." He slipped two pieces of paper from his pocket. "Trust for trust, Agent Royce. This is Rhana's Cayman account number. The bank, we are led to believe, is secretly controlled by your government. This morning Rhana gave Hesam al-Farouz access to the funds. We urge you to track the money and see where it goes."

He handed over the second slip. "Rhana uses a new phone each time she contacts Hesam. The next time she speaks with him, she will call from this number. Tell your people to be ready. We will be able to give them only a few moments' notice."

Marc opened his door. "I'm on it."

Chapter Sixteen

Early that evening, Kitra accompanied Rhana to a gallery opening. She had no interest in attending, but even less in being left alone and reliving the previous day's aftershocks. She had spoken briefly with Marc, just long enough to hear that the police inspector had awakened and was expected to make a full recovery. As though the policeman's condition was what she had been waiting all day to hear about. Afterward she sat in the chair by her balcony, gripping the armrests, waiting for the shudders of fear to subside.

Rhana clearly remained shaken by the attack as well. As they settled into the Mercedes limo to go to the gallery, the woman drew in close and said, "Thank you for not making me do this alone."

"Why are we here?"

"Because I was asked. Told, actually." She lifted a finger as the driver slipped behind the wheel, and did not speak again until they arrived. As they rose from the limo and entered the elegant gallery, she went on, "I received a call from my contact. I was to be here, at this hour."

"He wants to meet you?"

"If so, it will be the first time I have ever seen him. I do not even know what he looks like." She glanced swiftly about the gallery, then sniffed her disdain. "I have no knowledge of this painter, nor do I care. I do not deal in modern art. Normally I come to such events merely to be seen."

Kitra had difficulty focusing on anything. The noise battered at her. She felt disconnected, and her mind kept replaying the distant ripple of gunshots. She jerked with fear when a waiter suddenly appeared and offered her a glass of champagne.

There was no evident shift in the elegant woman's demeanor. She still surveyed the gathering with a cool, dark gaze. But Kitra sensed the change. An instant's fear sliced through her calm. "What is it?"

Rhana waved and smiled to someone neither woman actually saw. "Phone your young man. Where is he now?"

"With the agent. Behlet." Kitra was already reaching for her purse. "He said he would join us—"

"No, no, don't make any sudden movements. Your every motion must carry a languid ease." Rhana motioned to the painting with her untouched glass. "Tell him to come. Tell him . . ."

"Yes?"

A faint tremor rippled across Rhana's features, the slightest indication of all she struggled to hide. "I can't be certain. But tell him I think death has just entered the room."

Kitra watched Rhana step into the tide of people and drift away. She made no attempt to follow. Instead she moved to the side window, where the night formed a dark mirror. As she coded in Marc's number, she watched the reflection of a tall man slip through the crowd with a predator's ease, taking aim for Rhana.

When Marc came on the phone, she discovered she had

lost the ability to breathe. She gasped once, twice, then managed, "I'm so afraid."

Rhana stopped before another painting, pretending she had not even noticed the gentleman moving toward her. He was Persian, she knew this instantly, a pure-blood Aryan, a member of the world's most ancient race. And he fit the one bit of description she had of the man whose voice she heard in her nightmares yet had never met.

She stepped to the next painting, moving slowly, drawing farther away from where Kitra stood by the front window. Then the man stepped around the nearest guests and smiled. Rhana could almost imagine the blade slip between her ribs as the man said in French, "Madame Mandana, a pleasure."

She took great assurance from how her voice remained steady. "Do I know you?" She cocked her head, eyebrows raised.

"We share numerous mutual acquaintances. Although one of them, Sylvan Gollet, sadly is no longer among us."

She gave him the most brilliant of smiles, as though his latent rage remained unnoticed. "How very nice to finally make your acquaintance. What shall I call you?"

"Your doom, if I do not like your answers." He had the olive complexion of most Middle Easterners, but his features were perfectly aquiline, like a Renaissance sculpture of a young boy. He would have appeared effeminate were it not for his razor-edged strength. And the blaze of fury in his gaze. "Tell me what happened at the spa." The words came from lips that barely moved.

Rhana turned and walked slowly toward a rear alcove, astonished that her legs managed to keep her upright. The scent

151

of dread and some ghastly cologne he wore threatened to cut off her air. She waited for him to join her, then answered, "That's simple enough. Your men botched the attack."

He stood against the rear wall, forcing her to remain with her back to the room. "Four men in two cars, a seventh assailant embedded among the guards, all of them highly trained. They failed. Do you know what that suggests to me?"

"That you should have prepared for greater opposition." She managed to transform her fear into an outraged tone. "There were nineteen security personnel on duty!"

"Bored guards, most unarmed, who should have been overwhelmed by my men."

"I always assumed you were too much a professional to make such an assumption," she snapped.

"I am the *consummate* professional. Your life depends upon that."

"There were *six* former Swiss special forces among the nineteen. Not to mention a former agent of the FIS, a former member of U.S. intelligence, and a police inspector."

His gaze tightened. "And how do you know this?"

"The U.S. agent is that young woman's bodyguard. He told us afterwards." Then she amended, "Actually, he was formerly an agent. He was fired. Now he freelances."

"Who is that woman?"

"Daughter of a French industrialist. I suspect she has Jewish blood."

"Her arrival at this point did not raise your suspicions?"

"Of *course* it did. Why on earth do you think I brought her here? I need to know what is happening. For all our sakes!"

"Keep your voice down. Why was there a police presence at the spa?"

"Some rumor of a robbery. He interviewed several of the patrons, asking if any—"

"Yes, yes, I know all about that." He was dressed in a suit that fit him like a second skin, black with a black woven pinstripe, and a black shirt. His cuff links held diamonds, as did the face of his watch. They caught the light as he adjusted the knot of his woven silk tie and shook his head. "Rhana, I am wondering what I should do with you."

"You seek to punish *me* for *your* failure?"

"You were the one who suggested the spa as a location for our trap."

"And you were the one who came unprepared." She started to turn away. "You have your money. Leave me—"

"Stay where you are."

Reluctantly she turned around. What choice did she have? He did not merely command. He *dominated*. She had known such people all her life. Persians who had taken control not just of her nation, but her soul. "I do not know why you risked coming here." She was shocked at her own temerity in the face of the evil power in front of her.

"And you will *never* know. It is not your business to know. And that is not the issue here. I am wondering how to punish you. How to ensure you realize just how close you are to death." He studied her. "Rhana Mandana, you stand there with your fine jewelry and your poise. Do you not feel the cold breath upon your neck?"

She met his gaze and did not speak. She knew he expected her to beg. And that was her first inclination. The plea took shape in her frantically beating heart and rushed up her throat, a silent scream for mercy. But Rhana clenched her jaw and held it trapped inside. She would not give him the pleasure of even a glimpse of her terror.

Something in her gaze caused him to concede, "No, not this night. You still have a role to play. Perhaps. If indeed you are to be trusted. But you must be made to see just how close death has come to you. How there can be no further mistakes."

"I have made none."

"No mistakes," he repeated. "All missions must lead to success. Even the ones you know nothing about. There are no innocents in this world." He smiled at some passing patron behind Rhana, probably a woman who had given him the eye. His voice was almost musical. Killers often took this tone, she knew, when the blade was about to be inserted. "I am taking your commission from the sale of these articles. The entire fifty million dollars is now mine."

She dared take a half step toward him. "I have earned—"

"I am taking all of it, Rhana. Every cent. Take what consolation you can from the knowledge that much of it will go to the families of those who took part in the debacle at the spa." He smiled. "And the young woman who accompanied you tonight, she will be placed on the altar in your stead."

"Ridiculous! It risks everything—"

"Turn and relish the spectacle of her death." He tracked an unseen ally with his gaze, then lifted his chin, indicating Kitra. "And if I experience any further failure of any kind, I will come looking for another sacrifice."

They were already in the Ferrari and leaving Remy's hospital parking area when Kitra's panicked call came. From his position behind the wheel, Bernard ordered Marc to phone

Remy and request backup. Now they raced down the highway that rimmed the lake's southern edge, the engine roaring in their ears. The Ferrari was made for this, pushing beyond the limits of normal cars. They started off alone, then a pair of patrol cars slipped in via an autoroute entrance. Bernard slowed enough to allow the supercharged Renaults to box him in, but when they attempted to temper his speed, Bernard shouted something Marc did not need to understand, swerved around them, and blasted on alone.

At this point, Bernard's phone rang. He slipped it from his pocket and tossed it over. Marc answered, listened to the tirade in French, and replied, "Whatever you have to say, it needs to be in English."

The policeman's accent was atrocious. "We are instructing you to slow down!"

"Check with your superiors." Marc cut the connection and told Bernard, "Wrong number."

Bernard shouted another phone number to Marc. He called and reported his findings to a woman who felt no need to identify herself. When he was done, the woman had responded with, "We will alert the Geneva Police."

"Negative! No cops! Repeat, no police! If the enemy sees them, my friend is dead. Tell the police trailing us to cut their sirens and play by our rules."

It was far from the clearest summary Marc had ever given a superior, but it had apparently worked, for the woman simply said, "Stand by."

Ten seconds later, the Renaults both cut their sirens. One moved in close to Bernard's rear, the second soon vanished. The Ferrari's speedometer held steady at 230 kilometers per hour, which Marc did not even bother to convert. Fast enough to scare him silly. Even though he wished they could go faster still.

The woman on the phone said, "Tell Monsieur Behlet that detectives in unmarked vehicles will be standing by, awaiting his orders. Good hunting."

Marc cut the connection and said, "I need a boss like that."

"You need to alert Rhana's ally, is what you need."

"Roger that." Marc phoned the number Amin had slipped him. The Persian was definitely not pleased to hear from Marc. "That number was for dire emergencies only."

"My friend, Kitra Korban, just phoned. She is with Rhana—"

"At the gallery opening. I know all this. Rhana's bodyguard is one of us."

"Kitra says Rhana told her to call. She said death was there."

The man's tone shifted to full-on alarm. "From where?"

"That was all she said. I'm assuming Kitra was being watched when she called. Give me the gallery address."

Amin fed it to Marc, who passed it on to Bernard. The agent told Marc, "I know it. Tell him, no alarm and no movement until we arrive. We handle the police."

Marc repeated the instructions, then added, "If your man calls for backup or does anything else out of the ordinary, it will alert the enemy."

"Where are you now?"

"Autoroute, outskirts of Geneva."

Bernard said, "Six minutes and closing."

"I will alert my man. He will find you."

"Red Ferrari." When Marc cut the connection, Bernard fed him the police number. Marc asked, "They speak English?"

"Probably, and badly."

Marc gripped the dash and the door handle as they left the

autoroute in a swooping maneuver that left burned rubber and squealing tires and a hundred blaring horns in their wake. He passed on the information to the cops, then cut off just as Bernard took a corner at an impossible speed and hammered a lamppost. The police car lost control entirely and slammed into a parked van. Bernard downshifted and burned rubber around the wreck. "Tell the police we are four blocks out."

"Slow it down. Where that crowd is, is that the gallery? All right, stop now. Block that alley." Marc was up and moving before the car halted. He raced forward, saw a man with a fighter's bulk beneath a dark suit, and said, "You're with the good guys?"

"As God wills."

"Okay. Follow my lead." He heard footsteps rushing to catch up and said, "This is another friend."

"I have no weapons."

"Yeah, I know how that feels." Marc arrived at the door. "You two find Rhana. I'll cover Kitra."

The entrance was guarded by a slender young man who demanded something in French. Marc shot past him, ignoring the protest and Bernard's retort. Because he spotted Kitra then, beautiful in her midnight-blue evening dress. And then he saw the killer, and knew he was too late.

Chapter Seventeen

The assassin stood out like he was being tracked with Klieg lights. He did not belong in this crowd, nor in this elegant and refined world. He wore his expensive tailored suit like he would the furs of a captured enemy. His shoulders were hunched, his jaw tight, his gaze fixed upon Kitra. His target.

Marc moved through the guests as though they did not exist. As though only three people stood in this place, and the space itself was nothing more than a kill zone. He did not actually run. He moved like a river flowing into the sea. Doing what he did best. Heading straight for peril.

The attacker could have taken her. Marc was still half the chamber's width away. But the killer made a mistake. He wanted her to see him. He gave himself time enough to be spotted, for Kitra to look into his face and see her end.

Marc leaped and roared all at the same time. "Down!"

Kitra did not fall; she wilted. Her body went boneless and she dropped.

The gunner gaped at the empty space where his target had once stood. Mistake two. It was only an instant, half a heartbeat of indecision. But long enough for Marc to strike.

There was no subtlety to his assault. He rammed the attacker with all the force he had in him. Knowing the man carried a knife. Possibly a gun. Not having any idea where the weapons were, as the attacker's right side had been blocked from Marc's view. So he did what he could, the only thing that occurred to him. Slammed into him and found a grip with his feet and just kept shoving, ramming the attacker into the wall. Into the painting, actually, which folded around them like a smelly shroud.

"Kitra, get away! Move, move!"

Marc reached up and flattened the smashed painting around the attacker's face. The enemy snarled and flung outward with both hands, using the dark carbon blade to clear away any threat. He shouted in a foreign tongue that sounded both savage and melodious.

Something about the way the man kept shouting told Marc he had not come alone. Marc yelled, "There's a second attacker! Bernard!"

But the Swiss agent's approach was slowed by the screaming horde of well-heeled clients now streaming up, down, anywhere but near the fray. The second attacker was squat and agile and far closer. He too carried a knife, and he headed straight for Marc.

Bernard shouted, "Federal police! Halt!"

Marc feinted left, then used his superior height to leap up and strike heel-first, down upon the second attacker's head. The man was swift and managed to jerk away, but still caught the strike on his blade arm. The knife clattered to the stone flooring.

Marc landed and kept falling, covering the blade with his body. The first enemy ripped the painting off his face and struck with his nearside boot. Marc scrambled away just in time, leaving the knife behind and coming up empty-handed.

As the squat attacker turned to face Bernard, the original foe swiped at Marc. The blade hummed a song of black death, the man's reach great enough for Marc to feel the wind across his chest. He began backing away but was blocked by some great mass of screaming, writhing people. Marc saw Bernard grip Kitra's arm and fling her back toward safety. He felt his focus tightening now, released from fear for the woman he loved.

Yes, loved.

The squat attacker punched at Bernard, but the Swiss agent proved as swift as he was agile. Bernard countered with a savage kick to the man's ribs. He spun away, recovered, and reached into his pocket.

"Gun! Gun!"

Kitra scurried into a side alcove Marc had not noticed until that very moment. A terrified Rhana gripped her and drew her into safety. The stubby gunman tracked her out of sight, which was long enough for Marc to duck a second wild swing from the taller foe, then leap in and hammer the gunman twice, once to the neck and then to the temple. It was far from his best work, but the man wobbled slightly before turning and firing through the gallery's plate-glass window.

The window shattered in a blast of falling glass. The gunman shouted again, then leaped through the opening. The tall man moved incredibly fast for his size. They were followed by a third man that Marc had not noticed until then. The trio vanished into the night while sirens roared at them from all sides.

Chapter Eighteen

Marc was back in the Geneva police station. Same bullpen as his first night in Switzerland. He was just as tired as during the last visit. But the authorities' previous hostility and the suspicion were gone. In their place was a palpable respect, a desire to jump up and do whatever he requested. Which was not much, really. Give him a secure line and a private space and a coffee. Then he recalled how bad the food had been the last time, and amended that last request, asking someone to hoof it across the street and bring back a hot beverage and a sandwich from someplace that understood the word *fresh*.

The reason for the change in atmosphere had come in the form of a senior police officer who had arrived as Marc was coming in with Bernard and Kitra, basically offering Marc anything and everything he required. The officer had not needed gold braid or a fancy dress uniform to get his message across. The way the other police had watched, all standing at full alert, had said that this was a man whose words carried true power.

They set him up once more in Inspector Reynard's office, which Marc found good enough irony for a weary smile. Kitra was the only other person in the office. Bernard was on the phone next door, reporting to his own superiors. Marc ate his sandwich and drank his coffee. Kitra had declined repeated offers of both. She was seated in one of the station's hardback chairs, pushed over tight against the side wall, beside the inspector's three filing cabinets. She watched him with a hollow gaze. "What are we waiting for?"

"I need to report in. But I want Bernard to hear what I say." He bundled up his sandwich wrapping and dropped it in the waste basket. "You can go back to the hotel anytime you like."

"I'm not going anywhere without you."

When he put down the cup, he said, "I need to tell you something, Kitra."

She braced herself as much as her weary state allowed. "You want me to go home."

"If you want to stay, I want you to stay. If you want to go . . ."

"I don't know what I want."

He nodded, not in agreement, but acknowledging that now was a time for truth, however raw. "When my wife passed away, I made a decision. But to understand what that decision was, I have to back up. About two weeks earlier, I finally accepted that she was going to die and there was nothing I could do about it. I had hoped my prayers would be enough to save her. I had felt God very close to me at times when I prayed. I thought that meant she was going to make it. That we would see a miracle. And sometimes she was better, for a little while. Then she went into a serious decline, and even though I didn't want to accept it, I saw it in the faces of the doctors and the nurses at the hospital. She was never coming home again."

He was so involved in the memories, he did not even notice

Kitra was crying until she wiped her cheeks with both hands, the wetness now all over her face. "What was your decision?" she asked, her words no more than breaths.

"That I would not let this come between me and my God. It was so tempting to leave my faith behind. Bury it with my wife and walk away. The temptation was a burning in my gut, a hunger, a . . ." He stared at his hands, flat on the desk in front of him.

"Why didn't you?"

"Because my faith was all I had left." He met her gaze, glad he could keep his voice steady. "Just like now."

He waited for her to object, to come back with some sort of deflection. And he wasn't sure he'd have the strength to keep them on target. Even though this truth needed to come out. Tonight.

Instead, all Kitra said was, "I understand."

"I realized tonight that by letting myself turn so cold and distant, becoming cold to you, shutting you out, it has left me unable to pray."

She opened her mouth to speak, then closed it and nodded. The motion released another trickle of tears. These she did not bother to wipe away.

"I feel like we've been going at this all wrong, Kitra. We can't deny how we feel, any more than we can deny the obstacles that stand in our way. We love each other and yet our destinies lie on different paths. It's hard. I know."

"So very, very hard," she whispered.

"But it's also very real. And after the attack, when it came down to how close I had been to losing you, I knew this wasn't right."

"No," she said. "No. It's not. But—"

"But you don't know what to do. And neither do I."

She took on the thousand-yard stare he had seen so often in shell-shocked victims who could no longer find the strength to bring reality into focus. She opened her mouth and framed a single word, but could not give it volume. *What.*

"I think we should pray. Together."

It took her a long moment. But he waited it out with her. Until she could look over and really see him.

"Morning and night," he went on. "We come together and we ask for clarity. Vision. Purpose. Wisdom. Healing. Peace. For each other and for the two of us."

She said, "You don't know how hard that is."

"I think I do."

"No, you can't . . ." She stopped at a knock on the inspector's door.

Bernard opened the door. A single glance was enough for the agent to take in Kitra's tears, the distance between them. "I am interrupting."

"Five minutes," Marc said.

"I am just outside."

When the door shut again, Kitra went on, "I am my father's child."

Marc nodded like that made sense, glad at some level beyond logic that she was being open with him at all. Not closing him out. Not making a mockery of his suggestion.

"I have been raised to fight. To do. To challenge the status quo and bend the will of an entire nation. To force people who stand against us to accept us and give us a place. To claim what is ours by right. I would have gained none of this if I had submitted."

It was his turn to say, "I understand."

"But this is what you're asking me to do, isn't it? Submit?"

"No, Kitra. It's not about me asking you to do anything at all. Except pray."

"But don't you see?" Her face creased with pain. "What if God tells me to do that? Bend to a will that's not my own? Do something other than what I've spent my life building? The kibbutz is my life."

"Kitra, think about what I'm saying." There was no argument now. Which was beyond good. Marc had no energy for a quarrel. This was all about laying it all on the table. Even when it hurt. Even when they disagreed. He felt the rightness resonate in his weary bones. "This isn't about giving up on anything. This is about taking a new direction. Together. As believers who care deeply for one another. This is about us and God. Okay, we know our paths. They have seemed totally separate, but they've crossed here. In Geneva. So what comes now? We need to pray for direction, for a way ahead. Why shouldn't we pray for each other? There's no one on earth I feel closer to than you."

"Oh, Marc."

"It's true. So let's meet and pray. No agenda. No aim beyond seeking God's will. For each other. As friends." He waited. "What do you think?"

"I know you're right. I feel this is what we need to do." She studied him. "Why does that frighten me so?"

"I don't know. But I'm glad you agree."

She nodded. Once. Twice. Then she looked at the door. "The agent is waiting."

"You folks have certainly stirred up a hornet's nest. Several, in fact."

Ambassador Walton's voice sounded far more reedy than the previous day, his wheeze as pronounced as his words. "Agent Behlet, on behalf of my government, I offer my official apologies for causing further mayhem in your lovely city."

"Let us wait until we have successfully concluded this matter," Bernard replied. "Then we can worry about such issues as regret."

"Duly noted. Then there is the matter of trusting Rhana. Which I must tell you is facing considerable opposition here."

"It is happening," Marc said.

"You do not yet have—"

"I am front man on this operation. And I am telling you the woman is central to our operation."

Walton gave that a moment's silence, then went on, "And finally there is the matter of the new gentleman and his information. How, precisely, did Ms. Mandana come into contact with him? Does anybody know?"

"I checked on this," Marc replied. "Amin Hedayat is on the board of an Iranian refugee center based in Toronto. The newcomers arrive there, gain Canadian papers, then continue on to Persian communities in half a dozen different locations. Calgary and Montreal in Canada, the rest south of the border. Rhana started making sizable donations. She met Amin personally about a dozen years ago. Trust was built up over time."

"Hedayat operates a successful limo service in San Diego, and tax records show part ownership in four others around the country." Walton coughed noisily. "There is no record of the man on any international watch list. Which may mean nothing more than that he has managed to stay under the radar."

"What about his concerns over Iranian aims?" Marc asked.

"I have to tell you, this stranger's knowledge of what we thought was a highly classified operation leaves us seriously worried."

"We know there are leaks," Marc pressed. "We also know there's a ticking clock."

"There is serious disagreement over here. The majority opinion is that the Iranians have gone to the North Koreans because their own nuclear weapons aren't ready. But some are saying this doesn't make sense. If the North Koreans wanted to set off a bomb, they could annihilate Seoul and the two U.S. bases with one fell swoop. But they don't. And the reasons they don't are the same reasons it would be ludicrous for them to involve themselves with the Persians in an act of global terrorism. They'd be wiped off the map, and they know it."

"Our reports suggest the Persians lack crucial bomb components, such as detonators," Behlet offered. "Something the North Koreans now possess."

"Again, on paper it is all possible. But nine containers? You could build an arsenal with that many components." Walton coughed again, a wracking sound that ended in a wheeze and a struggle for breath. "I must warn you, the commander of DOD intel considers you and I to be his foes."

Behlet protested, "Your man is doing excellent work, Mr. Ambassador."

"That only heightens the admiral's concerns. The last thing he wants is a source over which he has no control throwing doubt into the mix. He has identified an enemy, and he is intent upon military action. He fears you will find some reason for our blockade to be put on hold. Make no mistake. Unless you find incontrovertible evidence, in four more days we close the Strait of Hormuz, and the world will be at war."

Chapter Nineteen

The next morning, Kitra called Marc's room as soon as she had washed her face. "Were you serious about what you suggested?"

"You know I was. Did you sleep?"

"Some. Not a lot."

"The whisper of near death can be very loud when you're alone in the dark. Next time call, and we'll get together and pray. It helps."

"Have you had breakfast?"

"I was waiting for your call."

"And doing what till then?"

"Looking for something in the Scriptures. Preparing for our time together."

That was what defined him, she knew. The willingness to make infinite effort and be prepared for anything. Even this. A dawn prayer time with a woman he should not love. "Give me ten minutes."

She ordered a breakfast for two, dressed, and was ready to greet him when he knocked. Breakfast arrived soon after he did. Both sets of French doors were open to the rising sun. The traffic was a constant rush somewhere out of sight. From where she sat, Marc was framed by the lake and the

171

hills and the growing light of day. The air was freshened by a sweet morning chill. Birdsong pierced the room's silence. The gilded ceiling and polished wooden floor reflected the beauty of another day. They ate from embossed china and drank fresh coffee from a silver thermos. Kitra tried hard to convince herself it was close enough to her dream come true.

When she declined his offer of more coffee, Marc said, "I was looking for a passage that might frame what we were going to be doing here." He pulled a hotel notepad from his pocket. "This comes from the twenty-fifth chapter of Proverbs. 'It is the glory of God to conceal a matter; to search out a matter is the glory of kings.'"

He shifted his coffee cup over and placed the pad on the table between them. "Sitting here in this amazing place. The fate of nations in the balance. I would say we're as close to royalty as we ever need to come, both in terms of beauty and responsibility."

She could see he had spent a long time on this, measuring out the words, taking aim at the objective. Curious, she asked, "Did you sleep at all?"

"Some. Enough." He touched the pad. "I don't mean to put you on the spot. But do you have a Scripture passage you've been thinking about?"

"Something I thought of just before I fell asleep. A prayer my father used to say when I was young. Every night when he tucked me into bed. It's a revision of the hundred and twenty-fifth Psalm. 'Lord, as the mountains surround Jerusalem, so surround my family and me, both now and forevermore.'"

"I like that. A lot." He turned to a new page and wrote it down. "I have an idea how we could proceed. But that's all it is. An idea. If you don't like it—"

"Tell me."

"It goes back to the passage from Proverbs. We don't know what to do, where to go, or how. So I thought we'd try and take this time to find out what we want, and what God wants, and pray for each other."

He was so handsome sitting there. The blue shirt accented the smoky depths of his eyes. His tanned skin was stretched taut over strong features. She doubted he had an ounce of excess poundage on his entire frame. And yet he comported himself with an immense gentleness. Something that did not come naturally, she knew. He was and always would be a warrior. Still, he had learned how to approach the moment with tenderness. She blinked against the burning behind her eyes and said, "I like this."

"So do I."

"Yes, Marc. It's an excellent idea."

"Okay, then I'll go first." He turned to another fresh page. "The issue we're talking about here is, what do I want most from life. I feel like we need to look at this honestly before we can work out what God wants. So far, I've only come up with two things. I want a new course in life. Right now it feels like I just tread water between assignments, until Walton calls and sends me out again."

"Go to Geneva and save the world." They both smiled.

"It's still somebody else's concept. After this is done, assuming we come out in one piece, I go back to Baltimore and sit in an office and bide my time. And wait for another phone call. It's not a life. It's not *my* life."

"That's one."

"I want a new reason to hope. A new reason to be fulfilled. I haven't felt that way since my wife died. I thought . . . you know."

"Yes." The unspoken was enough for another fierce blink. She hardly ever cried. And yet it seemed like it was all she had been doing lately, in those moments when she had not been assaulted by sheer, unbridled terror. She watched him turn to a new page and wait. She knew he would wait there all day. But there was no need. She knew what she needed to say. "I want to stop yearning for what I can't have."

His hand tracked slowly across the page as he wrote. "That's a good one."

"I want to be happy with my world and my purpose. I want the old ways to feel right again." She noticed that he had stopped writing entirely. "I want to stop seeing the kibbutz as a prison."

Surprise creased his features. "You feel that way?"

"I didn't. Not once. Not *ever*. Until . . ."

"Until I didn't come. Until I didn't join you."

"I know these feelings are part of the process. That's my prayer. To move on."

"I understand, Kitra. Thank you for sharing this. I'm so sorry."

"It's not your fault."

"In a way, it is."

"We're beyond all that now."

"Yes." The sadness was clear as the tolling of a bell. "We are."

She knew merely blinking would not be enough this time. She pounded her fist on her leg. "I want to stop yearning for the impossible."

He waited until she calmed to say, "Why don't we pray."

She bowed her head, which was good, because when he shut his eyes she could surreptitiously wipe her cheeks.

She did not hear his words so much as the way he prayed. The moment and his quiet appeal to God became a mirror. She saw with utter clarity that a part of her had hoped he would be insincere. There remained a faint and bitter mockery in her brain. Part of her had expected him to show up and give her the standard line of how they should still be friends, only add God to the mix.

But Marc was *real* in this. And she knew, in this moment of internal honesty, that was one of the things she loved so much about him. He was *always* real. He most resembled her beloved father in this, the integrity that was so ingrained, so much a part of him that no one even spoke of it or questioned it. Others followed him, even when they disagreed with him over one point or another. They trusted him, even . . .

At that moment, she realized Marc had gone silent. The internal clarity remained with her, such that she knew precisely what it was she needed to say. "Heavenly Father, I have never been good at asking you what I should do. Most of my time in prayer has been spent telling you what I want. Even speaking these words is an effort. It makes me scared. What if you want me to do something . . . ?" She took a long, hard breath. "I am asking, God, what do you want?"

She heard Marc say, "Lord, I join my prayers with Kitra's. I ask for us both the answer to the impossible question. This is the hardest thing a strong person can ever do, to be weak in the face of uncertainty. She has led me to the point I could not come to on my own. I ask for Kitra and for myself. In our weakness, we join in this prayer. Show us your will."

Rhana watched a lovely sunrise from the Hotel de la Paix's veranda. The morning chill was kept at bay by heaters flanking the retractable roof. Rhana considered this terrace one of the most beautiful settings in Switzerland. She would often come here to celebrate a sale or entertain a special client. When Kitra appeared in the doorway, Rhana nodded her approval. Kitra wore the raw-silk outfit, slacks and a high-necked blouse and long woven pashmina, all in shades of cocoa and cream. The color highlighted the golden glow of her skin. In greeting, Rhana tilted her chin, offering Kitra a cheek to kiss, and said, "You make me feel a decade younger, my dear, just by joining me here."

"Thank you, Rhana."

She liked how the young woman seemed unaware of the glances cast her way. "This morning we will be visiting two galleries before they open. We are being observed, of course. It is inevitable. For me to remain in your company after the warning is a declaration of sorts."

"I understand."

Rhana paid her tab and led Kitra from the café. Two bullet-proof Mercedes were pulled up in the hotel's front circle. Marc was stationed by the second car. Rhana led Kitra to the first vehicle, where both the driver and the guard held the rear doors. Rhana's Bentley was stowed away for the duration.

Beside Marc stood Agent Bernard Behlet.

"Your friend does not ride with us?"

"Marc wants to talk with Bernard," Kitra told her. "He asks if the driver is trustworthy."

"Utterly. And the guard. Both are allied to our friend. You understand?"

"Of course."

Rhana waited until they were under way to ask, "You are not afraid?"

"I was. Last night I hardly slept."

"And now?"

Kitra hesitated, glancing at the driver and the guard.

"My dear, if you are going to exist comfortably in this world, you must learn that either your guards are discreet or they are to be replaced."

Kitra nodded, but her voice turned soft as she said, "Marc prayed with me."

Of all the things Rhana might have expected this astonishing young woman to say, this was most certainly not one of them. "He prayed?"

"This morning. It helped. A lot."

"But . . . is this not the young man who broke your heart?"

"In a way. Yes. But it's not . . ." Kitra touched the window, which was almost half an inch thick. "Does this come down?"

"No. It is one of the unfortunate costs of traveling in safety."

Kitra settled her hands about her purse, a chalky pearl that matched her shoes. She described the events in Kenya, some of which Rhana already knew. Marc's venture with Lodestone, the rare earths, the relocation of the villages, the partnership between Kenyan tribesmen and Israeli followers of Jesus, the role of faith in their lives. She finished, "I wanted him to come join me on the kibbutz. I wanted him to lead it with me. I wanted . . ."

Rhana nodded slowly. She knew all there was to know about impossible desires. "His answer was no."

"Only after he had prayed about it for almost six months," Kitra corrected. "He felt God telling him to stay in America. As soon as he told me, I knew he was right. He is a patriot and a warrior. I could not ask him to simply give up his life's direction and join me."

"And you would not leave Israel?"

She shook her head. And yet Rhana detected a faint hint of doubt in her next words. "My brother and I lead the kibbutz my father founded. Our goal is to grant Jewish followers of Jesus a haven in a country where they are not welcome."

Rhana could tell this discussion interested the guard and the driver far more than was proper. But she could not bring herself to scold them. Which surprised her, in a mild and secret manner. For she had become very adept at keeping employees in their place. And yet these two men were far more than that. They were representatives of her ally, Amin Hedayat, the honest guide. They shared her heritage. What was more, they shared this young woman's faith in Jesus. Rhana decided to allow the two to listen and asked, "So what happened?"

"Last night Marc suggested we pray together and ask for direction. I expected . . ." She smoothed the purse in her lap. "I was half hoping it would prove false. That he was hiding his own desires behind this claim to faith. I was wrong. And it shames me that I thought as I did."

Rhana turned and stared. She was unaccustomed to this kind of transparency. It was not just the discussion of faith that felt so alien. No, it was Kitra's honesty.

Kitra continued, "Marc started with a Bible verse. Something to surround and structure the time. Then he asked me to say what I wanted most from life. Then he prayed for me. To have what I wanted. Even when it meant we would never be together, never have a future. He prayed for me."

Rhana nodded as though she understood and faced the front. The driver had shifted the rearview mirror so he could see Kitra. Rhana did not say anything. She understood their bewilderment. She felt it herself.

Rhana tried to tell herself that she had endured far more than this young woman could ever fathom. Rhana had herself been repeatedly wounded by life. She had been taught to trust no one, and now that included God. Her only way to punish God for all life's unfairness was to banish him. Politely. With elegant disdain. And in his stead, allow revenge to consume her.

She glanced over and realized the young woman was crying. Rhana opened her purse and offered a tissue. When Kitra did not see it, she pressed it into Kitra's hands. The connection was like an emotional fission. Rhana could not recall the last time she had permitted herself to have real feelings, real joy, real love, even real sorrow. She stared out the side window and tried to bring up the faces of those she had lost. The reasons for her lifetime quest for revenge. The hardened glass reflected nothing but the hollowness behind her gaze.

The guard cleared his throat. "Forgive me, mistress. But the passage of the Bible. The one your friend spoke of this morning. What was it, please?"

Kitra used the tissue to dab at her eyes, trying to keep the liner from smearing. "Something about mysteries and kings."

The guard and the driver switched to Farsi and spoke softly. The driver said, "Proverbs, no?"

"Yes."

The guard said, "The twenty-fifth chapter. The power of God to conceal, the power of man to discover."

The driver nodded. "It is a good verse for us and for our quest."

Rhana found it necessary to fumble with the clasp to her purse and draw out a second tissue. There was no reason why the words of two guards should affect her so.

Chapter Twenty

A s they pulled up in front of the gallery, the guard's phone rang. He answered, listened briefly, then halted the driver from opening his door. Rhana demanded, "What is it?"

The guard lifted his hand. "One moment, please, mistress."

Then he rose from the car and held his door while Marc slipped into the guard's seat. The guard shut the door and stood sentry. Marc turned around and said, "We have an idea."

"You or the Swiss agent?" Rhana asked.

"Both of us, and our ally in the United States."

Kitra gave her first smile of the day. "Which means it is Marc's idea, and the others agree. He dislikes taking credit."

Marc asked Rhana, "When are you expected to transfer the money to Hesam's account?"

"This morning as soon as the banks open. Why?"

Marc sketched out what he had in mind. But by the time he finished, Rhana felt the day had congealed into a solid lump of ice inside her. As though she could glimpse her demise lurking out there, beyond the sunlit city, hidden in shadows only she could see.

Then she felt something, and looked down to discover that Kitra had reached over and taken hold of her hand. She saw in those lovely features the same caring depths as she had heard in her description of the morning.

Rhana heard herself say, "I will do this thing."

Hesam al-Farouz parked a block and a half from the Pakistan Embassy, still smarting from the debacle at the gallery in Geneva. He loathed how he had been forced to flee on foot through the night, hiding like a refugee in the alley, skulking back to the main road, splitting from his men, flagging a taxi, watching every passing car in fear. The recollection burned like bile all through his abdomen and chest.

He sat waiting for the call from the Geneva banker, who was late. The banker had been given specific instructions to phone him precisely at nine. There were a dozen events that needed to take place in precise order. Beginning with this contact. The diplomat Hesam was meeting inside the Pakistan Embassy was nervous. The diplomat expected Hesam to soothe his nerves with a massive dose of ready cash. Which meant the banker's call was more than vital. It was the first step to victory.

The term *Aryan* came from Sanskrit, the oldest language still in use and from which the Farsi tongue was derived. This was completely different from the Arabic language, which was drawn from the same roots as Hebrew, the vile tongue of Persia's greatest enemy. Some of course would claim America held that spot, but in the view of many Persians, including Hesam, there was no difference between the two. Those nations marched in lockstep. To destroy one was to strike a killing blow to both. And that was precisely what Hesam intended.

The original meaning of Aryan was *noble race*. The Greek

word *aristos* derived from Aryan, and from this came *aristocracy*, referring to the upper class, the rulers, the elite. Aryan was also the root from which Iran was formed. A noble race that ruled a noble country. The elite of the world. The unspoken element to this term was that anyone who was non-Aryan was beneath notice, contemptible, created to serve the master race. Non-Aryans who disobeyed direct orders were to be punished with the utmost savagery. Just as he intended to do to this pesky banker, who was now twelve minutes late.

As if responding to Hesam's rising irritation, his phone rang. Hesam punched the connection and declared, "I *despise* tardiness."

"My sincere apologies, Mr. al-Farouz."

"You are *Swiss*. You are *paid* to be punctual."

"There was nothing I could do about the matter, I'm afraid. I can only offer you my earnest regret."

But the man did not sound at all sorry. If anything, his demeanor was indifferent. Hesam demanded, "You were to confirm the transfer of one hundred and fifty million dollars to my account."

"But it has not occurred, sir."

"Repeat that."

"No transfer of any funds has come through," the banker replied. "Because you were so certain, I called my associate at the bank in question. He reports that he has been instructed not to release a single penny."

"But I spoke with the account holder yesterday! She confirmed that the transfer would be made!"

"Perhaps so. I am unable to confirm any of this. All my associate at the other bank would tell me was, the account holder has placed a stay upon all transfers."

"What?"

"I too thought there might have been a mistake. At my request, the banker tried to contact his client. To no avail."

"Stay where you are."

"Naturally, sir. I am here until precisely five o'clock every—"

Hesam cut the connection and roared at the busy street, "I will *murder* that woman!"

He took a breath, another, then decided, no. That was not it at all. First he would crush Rhana's spirit. He would make her beg for death. Then and only then would he end her life.

Rhana was ready when the call came. She had sensed an inevitability behind Marc's words, as though his request had carried a hint of her own fate. All last night Rhana had lain awake and thought of how danger and even revenge had lost their appeal. She was so close to fulfilling her life's ultimate aim, and yet life itself no longer held any interest.

Rhana let Hesam scream at her in Farsi for a minute or so, then said, "Be quiet."

Hesam cut off. "How *dare* you—?"

"No, Hesam. How dare *you*? How dare you *fail* again. How dare you *threaten* me. After everything I have done, fulfilled your every wish. Last night you meet me in public, and you say you are going to *punish* me?"

"You have no idea what I am capable of. Yet. But you will. Very soon. I promise—"

"Oh, stop with your empty promises and your *failures*. Now you will listen to what *I* have done. I have written out everything I know about you and your organization and your plans. This morning I gave a sealed copy to my attorney. I have left another copy in the care of my bankers. And both have instructions to pass the information along to the CIA, to Mossad, to FIS, the instant I go missing, or die. If I am struck by a car, the information goes out. If I am struck by *lightning*. If a whirlwind lifts me from the face of the earth, it all goes public. Everything."

"You do not know everything."

"But I know enough, don't I?" Her voice was calm. Flat. She had practiced for this conversation all her adult life. Every negotiation to acquire a work of art, every attempt made by buyer and seller alike to wrest away her profit, it all came down to this. Facing death, and speaking with the calmness she would use to order her next meal. "I know enough to bring you down. Or at least to *slow* you down. Which would be the end of you as well. Wouldn't it, Hesam?"

"You talk nonsense."

"Do I? I know you urgently needed a hundred million dollars. Such an immense sum at such short notice must mean you have something truly enormous in the works. Something vital to your master plan. But you could no longer trust Sylvan. Because of his gambling and his debts and his forgeries, you knew he was a risk, you suspected he might sell your plans to the highest bidder. Is this correct so far, Hesam?"

The man did not respond.

"So you came to me. Your secret source. The one you used sparingly, the one you could always trust to be there for you, to be discreet. You off-loaded an entire gallery of stolen goods, and you demanded immediate payment of a hundred million dollars. Money you could get through no other source, because of the Americans and their choke hold on the Persian economy. And I succeeded. How am I doing, Hesam?"

The man was silent.

"So I supply you with the funds, and I give you a place and a time where you can wipe out all the loose ends. But you failed, didn't you, Hesam? Not me. I succeeded at everything. *You* failed. But you couldn't accept that. So you blamed me. And you threatened me with punishment. And then you failed again."

His voice was drawn low by the effort required to hold back. "I will not fail the next time."

"There will be no next time, Hesam. I hope you are listening very carefully. Because if you *dare* threaten me with *anything*, I will go public. If I have to walk through life looking over my shoulder, why not do what I can to exact a price? At least I will have the pleasure of taking you down. Which I will. Because we both know that *I do not fail.*"

The breathing was as ragged as the words, "What do you want?"

"Three things. First, you give me your solemn oath that you will *never* threaten me in any way, *ever* again."

A silence, then, "Agreed."

"Second, from now on you will treat me as the equal that I am, with the respect and admiration I deserve. You will not order. You will *request.*"

The silence was longer still. "And the third?"

"Yes or no, Hesam?"

"Very well. Yes. As an equal. With respect." The effort required to speak the words ground his voice to shreds.

"Now for the third item. My commission. I will have it. Every dollar. Fifty million. It is mine. And you will never seek to take what is mine, what I have earned, again."

This caused the longest silence of all, followed finally by, "Release the funds."

Rhana phoned her banker and confirmed that the account could be unfrozen and a hundred million dollars transferred to the Geneva account. The sum, she said, was correct. No, not the hundred fifty as initially instructed. One hundred million only. She would call later with instructions for the other fifty. She cut the connection. It required utmost concentration to fit her shaking finger onto the proper button. She found it harder still to draw a full breath.

Bernard Behlet now sat beside Marc in the front seat while the driver and guard stood duty on the sidewalk fronting the gallery. The Swiss agent said, "That was excellent work, Madame Mandana."

Marc asked Bernard, "You speak Persian?"

"The correct term is Farsi. And the answer is, not nearly well enough."

Kitra did not speak. But she reached over and took hold of Rhana's hand. And sat there beside her, offering far more than words ever could.

Rhana's cellphone was connected via Bluetooth to the speaker system of the Mercedes. The Swiss agent's phone was open on the central console, connecting them to the bedside of Inspector Reynard, who maintained his point position with the Geneva Police.

Marc raised his voice and demanded, "Ambassador Walton, did you get that?"

"Loud and clear. Hold, please." There was a silence, then, "We have a confirmation that our code is embedded in Hesam al-Farouz's phone. Even if he turns off his phone, unless he takes out the battery, it will continue to serve as our monitor and GPS. He is on a street in Bern." There was another pause, then the ambassador continued, "Our man has received a call from a bank in Geneva. The banker has confirmed that a transfer has been effected. One hundred mil."

More silence, punctured by the ambassador's labored breathing. Then, "Hesam al-Farouz has just entered the Pakistan Embassy."

Chapter Twenty-One

I despise the Swiss," the Pakistani diplomat declared. "They dress their world in cleanliness and smugness and superiority. But underneath their fine clothes and their arrogant talk, they are corrupt. They only hide it better."

Hesam al-Farouz flicked the dregs of his tea over the edge of the embassy's flat roof. He needed the diplomat too much to point out the absurdity of complaining about Swiss corruption when Hesam was here to deliver a massive bribe.

"I particularly despise Bern," the diplomat went on. "It defines boredom. The stench of cleaning fluid and smugness follows me everywhere. I was delighted to see them scurry about in fear after you bombed the gallery in Geneva. It was a proper blow for us all. Delighted."

They were seated in plastic chairs so overused the legs splayed like weary fat men. The plastic tabletop between them was supported by rusting metal legs. They were surrounded by a sea of satellite dishes and microwave antennae. A dingy cupboard held an electric kettle and an assortment of mismatched tea glasses, a jar of sugar cubes, and another of teabags. Hesam let the Pakistani man drone on about what a great moment this was, how wonderful to strike a blow against the West, on and on. The man loved the sound of his own voice. It was his only weapon. All oily talk and squabble and wasted actions.

But Hesam had years of experience at biding his time. He had endured endless hours of imams brooding and arguing. He considered most of Iran's religious leaders to be ridiculous. But he kept his sentiments hidden far down, in the secret recesses that every Persian was born with. The gift of selling lies as truth was never so important as now.

So Hesam fitted his face with a polite mask and let his thoughts roam over the havoc he intended to wreak upon that diabolical woman. The very instant this mission was successfully completed.

The Pakistani invaded his thoughts by placing a hand on his shoulder. "It is an honor and a delight to assist you in this great task. We are all brothers in the battle, yes?"

"Indeed so." Hesam knew his expression was as sincere as his voice. The life of sincerity was how he had managed to survive the years of serving the imams and enduring their endless drivel. But deep down in his heart, he boiled. To have this flunky official of a failed state call him brother was the worst of insults. "I would have it no other way."

"Thanks to Agent Behlet, the Swiss authorities report that we have movement on the account." Walton's wheeze had grown worse in the passing half hour. His labored breathing followed every word over the car's central speakers. The vehicle held Bernard, Kitra, Rhana, and Marc. The guards remained stationed outside. "A hundred million has been transferred into the Geneva accounts of one Helmut Schmidt. I think we can all assume they don't belong to the former leader of West Germany. The funds were then split into seven blocks of ten million dollars, and one of thirty. All have been dispersed into numbered accounts around the globe. Luxembourg, Singapore, Guernsey, Liechtenstein. Our money trail goes cold there. It would take years to ferret out who owns those accounts. If ever."

"Where is Hesam?" Marc asked.

"Still in the Pakistan Embassy. The Swiss have forwarded a video link. I'm looking at him and a senior consular official seated at a rooftop table, drinking tea."

"Can we hear what they're saying?"

"Negative. They are surrounded by a battery of antennae. It's a perfect location for a private little chat. The microwave transmissions cut our ability to link up from any angle, including a drone."

"I don't understand," Bernard said. "Why would they hold their conference out in the open?"

"That is simple enough," Rhana answered. "To be seen."

Bernard frowned. "But why?"

Marc pondered that. His cellphone was connected to the Mercedes radio by Bluetooth. He asked Walton, "Any chance our missing containers have been transshipped to Pakistan?"

"Most certainly. Our senior decision makers are fixated on Pakistan's involvement in preparing a dirty bomb. I am concerned over their single-minded focus. What has me awake and sweating at night is the risk that they're wrong."

"What do you want from us?"

"Concrete intel. A clear answer to the key question." Walton's words sounded almost strangled. "Intel. Evidence."

"We're on it," Marc replied, though he had no idea how.

"And fast. We are down to seventy-two hours. The warships

are now moving into position." A muffled voice drifted over the loudspeakers. Walton said, "Hold one."

They waited in tense silence until the intel chief came back on the line. "Hesam al-Farouz has left the embassy. We are tracking his vehicle."

"He was waiting for something," Marc said. "Confirmation that an event has taken place. Something big enough to justify a ten-million-dollar bribe."

"I agree," Walton said.

"Can you see if a ship has left a Pakistani harbor in the past few minutes?"

"We have been monitoring all shipments to and from Pakistan's ports since Hesam stepped inside the embassy. One container vessel just slipped from its moorings, next port of call . . ."

There was the soft muttering of numerous voices, then, "No dice. Rio." Walton coughed hard. "I'm due at a White House briefing."

Marc cut the connection. And sat there. Thinking.

Finally Kitra asked, "What do we do now?"

Marc saw no reason not to give them the truth, which was, "I don't know."

Everything went silent. The two women and Bernard retreated to Kitra's suite and ordered room service. The balcony doors were open to a beautiful afternoon.

At three thirty, Marc joined them to report on a call from some White House assistant, who informed them that Hesam al-Farouz had returned to Geneva, where he had spent ten minutes in yet another faceless private bank, then driven to the airport where he boarded a private jet, the manifest claiming it was headed for the Paris Roissy Airport.

At four, Bernard left to pay the injured inspector a visit. At four thirty, Rhana requested tea, which she drank seated in a high-backed chair that took on the aura of a throne as she gazed out the doors into the setting sun. At five, they received a call from her friend Amin Hedayat, who was downstairs and asked if he might come up. Three minutes later he knocked on the door and joined Rhana for tea. It was all very calm, very civilized, at least on the surface. Marc sat at the parlor table and resisted the urge to pace. This was the worst part of his job, the moments of sheer helplessness when boredom was only heightened by the ticking clock.

Ten minutes after Amin's arrival, everything changed.

Three phone calls came through simultaneously. Amin's cellphone might have rung half a second before Marc's. "This is Royce."

A deep, grating voice said, "This is Admiral Willits. We spoke soon after you blew up half of the Geneva lakefront. Remember?"

Marc knew there was nothing to be gained from pointing out that he had been the victim of that blast, not the cause. "You're head of DOD intel?"

"One of them. All right. Here's how it's going to play. You are hereby ordered to stand down. Do not, I repeat, do not engage in further actions of any kind. Send your lady friend back to her desert kibbutz. You will return to the U.S. immediately. That is an order."

Marc heard another phone begin to ring. Across the room, Kitra fumbled in her purse, saw the readout, frowned, and carried her cell out onto the balcony. Marc said, "Admiral, we have clear evidence—"

"I'm not interested in what you may or may not *think* you

know, Royce. I am telling you how it is. The man you were tracking, Hesam al-Farouz, has cleared customs at the Paris Airport and is boarding a flight for Abu Dhabi. Your high jinks have done nothing but endanger lives and property. Your remit is suspended. Permanently."

Marc watched as Amin set down his phone and stared across the room. Straight into Marc's eyes. Marc said into his phone, "Abu Dhabi would serve as a perfect gateway to the Iranian ports, sir."

"We're all over that." The man's tone carried the deep resonance of a long-ingrained command. "We've completed a full work-up on al-Farouz. He's a rising star in their nuclear program. Which is all the confirmation we require."

"Sir, with all due respect, continuing the hunt at this end—"

"Would only risk clouding the picture. Brains a great deal sharper than yours, and who are *authorized*, are taking care of this as we speak. We've wasted valuable time chasing our tails here. There are nukes on the high seas. We're going to board all suspect vessels entering the Strait and eliminate this threat to our nation."

The admiral was as one-track as every other senior defense intel officer Marc had ever known. Willits had his sights on the target. With officers like him, evidence played less of a role than his own conviction. The man had identified his enemy and was looking for a reason to take him out.

Marc nonetheless felt a need to say, "Sir, evidence suggests the funds we've been tracking are playing a significant role—"

"Royce, I am ordering you to *stand down*. In my book, that means you zip it tight. You're on your way back home when this conversation ends. You lay low. You hope against hope that we don't find a reason to lock you away."

"Sir, I was sent into the field by Ambassador Walton. He would need to issue my return orders."

"Walton is out of the picture."

"Sir, he is the only one authorized to order me anywhere."

The man gave two quick grunts. "We'll see about that."

As Marc ended the call, Kitra reentered the room, her expression one of worry. Marc quickly asked, "Problem?"

She looked over without really seeing him. "My brother says I need to return to the kibbutz. There's a problem at the plant."

"Maybe you should go."

She gradually drew him into focus. "What is it, Marc?"

"Washington wants to shut us down."

"But why?"

"They're totally focused on a nuclear threat riding the high seas. They're readying for the attack." Marc relayed the conversation. He knew he was breaking protocol. As far as the admiral was concerned, Amin belonged well inside the enemy camp.

The man summed it up. "The admiral considers you to be nothing more than a distraction."

"I don't understand." Kitra looked from one to the other. "With Hesam gone, what good can we do now?"

"None at all." Rhana rubbed a weak hand across her forehead. "I have put my life on the line. I have prodded the tiger with a blunt spear. And for what?"

Amin rose from his seat. "All is not lost."

Rhana looked at him. "I have signed my own death sentence."

"Not necessarily."

"He will achieve his deadly aim, this Hesam. And then he will come for me."

"We must stop him," Marc said, watching Amin.

"How?" Rhana asked, her voice catching.

Amin said to Marc, "My associates told me of Ms. Korban's conversation with you this morning. Of how you meet together and pray. Of the passage in Scripture that you found. They were very moved."

"Where are we going?" Marc asked.

"A place that may hold the answers we require." Amin gestured to the door. "Come. You will see."

Chapter Twenty-Two

They drove along the lake and entered France by the Divonne border, joining a line of elegant vehicles—Rolls and Maseratis and Daimlers and Porsches all headed for the palatial casino, the surrounding bars, dance clubs, and restaurants. Then Amin's car ahead of them turned to the right and wound through an industrial zone, finally entering a slum. The markets and the shop fronts turned tawdry, the people not so much furtive as bowed. The eyes that glanced their way were mostly dark and very angry. And why not? They rode in a pair of armored Mercedes, the vehicle of oppressors everywhere.

Amin pulled up in front of a nondescript apartment building. Three dark-suited men stepped across the sidewalk. Two opened the doors while the eldest waited for Amin to rise from the lead car. They embraced in the manner of Middle Easterners, smiling as they met each other's gaze, speaking softly for a moment, Amin touching the spot by his heart before turning it into a gesture that encompassed everyone rising from the cars. The elder responded with a smile that Marc found almost moving, a gentle reminder that here in this one corner of a French slum, there was hope. There was light.

Amin escorted the older man to each person in turn. When

they came to Marc, he turned to Amin and asked in English, "This is the American of whom you spoke?"

"His name is Marc Royce," Amin said. "Mr. Royce, this is the elder Mina. From Cairo."

"A very long time ago." The man spoke with a distinct American accent, overlaid by his strong Arab roots. "I hear from my brothers that you and this lovely lady know a time of study and prayer, morning and evening."

"To seek God's will," Marc confirmed.

"Then you will please come." The elder gestured to where a fourth man held open the door. He scanned the dusk in every direction. "Let us seek and pray as one. You are all welcome."

The third floor held three apartment doors. There was no name on the doors, nothing to suggest anything other than families residing within. Once inside, Marc saw how most of the interior walls had been knocked down. A very large room ran the entire length of the building. In the back was a small alcove holding a crèche, with several chambers for a kitchen, a narrow dining hall, and three offices. At the front of the main hall was a small dais, and on it was a podium, a table, and on the front wall a carved wooden cross.

Amin led them through rows of folding chairs toward seats near the front. As they settled, many questioning glances were cast their way. But the looks did not carry any hostility that Marc could tell. No doubt the attendees were simply being cautious. It was ingrained, probably a response that greeted every stranger who joined them. Amin said to Marc, "The apartments above and below us are occupied by members of this community. The windows have been replaced by reinforced glass. The other rooms stand between this hall and all the entrances."

"You're saying we can't be overheard," Marc replied.

"What I am saying, Agent Royce, is that all these precautions were taken for a very specific reason. Now I ask that you take a look around and tell me what you see."

Marc turned in his chair and inspected the gradually filling hall. He was still searching when Kitra said quietly, "They are from many different cultures."

"Very good, Ms. Korban. You are correct. What you see here is an impossibility. We are Kurds. We are Turks. We are Syrian and Lebanese and Ethiopians and Iraqi. We are Persians."

"And enemies."

"We *were* enemies. Our countries still are. In many cases, so are our tribes, even our families. Sworn to carry the burden of hate for all our lives, and then pass the weight to the next generation." His dark gaze flickered to Rhana, then away. "You know what has happened here, yes?"

"Jesus," Marc said.

"The gift of salvation carries a very special significance to such as these. They have spent their entire lives learning to hate, to seek revenge, to fight and die for a cause they often cannot even name." Amin pointed to the rear of the room. "Look there."

Seven Westerners had entered and were swiftly enveloped by a cluster of well-wishers. The four women all hid their hair beneath colorful scarves. Marc asked, "Missionaries?"

"Only if they are approved by this group. They come here for a year. They are housed with families from the cultures where they intend to live. They learn the language and the customs. They are anointed and prayed over. Then if they are deemed worthy, they are sent on their way."

"Where?"

"That is a question we never ask. Not even the families with whom they live. It is safest that way. Especially for them."

"I understand."

"Many of the people you see here have lost everything. Some are still hunted by their clans. If they are found, they will be taken back, and for most that would mean their end." Amin settled back as the elder approached the podium. "We will talk later, yes?"

The elder greeted them in a rainbow of tongues. The words in English were clear enough: The blessings of Jesus upon you and yours. Then he began to pray, switching back and forth seamlessly between the languages. This was followed by a swift homily, and then one of the missionaries was invited forward. The elder explained that the young woman would soon be leaving them, to go and serve. The family with whom she had lived for a year was brought forward, as were the church deacons. They placed hands on the young woman and they prayed. Marc studied the faces of those standing and kneeling on the dais. He saw the intensity, the concern, the tears, and the determination. He closed his eyes and prayed with them.

When the group at the front dispersed, the elder motioned toward Marc. "We have several honored guests with us tonight, one visiting from America."

At a signal from Amin, Marc rose and walked to the dais. The elder asked, first in English, then the other tongues, "Where are you from, Marc Royce?"

"Baltimore."

"And you travel a great deal with your work, yes? Where have you been recently?"

"Kenya. Before then, Baghdad."

"You have visited with communities of the faithful in both places, yes?" The elder gestured toward the podium. "Please. Come and tell us what you have learned. Speak with us of your faith. Let us hear where you stand. What issues you find before you this day. Let us see your heart."

Marc stared out over the gathering for a time, before allowing his gaze to rest upon Kitra. And in that moment he knew what he needed to say. "There is a word I hear in many churches these days. That word is *discipleship*. It is something I have studied, and something I thought I understood. But until this week, I do not think I ever truly lived the word. Now I feel as though I have only glimpsed one tiny fraction of what discipleship truly means."

He waited for the elder, then Amin, to translate, and continued, "There is no single meaning to discipleship. There is no single lesson. It is a series of stages that I must go through for the rest of my life. How can I love better, serve better, and understand more? How can I grow in wisdom, help others, give more?"

The elder translated, then said, "And now, my brother— you do not mind if I call you that, yes? For I feel a kinship between us. You and I, we are both seekers of truth. Tell us, my brother, what lesson are you now facing on the path of discipleship?"

"I must learn to follow Jesus even when it is painful to do so," Marc replied.

The murmur among the congregation started before the translations were complete. Marc went on, "I have spent my entire adult life training to be a warrior. To analyze and fight and succeed. To control risk and battle danger. And yet there comes a moment when I must go against my training. When I must accept that events are not to be fought against, but rather accepted in prayer. That at such times I cannot retreat into the safety of coldness and anger and still remain a faithful servant." He waited for the elder and Amin to translate, then finished, "There is no harder lesson for me to learn than to recognize the moment when I am called to be weak."

The group was quiet for a long moment, then several began to nod, to whisper to each other.

The meeting was followed by a meal, when any number of people came over and thanked Marc in a myriad of tongues. There was another time of prayer and singing, and afterward they departed, slowly, reluctantly, until the hall had emptied.

Nine of them gathered in the elder's office. He made tea and served them by his own hand. When all held a steaming tulip glass and the room was filled with the fragrance of boiled mint, he said to Marc, "I thank you for the gift of your thoughts put into words."

"It was an honor to be asked."

"We have seen into your heart, Marc Royce. We have glimpsed the soul of a brother in Christ." The elder paused to sip noisily from his glass. "Now tell us how we can help you in this hour of weakness."

Chapter Twenty-Three

That night Marc slept in snatches. He woke countless times, hoping against hope that Amin would call and report the impossible. That the fragmented clans, the secret connections, the unnamed allies had come up with the news he needed. Either that, or Walton would phone him and say all was well, stay where he was, do the work, complete his assignment.

Finally in the predawn gloom he rose and went down to the hotel gym. He attacked the weights and the heavy bag with a ferocity fueled by grim desperation. He returned to his room in the gray light of a windswept dawn. Rain rattled the window as he showered and dressed. Knowing all the while he was just marking time.

He phoned the three numbers he had for Walton, his home and office and cell. He left messages in all three places, not bothering to hide his anxiety.

As Marc finished dressing, the hotel phone rang. There was a bleak mockery to the sound, for he assumed it would be Kitra. Telling him it was time to meet. Marking the start of another day, the one that would probably tear them apart, wreck the myth of their being together, even in prayer. She would leave when he did, return to the kibbutz, resume her life, and meet a man . . .

His hand remained poised over the phone, halted by a sudden thought. Why didn't he simply go? What was keeping him? Loyalty to a man who wasn't there when Marc needed him most? Allegiance to a cause? How was that possible, when a superior officer had said his work was useless and he had nothing of value to offer?

The phone stopped ringing. Marc remained where he was, his hand holding empty air. Kitra would accept him with open arms. She *needed* him. What held him back?

The answer was there as well. Dismal as it might seem on this rainy morning. He was that most unfashionable and outdated of souls, a patriot. Even when he was excluded from the fight. Even when he had nothing of value to offer anyone. He remained at his core a man who would lay his life down. Not for Israel. For America.

The phone rang again. Marc picked it up and said, perhaps for the last time, "Good morning, Kitra."

"Hello, Marc. How did you sleep?"

"Not well. You?"

"The same. I have just received a call from Rhana. She is downstairs and wants to join us in our prayer time." When he remained silent, she added, "I hope I did right, telling her of our meeting."

"Yes. Of course." But he had no interest in sharing his time with Kitra. Even so, he could think of no good reason to refuse. "Tell Rhana she is welcome." As he started to hang up, he heard Kitra call his name. "Yes?"

"There's something else," she told him. "Amin is with her."

Rhana had no idea why she had come. She did not regret her decision so much as loathe her own need. And that was what had driven her to rise the hour before dawn. To her surprise, she found Amin in the hotel lobby, apparently drawn by the same remarkable desire. To join with two Westerners they hardly knew. And pray. Something Rhana had not done in years.

Rhana and Amin were welcomed by Kitra. Rhana was offered the nicest chair facing the parlor's rain-streaked French doors and the gray morning light. Marc arrived and helped Kitra serve them coffee. Then Marc began, "Last night I learned that my closest ally in the intelligence field is gravely ill. You heard him on the phone yesterday. His name is Walton. I've always had trouble calling him my friend, because when I was at my lowest, he fired me. But I know now that this is who Walton is. He is defined by his work and his mission. He has sacrificed men to the cause before, and he did it again with me. He never apologized for his action, and now I understand why. He did what he had to do. Only it may be too late for me to tell him . . ."

Rhana turned her face away. Marc's raw honesty *threatened* her. He represented everything she had drifted from. Everything she was not. Everything that had frayed her night, drawn her to this place, almost against her will.

She turned her gaze to the French doors. She had stared at her lifeless reflection in the glass of her own room most of the night. It seemed but a faint tracing of all she had once been. Of course she had come and joined them this morning. What choice did she have?

Marc went on, "Towards dawn I was hit by something I've been avoiding. What am I going to do when Walton is gone? I'm not in, and I'm not out. But the truth is, I love this situation. I was born for this. I am an outsider to my core."

Many of the events that had scarred Rhana were the fault of others. But it did not change her mistakes. It did not excuse her choices, so many of which had been self-serving and wrong.

Marc Royce sat across the low table from her, his strong shoulders bowed. Kitra Korban sat closest to the balcony doors, her face creased by sorrow and regret. They were caught up in forces beyond their control. They were not merely sad, they were wounded. Just like she was. And yet they did not use these torments as a reason to turn from God. Just the opposite. They were seeking him. They prayed to know his will.

Marc said, "I know this is not what we're supposed to be talking about. I should—"

Kitra interrupted, "This is exactly what we are here to discuss."

"We were going to ask about God's will."

"Which is precisely what you are doing. Your world is in upheaval. You have been ordered home. You feel called to stay. You have a job to do. Even when no one wants your help. And the man you feel closest to professionally is gone. You are alone." Her voice seemed wrenched by Marc's pain. "We have come back to the same issue. Only from a different direction."

Marc nodded slowly. Taking in her words. "Do you have anything further to add?"

"Not today. I have nothing to say about myself." She waved it off. "Finish with your thoughts."

"I've finished. You said it all. I am in desperate need of God's guidance."

Amin spoke for the first time that morning. "As are we all."

Rhana opened her mouth, but it was as if the words were denied her. The thought took shape in her mind, *I want to confess.* But where to begin? How she had spent an entire life using her losses as an excuse for self-indulgence? How she had defined herself by luxury, surrounded herself with every conceivable extravagance. She had claimed it was all for revenge, for this one moment when she could treat her enemies as she and her family had been treated. And for what? So she could gather in a ratty third-floor apartment in a Divonne slum, surrounded by Christian outcasts from all over the Muslim world, and know that they were the rich and she the one who had nothing?

Marc said into the silence, "I suggest we pray. I'll start. Anyone who wishes is welcome to speak."

In the end, though, his was the only voice. Why neither Kitra nor Amin prayed, Rhana did not know. She could scarcely make out a single word that Marc said. For as she shut her eyes, Rhana found herself filled with an all-consuming fear. That she had left it too long. That she had taken it too far. That she was lost. That there was nothing for her but to continue down the opulent road she had set for herself, until it ended in a gilded tomb—or merely an undiscovered body. Forlorn, abandoned, and unsung.

Marc gave the silence a few beats, then spoke the Amen and everyone lifted their heads. But Marc continued to study his hands. Rhana inspected him. Everything about Marc Royce was strong and hard, except for his eyes and his voice. Marc Royce was not built with the perfect angles of a gym rat. He was hard because his work required it. He treated his body as an instrument that could be applied to a particular task. She admired him. What was more, she trusted him. She wanted to open up to this Westerner and confess just how lonely and frightened and empty she felt, how much she longed for what he had—the ability to remain open and vulnerable and caring. Even when it hurt, even when . . .

Amin broke into her thoughts, asking Marc, "Why are you still here?"

"My job isn't done."

"But if you stay, you endanger your career. You risk losing any chance of returning to the intelligence services. You make enemies you cannot afford."

"It's what I've been wrestling with all night." Marc's voice was so low his words were almost lost to the rain. "But my job here is not done."

"What, then, is your job?"

"The same as it has always been. To protect the innocents. To serve my country."

Kitra's slight gasp was the sound of a woman on the verge of a sob. Marc lifted his head finally, revealing the depth of his pain. Rhana could see how much he loved Kitra, and yet knew he accepted the loss of her. He prayed not for what was denied, but rather for wisdom. Rhana had never felt more ashamed.

Marc forced his gaze back to Amin. "Say I go home. They close the Strait, they invoke an act of war, they make their assault. Then the Iranians still manage a successful assault. From a different angle. And say I am proven right. If there is even a shred of hope that I might have prevented it, how would I live with myself?"

Rhana kept her gaze upon Kitra. The young woman stared across the parlor, seeing nothing. Her eyes blinked and blinked, as though struggling to clear away the interior reality that attempted to blind her. Rhana knew exactly how she felt.

Amin said to Marc, "Do you recall what you asked of the elder last night?"

"Of course."

"Remind us. Please."

"I asked for cold, hard evidence of what is inside those North Korean containers, and confirmation of where they are headed. We need to obtain a clearer sense of who our enemy really is. What is Hesam al-Farouz's role in all this? Washington is sold on him being tied to Iran's secret nuclear program. Is that true, and if it is, is that the *only* truth? We need to assume Washington has the nuclear side down cold. The question is, what *else* is there? In taking their single-minded approach, what could they be missing?"

"Your questions are good ones," Amin said and rose from his chair. "Come, let us see if we can find some answers."

They left the hotel together, Amin ushering them into one Mercedes, the second one following. Marc sat with Kitra and Rhana in the back, Amin up front with the driver.

Rhana said, "What possible good does it do us to be crammed into this one vehicle?"

"Patience," Amin replied.

Marc guessed, "We're being followed?"

"So it appears," Amin said. "We will soon know."

They joined the early rush of traffic headed toward the industrial zones beyond the airport and the UN district. Amin lifted his phone, spoke briefly, then nodded to the driver and said a single word, which Rhana translated as "Now."

They turned into a narrow cobblestone lane. The second

Mercedes swung wide, which required it to reverse in order to take the corner. Horns blared and brakes squealed. Their own vehicle exited the lane and rejoined the flow, now moving back toward the lake. Two blocks later, their Mercedes pulled to the curb. Amin said, "Everybody out, please, and swiftly."

An SUV taxi halted in front of their parked vehicle. Two men and two women climbed out and wordlessly took their places in the Mercedes. Amin gestured his group into the taxi. Fifteen seconds later they were off again.

Geneva's high-rent commercial district was at the tip of the lake, where the Rhone flowed out and meandered back through the city and finally entered France. A series of medieval bridges crisscrossed the three outgoing flows, creating fanciful islands that once had housed the guilds and the royal palaces.

They halted before a building whose ancient stone walls had been hollowed out and rebuilt to house one of the city's many private banks. They followed Amin to a side portal. He spoke into the intercom, and they were admitted by a burly guard. As they waited for the man to call ahead, Amin explained, "This is the unseen face of Swiss banking, the door that only opens to the wealthiest of clients."

An elevator silently took them up several floors. As they entered a penthouse office suite, Marc's phone rang. He checked the readout and said, "It's Bernard."

The Swiss agent greeted him with, "I am at the hotel. You are not."

"We got called away to an early meeting."

"And you did not wait for me."

"No time. We're being tracked." Marc described Amin's strategy for freeing them from their tail. "Can you help?"

"Most certainly." Bernard surprised him by chuckling. "My

nose is itching. My nose rarely itches. It waits for moments when I sense my team stands on the verge of something big. Let me speak with Amin so we can arrange for the trackers to be tracked."

As Amin finished speaking with the Swiss agent, a secretary ushered them into a vast corner office. One set of windows overlooked the lake turned slate gray by the weather, another showed the Parc des Eaux Vives, the most exclusive residential area of this opulent city. The gilded ceiling held three crystal chandeliers. The carpets were silk. Rhana took a long moment to inspect the three oils, none of which Marc recognized, but when she finally allowed their host to usher her into a seat, she declared, "Monsieur has exquisite taste."

"And you, Madame Mandana, have been known to me for years as a purveyor of only the finest and most exquisite of works." He was as refined an older gentleman as was humanly possible, every inch of him a work of extensive effort and money. His small feet were housed in polished loafers as delicate as ballet slippers. He bore a frosting of silver hair, two streaks that joined in the back forming a white crown. He barely reached Marc's rib cage, his handshake had the fragile quality of a butterfly's wing, and yet his presence dominated the room. "Sayed Al-Rashid at your service."

He shooed away his assistant and served them coffee by his own hand. Marc guessed his age as early seventies, and yet he moved swiftly about the low table. Once he was assured that they were comfortable and served, he took the seat next to Marc and asked Amin, "How should we proceed?"

"Allow me." Amin put down his cup and looked around the group. "I have known Sayed Al-Rashid for twenty years.

He is a principal backer of our efforts. I trust him with my life. I urge you to do the same."

The little man showed the ability to bow elegantly while remaining seated. "I and my family have been followers of Jesus since many years. I am Lebanese by birth, raised in Canada. We Lebanese are merchants and travelers by nature. I am a specialist in finance law. I work with clients from all over the globe."

"Including Pakistan," Amin inserted.

"Indeed so. But there is another layer to my commercial activity. A secret layer. One that very few people can ever know about."

"We will never divulge your name," Marc assured him.

"Very well. You must understand, Mr. Royce, that the community of Arab believers shares a very rare trait. We are supporters of the West. We admire your lofty aims, even when we despair over some of your actions. We yearn for what you so often take for granted, the freedom to practice our faith, to live our beliefs, and to be treated with respect and equality by our neighbors. This can only come through a true Western-style democracy. This is why so many Arabs fear and despise you. Democracy carries with it not only freedom but *choice*. You have the ability to choose your lifestyle and direction. We envy you this freedom. We seek it for ourselves. We are, in short, your natural allies."

Sayed could no longer remain seated. He bounded to his feet and began pacing back and forth between them and his desk. "There is a new phenomenon rising in the Arab world. One that many oppose. People within the Muslim community are coming to recognize Jesus. Yes. There, it is said. The impossible is happening. And with this comes a dread realization among our opponents, that the message of Jesus and the gift of salvation carries significance for *all* people in *all* nations."

The man, Marc decided, would have made an amazing pastor. His energy was captivating. He invited the listener to agree with him. He *willed* it.

Then Marc noticed Rhana.

The elegant woman appeared to have shrunk inside herself. Her features had become hollowed, as though the banker's words pummeled her. Her gaze flickered about the room like a captured animal, desperate for escape.

Sayed went on, "So they call the West their worst enemy, and they persecute the believers they can identify. But they cannot locate most new believers. If they could, they would wipe us out. That is why our secret is so precious, Mr. Royce. That is why confidentiality is so vital. What I am about to tell you carries the lives of many, and the hopes of even more."

Marc forced himself to turn from Rhana. "I understand and will respect your need for secrecy."

"I believe him," Amin assured their host quietly.

"Very well." The man plucked a file from his desk and returned to his seat. "Here is the manifest for your missing containers." He reached toward Marc with several sheets of paper. "As you can see, everything is very clear. Machine parts for oil pumping stations. The North Koreans manufacture them under contract for a Chinese conglomerate. They are sold all over the world. Everything is aboveboard."

Kitra asked, "So why are the Western governments so concerned?"

"Because, my dear, these containers come from a cluster of factories that form the center of all North Korean nuclear activity. That is the only reason the West was alerted at all. Because of their point of origin."

"And then they went missing in Singapore, and everybody went ballistic." Marc studied the pages before him, the originals in Korean, the second set in Arabic script, the third translations in English. All of it gibberish. "What if it's all a ruse?"

The banker settled back in his seat. And smiled.

"What if it's all an elaborate hoax," Marc went on. "What if they planned this from the beginning, playing on our greatest fears, *willing* us to look in the wrong direction?"

Their host nodded agreement. "A shell game would be ever such a Persian gesture. Slipping the dagger into the Western heart while the eyes are watching the wrong hand."

Amin asked, "How do we proceed?"

Marc could come up with only one slender thread. "Hesam al-Farouz. My sources in Washington have been shut down. I need a full work-up."

Sayed and Amin began speaking softly in Farsi. Amin nodded at something the banker said, and announced, "Sayed has an idea."

"A possible contact," Sayed confirmed. "A friend in the cause. Someone who might aid us in glimpsing behind the veil. Because I for one believe your fears are justified, your theory correct."

Chapter Twenty-Four

As they left the bank, Bernard called with the news that all those tailing them had been arrested. "There were, in fact, four teams. Two watchers each. Very professional. Here is a strange thing. Two of the teams are Iranian. Two are Pakistani."

Marc thought of the Divonne chapel service and standing at the podium, looking out over the sea of faces representing so many different ethnicities, yet a thread stronger than steel pulling them together. But what his little group was facing now was the flip side of the equation, he knew. Nations bound together toward the common intent of spreading darkness. "How long can you hold them?"

"A few hours only. All have diplomatic passports. Their embassies have already lodged protests. Consular officials are now rushing down from Bern. I am personally supervising their questioning. It is doubtful we will learn anything. But we will have sent a clear message to the embassies that these actions are unacceptable. They will be escorted to the airport, and there they will remain until their flights depart."

"Thank you," Marc said. "For everything."

"I assure you, my friend, the people I answer to are increasingly irate over the actions of our foes."

Amin had stepped away from the others to take a phone call. He approached Marc to say, "Sayed has located us a source. We need to leave now."

Marc related this to Bernard, who replied, "You will report back to me immediately, yes? In the meantime, I will return to the useless interviews."

Amin drove the Mercedes, with Marc settled into the middle of the rear seat, Kitra on his right, Rhana to his left. The woman bore the same haunted expression as the previous night. He said softly, "Perhaps you would want to go back to your hotel?"

She seemed reluctant to meet his gaze. She responded only with a quick but firm shake of her head.

He hesitated, then decided he owed her a final warning. "Things could get intense, Rhana."

"How do you describe events up to now?"

"We've kept you safe. We've shielded your involvement. If you stay, they'll know you are with us." He let that sink in, then repeated, "Intense."

She turned to him, her eyes red-rimmed from too many sleepless hours. "I owe people who are gone. I will be staying."

He nodded. He had done what he needed to do. The decision was hers.

Marc savored Kitra's closeness. She smelled of a lovely blend of lemons and sage and youth and feminine allure. He knew he should not let her invade his concentration. But then she shifted slightly and seemed to melt to him, just for a moment, before drawing away again. And he was glad he sat where he did. Very glad.

The village of Meyrin was located on the border of the

Canton of Geneva, still containing remnants of its farming origins. The outskirts were dotted with vineyards and orchards and traditional wooden chalets. But the more recent portion of the town had overwhelmed its origins. Meyrin was a faceless commuter city, filled with bland apartment blocks and tight little postage-stamp parks and new shopping streets and office buildings. The only standout feature of the nondescript new city were the signs for CERN, the world's largest particle physics laboratory headquartered in Meyrin.

They entered a bland café situated across the street from a dozen identical office buildings. The compound was ringed by a park, and between the park and the street was a security fence topped with warning signs. Marc spotted nine different patrol vehicles in less than fifteen minutes. Sentry cameras stood atop tall poles. The guards manning the front gate were armed and extremely alert.

Most of the people seated in the café bore an air of preoccupation. Many of the tables held worksheets covered with indecipherable mathematical symbols. The conversations were muted and intense.

The man who approached them was dark-skinned, dressed in the garb of a professional nerd—shapeless jacket over a gray T-shirt, corduroys, Birkenstocks. He moved swiftly between the tables, shook Amin's hand, surveyed the others, and demanded, "We are safe?"

"These are friends," Amin assured him. "There are more friends guarding our perimeter."

The man dropped into a seat, declined Amin's offer of tea, and said, "I have only a few minutes."

His accent was a peculiar blend of many cultures. Marc had known this in other scientists. They were born here, studied there, did their postgraduate work somewhere else, accepted appointments in a fourth country, and learned languages with an impatient facility. Their real focus never changed. Their first language was the impossibly difficult tongue of higher mathematics.

Amin said, "We are most grateful that you agreed to join us."

"Our contact tells me you wish to know about Hesam al-Farouz."

"That is correct."

"Yes, well, so do I."

Amin glanced across the table at Marc, gestured with two fingers, inviting him to take charge. Marc shook his head. The scientist had not looked directly at anyone except Amin. The scientist sat with his back to the rear wall, studying every face that went by, as well as the street and the misting rain. He did not want to know them.

Amin said, "Could you please explain what that means, you want to know him?"

"My field is high-energy physics. I know everyone who is involved in this. By know, I mean I have read their work, or heard them speak, or met with them."

"You know their research," Marc said.

The scientist shot him a quick glance, tight and worried, then away. He continued to direct his words at the empty space before him. "It is like a signature. A fingerprint. And Dr. al-Farouz has none."

Amin's voice held the gentle tone of a supplicant. "What exactly do you mean?"

"Two years ago, he abruptly appeared. Before, nothing. Suddenly he was everywhere. So I asked. Of course I asked.

Who is this man? His credentials were impeccable. He completed his doctoral research in applied high-energy particles at age twenty-two. Twenty-two. That is astonishing but not unheard of. According to my research, Hesam al-Farouz did his postdoctoral research at Tehran, then vanished. For almost twelve years, there was nothing. Then two years ago, he pops up. Like I said, now he is everywhere. I spotted him at conferences in Paris and here and Zurich and Bonn. Never America. Never England. But elsewhere, yes, he comes and he shakes the hands and he smiles his handsome smile. The conference list of attendees state he is now on the faculty of Isfahan University."

Amin frowned. "But this would be a normal cover for a scientist attached to a secret nuclear weapons program, no?"

"Of course it would. But why has he suddenly popped up again? There is no other such person anywhere in Iran. If a person enters into their secret work, they *remain* secret."

"You have checked?"

"Of course I checked." He wiped at a faint sheen of perspiration. "I spoke with an associate at Isfahan. There is quite a good department there. Not cutting edge, but they know things. They are focused on applications. Medical, communications, cryptography, like that. I ask someone I know. I was told not to ask. My contact refused to even speak with me again. About anything."

Marc said, "You think the man's background has been manufactured."

"It is all so *perfect*. And that bothers me. Nothing in physics is perfect. If it was, we would all know the answers and we would all agree. But we don't agree, and the answers take generations to become clear. And here is this man. He has never taken a wrong step. But there is no research bearing his name, no one who will speak of his work, nothing. If you wanted to make a man appear to be a bomb maker, what would you say? He is brilliant and he is well trained and he has spent his life never making a wrong step." He met Marc's gaze with worried intensity. "This Hesam al-Farouz is perfect. And he also is a ghost."

Chapter Twenty-Five

An hour later, they were joined by Bernard Behlet and headed out in both Mercedes. Bernard grew distinctly uncomfortable as they crossed the border into France and turned away from the glitz and glamour of central Divonne. "Why are we here?"

"I told you," Marc said. "You need to understand how certain sources have come to us."

"I trust you." Bernard scanned the rain-swept slum, his uncertainties apparent. "I trust your sources."

"In this case, it's not enough. You need to be convinced enough to satisfy your superiors."

"Without ever telling them precisely what you observe this evening," Amin cautioned. "Or even where it is located."

"How can I say that when I don't know where we are?" Bernard took in the dank surroundings and the kerchiefed women and the suspicious glares of passersby. "I have lived across the border most of my life and I have never been here."

Marc motioned toward the building's entrance. The two vehicles pulled over, and the occupants climbed out. The men walked up the three flights while Rhana and Kitra shared an ancient elevator with two ladies in Pakistani scarves. Marc waited on the third-floor landing with Amin and Bernard, and pried open the rusting accordion doors. They entered the chapel together, but once inside, Kitra said, "Rhana and I need a moment."

The elegant woman had scarcely spoken a word all day. She seemed to drift, carried along by swirling currents.

Marc drew Bernard into the chapel, and they found places in the back. Bernard joined in the singing, but faintly. When it was over and the people had dispersed, Marc asked, "Do you understand what is happening here?"

"An astonishment," the Swiss agent said, staring at the front of the room toward the cross. "Never in all my days did I think I would witness such a thing."

"You also understand why you can never tell anyone about this," Amin warned. "You would not just be risking their lives, but the lives of clansmen and families, reaching thousands of miles."

"I accept this," Bernard replied solemnly. "No one will know."

Marc related what they had learned from the Lebanese financier. He then described their meeting with the physicist at CERN. Bernard listened in silence, then asked, "What do you need from me?"

"I want you to take another look at Hesam al-Farouz."

Bernard nodded slowly. "My superiors have learned precisely what you already have heard. That the man is recognized as a nuclear physicist. He is a member of the ruling council. But if what you tell me is true, all of this is a ruse."

Amin agreed. "If Hesam al-Farouz is the public face of a myth, it changes how we must look at all that has transpired."

"Everything changes," Marc confirmed. "Including the

attack at the spa. He wants us to look in this direction. Hunt him down. Stop the ship. Expect an attack, one that he leads."

"So while the West's armed might gathers in the Strait of Hormuz and takes an action that defines international war," Bernard countered, "what do you expect our ghost to do?"

"I cannot tell you that. Yet."

Marc waited, fearing the Swiss agent would demand more information. Which he did not have. It would be right for Bernard to question his assumptions, and dismiss the information gained from a Lebanese banker and the physicist. Both of whom had been drawn together by the invisible thread of faith. It would be a thoroughly Swiss response to say the logic did not stand up.

Instead, Bernard turned to Amin. "Why are you involved in this?"

Amin smiled thinly, as though having long waited for this very question. "You are right to ask."

"I mean no offense."

"None is taken, I assure you."

"But you also have remained hidden. Why do you now reveal yourself? Why do you risk your associates, your—"

"The correct term," Marc offered, "is members of his faith community."

"My brothers," Amin added. "And my sisters. In Christ Jesus, the risen one."

"Amen," Marc said.

"Understand this," Amin explained. "Our aim is not to stop a single terrorist act. No matter how bad. For by revealing ourselves, we risk having word reach the people who seek to destroy our communities. To rip apart the churches that are rising up in all these nations. To demolish the hope we offer, to pretend that our faith has no place in their realms."

"Then what . . . ?" Bernard caught his breath. "Ah."

"You see, don't you, Agent Behlet? Our aim is much higher. There is one purpose great enough to justify such a risk. We seek to bring down the Iranian government. We want to end a regime that has lost its right to rule." The man's words carried no additional volume. But the burning flame in his gaze ignited a flame in Marc's heart. "We seek to establish the impossible. A regime that welcomes our presence. A nation that is open to the presence of Jesus. A democracy. In Iran. At the center of the Muslim world."

"There is more," Marc said, "isn't there?"

Bernard said weakly, "More?"

Amin's eyes fastened on him with the force of a blow. But he did not speak.

"You want to establish yourselves as allies of our governments," Marc said. "You want them to see you as people who can be trusted. A network worth preserving. You want our protection. You want us to treat you as allies, and your cause as worthy."

"Dreams," Amin said quietly. "Goals we have carried for twenty-five years. And never spoken of to anyone beyond our community before this night."

Bernard nodded. "Tell me what you need."

"Marc has already told you, Agent Behlet. A new work-up on Hesam al-Farouz."

The Swiss agent's brow furrowed. "I have already given you what I obtained. The man is—"

"Totally clean," Marc finished for him. "Made to lead a nuclear attack on the West. I know. Like he's got a target painted on his chest. Forget all that. I want you to do a *new* scan. One that totally discounts the obvious."

"And look for what, exactly?"

"Like I said," Marc replied, "I don't know yet what that is. But I beg you to put this pursuit in motion."

Chapter Twenty-Six

Two women with the finely sculpted bones of tribes from the Horn of Africa were slicing bread and mixing salad as Kitra and Rhana slipped into the kitchen. They offered a musical greeting and returned to their work. Clearly the arrival of visitors seeking a quiet corner was nothing new, though these particular ones drew second looks from under their headscarves. Kitra drew out a chair from the long central table and directed Rhana into the seat. "Would you like tea or something?"

The older woman looked around in confusion. "Why am I here?"

Kitra took that as a no and sat down across from her. "I thought it might be nice if we had a moment away from the others."

"No, I mean, why am I *here*? In this place?"

"Because you chose to stay. To come with us. Marc said you could go back if you wanted."

"Go back to *what*?" The last word almost broke her.

"Do you want to tell me what is wrong?"

Rhana dropped her head. "I can't."

"I understand."

Rhana shook her head. "How can you possibly know—"

"You fear your entire life is one giant mistake. And every direction you might choose would only take you deeper into the mire."

Slowly the woman lifted her gaze.

Kitra went on, "You have spent a lifetime building walls to hide your secrets. And suddenly the walls are gone. And nothing is as you expected. You thought . . ."

"I thought I would have won," Rhana whispered.

"Yes. Yes. I do understand."

This time, the words were a plea. "But how *can* you?"

"Because I have done the same. Oh, not your exact mistakes. But I too have done many right acts for the wrong reasons." It felt to Kitra as though she were breathing in glass fragments. "I received a phone call from my brother. Serge called to say . . ."

When she stopped, Rhana pressed, "Yes? To say what?"

"It doesn't matter. Well, it does. But not to this . . ." Kitra dragged in another painful breath. "In the middle of our conversation, I remembered something I had done my best to forget. How I manipulated my brother. My good, trusting brother. My closest friend, the man who would do anything for me and always has. A few years ago, I told him I was going to Kenya. And I waited for him to insist that he was coming with me. When he did, I argued and I fought, but all the while I was doing it to protect *me*."

"So that you could say you did your best to shield him from whatever came next." It was Rhana's turn to say, "I understand."

"I almost got Serge killed. If Marc hadn't risked his life to identify and hunt down the kidnappers, my brother would have been lost. Forever." She looked at her hands clenched on the table. "And then I tried to do the exact same thing to Marc."

"How can you possibly think such a thing?" Rhana sat forward, her face wreathed in genuine astonishment. "Marc Royce came to Geneva because of his government. You traveled from Israel to *save* him."

"But it's the same thing. The truth the world sees is built on lies. I came because I want him to change his mind. To make him see me and want to return with me to the kibbutz."

Rhana gave a soft breath of understanding. And nodded.

"I manipulate. I manage. I control. I fight. I say it's for the kibbutz. But it just gives me a reason to be who I am, to steer things my way. And now . . ."

Rhana's gaze focused on the distant unseen. "Now you see the lies for what they are."

Kitra reached over and took the woman's hand. And waited. She was not going to ask Rhana to talk. It was the older woman's decision. Besides, she needed a moment to fit her heart back into the hollow space at the center of her being.

Rhana whispered, "I cannot any longer remember my father's face."

Kitra freed one hand to wipe her eyes. The prospect of telling her own father the truth melted her resolve. And she would tell him. She had to. And Serge. They all had to know. So she could ask their forgiveness. She wiped her eyes a second time.

Rhana said, "It does not matter any longer whether I exact my revenge. The act has lost all meaning. Everything has." She focused on Kitra. "I did as you just described. I turned my loss into an excuse to live a life of shameful indulgence."

"Would you like to pray with me?" Kitra asked. "Two lost and wandering souls, asking for forgiveness and wisdom?"

"It is too late for me."

No smile should dislodge so many tears. "With all my heart and mind, I tell you, you are wrong."

Rhana looked at the hand holding her own. "How can we know if God hears? Or if he even wants us to speak?"

"Because," Kitra replied, "everything we have done has been leading to this moment. When we confess our helplessness. And ask for help. Strength. Wisdom. Healing."

"Impossible. What you say . . . it cannot happen."

"By man, by logic, by what we deserve. Yes. You are right. But with God, all things may come to pass. Even this."

Chapter Twenty-Seven

Clouds reduced the sunset to the gradual darkening of the already dull sky.

They sat in the apartment assembly hall, sipping mint tea from tulip glasses, isolated by choice and a sense of helpless foreboding. Another group of believers filtered through the rear entrance, and preparations began for the evening service. Marc was about to admit defeat and suggest they return to the hotel, but his phone rang and the diminutive banker asked, "Where are you now?"

"Sitting in the Divonne church hoping against hope." Marc covered the phone and told Amin, "It's Sayed."

The Lebanese banker could not have sounded more pleased. "And where else on earth could you find a better place to do just that?"

Marc did not attempt to hide his desperation. "Please tell me you have something."

"Two things. Perhaps neither are important. But I and my friends thought it was worth passing on. First, you asked me what the other factories in this North Korean compound produce. One older facility produces agricultural machinery. It is best known for industrial blowers."

"Blowers," Marc repeated. Hunting the floor by his feet.

"Great beasts of machinery. Used for drying grain, I understand."

Marc rose and crossed to the window, his mind scrambling for answers. "And the other matter?"

"I have just learned that a second ship set off from Karachi on the same day as the vessel carrying the suspicious containers. Which is not important, except that both set sail hours after the money was transferred to our enemy's account."

Marc began pacing up the side aisle. "I don't follow."

"It is actually quite an old vessel, but newly refitted. As a research vessel. Licensed to the University of Hyderabad. I am looking at a photograph of the ship now. It appears almost intentionally ugly. The long bow is equipped with two cranes."

"Tell me more—why is this significant?"

"First, the size. At two hundred and sixty feet, it is extremely large for a relatively poor university. Secondly, its purpose. The vessel is licensed to study coral-reef formations and fishing habitats."

"And?"

"The University of Hyderabad does not have a marine studies department."

"You are sure of this?"

"I checked," Sayed replied. "Most thoroughly."

Marc felt the heat of the chase begin to boil up inside him. "This is it. Our target. This vessel is what we're after."

"That was precisely my own reaction upon receiving this news. The ship's destination is Mauritius."

"It's a decoy, and it's a good one." Mauritius was surrounded by vast stretches of the Indian Ocean, thousands of miles of nothing. Marc said, "Hold one moment," then hurried across the sanctuary to Bernard and Amin. He summarized the discussion, put the banker on speaker, introduced Bernard, and said to them all, "What does a research vessel have onboard?"

They were all silent for a long moment, then Sayed said, "I am sorry, but I do not see—"

"A lab," Marc replied. "The vessel will be equipped with a lab."

Bernard rocked back in his seat. "Of course."

Marc asked, "What else does North Korea have in spades?"

"Chemical weapons," Bernard breathed.

Over the cellphone's little speaker, Marc heard the banker's gasp. He demanded, "Iran has a chemical weapons operation, right?"

"Most certainly," Amin confirmed. "Very secret. But present."

Bernard said, "My superiors will want concrete confirmation."

Marc's adrenaline-amped mind had already reached that conclusion. "Hesam al-Farouz may be our answer."

Amin frowned. "I do not follow."

Marc said, "Look for a top scientist within the chemical weapons division, a manager, a Revolutionary Guard overseer, who was there one day and vanished the next. Someone who with a bit of plastic surgery could be made to look like our guy."

An hour later, Marc was seated in a vehicle driven by Amin and parked at the curb in downtown Geneva. Marc turned in his seat and said to Bernard, "Please thank your superiors for setting this up."

"They want their pound of flesh in return," Bernard

cautioned. "They want regular reports. They want to be involved. They want discreet recognition. They dislike being treated as a pariah by the international intelligence community. They want to use you as a lever to open the door."

"No problem," Marc replied, and saw no need to add the obvious, that first the group had to succeed.

The Geneva station of the United Nations was, after New York City, the second largest of its four major sites. The UN's central offices were housed within a mock Grecian structure known as the Palais des Nations. The UN's Geneva arm oversaw a myriad of programs and funds, including the European Economic Commission, the Office of Humanitarian Affairs, the International Trade Center, and fourteen other august bodies. The top representative of the U.S. government to Geneva held the same senior level as the UN ambassador in New York.

Bernard's phone rang. He listened, then announced, "The ambassador's limo is pulling up now."

When Amin started to open his door, Marc said, "Not yet."

They watched as the driver rose from the armored Caddy, opened her door, accepted her umbrella, and shut her inside the vehicle. Then he remained standing there, waiting in the rain.

The Swiss-based U.S. Ambassador to the United Nations was a stern, gray-haired woman named Samantha Keller, Bernard had told Marc. The diplomat had served as professor of international law at Columbia University before becoming a UN assessor of human rights violations in Bosnia and then a director of the World Bank.

"All right," Marc said. "Let's move."

The driver watched them approach in stony silence. Marc

stopped in front of the man. "I believe the ambassador is expecting us."

"She's due at an event in twenty."

"Understood." Marc walked around to the car's other side, opened the rear door, and slipped inside. Bernard settled himself on the jump seat, Amin in the front on the passenger side.

She had a linebacker's jaw and an energy that punched through the dusk. The woman's gaze, hard as sword steel, matched the voice that barked, "Which one is Royce?"

"That would be me, ma'am."

"I've worked with Ambassador Walton on three occasions. He impresses me. I expect you to do the same." She leaned forward a fraction, enough to look around him at Bernard. "You are Agent Behlet?"

"Correct, Madame Ambassador."

"Your superiors at FIS could not have stressed the importance of your information any more highly. I hope they're right in their assessment." She indicated Amin. "And who is this?"

"He is not here," Marc said.

She was singularly unimpressed. "You cloak-and-dagger boys are all the same. All right. Tell me why I'm going to be late for a meeting with the NATO chief."

"Does the name Hesam al-Farouz mean anything to you?"

She glanced at her watch, a diamond Rolex. "I'm waiting, gentlemen."

Bernard unzipped his pouch and handed Marc a file, which he passed on to the ambassador. "The man is a myth from beginning to end. He has been manufactured by the Iranian authorities. He is part of a larger ruse."

"I've been granted access to the White House file," she snapped back. "Al-Farouz is a nuclear-weapons expert."

"He did not even exist until three years ago. They have put together a fictitious history designed to entrap us and draw us in." Marc tapped the file. "This is the man's true legacy. His background is not nuclear."

She started to open the file, then decided against it, laid her hand on the cover, and stared at Marc.

"The man detailed in this file went straight from university into the elite Revolutionary Guard force known as Quds. That was nine years ago. He moved to Qom. Three years ago, he died in an automobile accident."

"Then why are we discussing him?"

"Because," Bernard said, "this supposedly deceased officer bears a striking resemblance to Hesam al-Farouz. If one removes the beard, applies face-recognition software, and factors in what could be done with plastic surgery, the two men could be twins."

Marc nodded to Amin, who said, "The Quds is the elite element of the Revolutionary Guards, sometimes described as the successor to the shah's Imperial Guards. It is very small, very tightly organized. All but three of the current Revolutionary Guard senior leaders come from the Quds force."

Marc added, "The Quds are responsible for protection of the ayatollahs. They have a second role, seldom discussed. They hold control of what is known as unconventional warfare."

"Meaning nuclear," the steely woman said.

"No, Ambassador Keller. Nuclear is controlled by the Missile Division."

"Then what—?" But she stopped abruptly as Marc reached to his left. Bernard had the second file ready. "The Revolutionary Guard is not just working on nuclear arms," he continued. "For the past eight years they have brought a secret facility online near Damghan. This facility falls under the direct control of the Quds. The Damghan base is producing chemical weapons."

The woman breathed a quiet breath, a huff of what could have been surprise, or concern, or both.

Marc went on, "These weapons of mass destruction are focused on smallpox. According to UN regulations, usage of smallpox in offensive weapons is universally outlawed. What makes the Iranian efforts especially lethal is, they are mixing smallpox with biotoxins. The problem with biotoxins is that they must be ingested directly. An infected victim cannot make anyone else sick. But when joined with smallpox, this means an entire population could be eradicated. They—"

"All right. Enough. Are you telling me the missiles are intended to carry biochemical weapons and not nukes? If so, what difference does any of this make, except to add further urgency to our efforts on the high seas?"

"Madame Ambassador, we don't think the container vessel the U.S. Navy is tracking contains anything related to this attack. We believe it is all part of a complex smoke-and-mirrors ruse, designed to embarrass the U.S. government and sow confusion. So that when the true attack is carried out, our response will be slower, and the enemy will be hard to identify."

Her horror was genuine. "Where are they attacking?"

"We don't know yet."

"Gentlemen, that is not acceptable." She was sitting forward on the seat, hands gripping the files in her lap.

"We agree."

"The initial intel suggested an assault on an American port city. You're telling me there is a *different* vessel out there, loaded with biochemical weapons *and* a reasonably accurate delivery system?"

Marc started to confirm, then stopped. Snagged by a half-formed thought. Something so vague he couldn't even name it for himself. Hovering just out of reach.

When he remained silent, Bernard answered for him. "Perhaps this is the case, Madame Ambassador. Only perhaps."

"While our entire defense system is looking in the wrong direction. Hunting for the wrong threat." She tapped the files with a bloodred fingernail. "When can you deliver something concrete enough for me to run up the flagpole?"

"We think we have a lead," Marc replied slowly, still trying to capture whatever that flash of insight might have contained. "But pursuing this further places us in jeopardy. We needed someone to have this information in case we go off the grid."

"Gentlemen, you are hereby ordered to deliver the goods and remain safe in the process. Now, what further do you need from my end?"

"As of this moment, I am officially not reachable." Marc told her. "It's the only way I can remain beyond the control of Admiral Willets and his orders for me to return home." He handed her a slip of paper with his new cellphone number. "Any fresh intel without doubt would be most useful."

"But be careful who you tell about us and what we are thinking," Amin put in. "There are leaks within your system, and—"

"I'm well aware of this. All right. Find the *real* boat, gentlemen. Fast."

Marc motioned for Bernard to open the door. "Thank you for your time, Madame Ambassador."

Chapter Twenty-Eight

It was the strangest telephone call Kitra had ever made. Bernard, Marc, and Amin sat with her. Inspector Remy Reynard had been delivered to the Geneva hotel by police ambulance and was now seated in a lounge chair drawn up by the balcony, his injured leg supported on a padded stool. Rhana sat to Kitra's left. She hadn't spoken more than half a dozen words since leaving the Divonne church and ate little. But she was there. Emerging from time to time from her internal struggle. Like now.

Kitra turned on the new cellphone Bernard had supplied. He had also provided six pages containing their names and new phone numbers, then asked them to destroy all other electronic devices they carried. He explained that these new phones were specially designed so that no viral software could be inserted.

Amin had asked, "Are we now being monitored by the Swiss?"

Marc replied, "Every gift in the intel universe comes with its *quid pro quo*."

Bernard smiled and gave Marc a second sheet of paper. "Always a pleasure, doing business with a professional."

Marc passed the paper to Kitra. "You understand what you need to do?"

"Yes, Marc. We have gone through this. More than enough," she added, eyebrows quirked upward.

"Sorry. It's a habit from my training. You repeat and you repeat and you repeat. That way, when the bullets start flying and people are on the verge of panic, they can still remember what needs doing. Hopefully."

She caught the warning in his casual response. She was not just making a call; she was opening the door to whatever came next. And everything beyond that doorway shrieked with peril. She looked into Marc's eyes and saw what he wanted her to see. That he was strong and ready and there for her. Which gave her the strength to nod. "I'm ready, Marc."

"All right. Here we go."

She dialed the number.

A man's voice answered in Hebrew. A sharp, simple yes, tight as a bullet.

She responded in the same language. "My name is Kitra Korban. Recently I was visited by a man from your organization. He asked me to do something for him. I have done it. I need to speak with him. I have something to report."

The man replied instantly, "You can give me the information."

"That is not possible. I speak only with him."

"What is his name?"

"I do not know. He did not tell me."

The man scoffed. "You expect me to run around looking for a man without a name?"

"Yes, that is precisely what I expect you to do," Kitra confirmed, looking at her paper.

The man hesitated, then said, "Describe this man."

"Not tall. Maybe sixties. Very stocky. A birthmark or sun blemish on his forehead. He walks with a cane."

"The man you describe has been retired. Since two years, he officially holds no position."

Marc had warned her this might be the response, as there were clearly opposing forces at work in her country as well. "He came to me regarding a possible threat. I am calling to say he was correct, and that the threat is imminent."

The man was silent a moment. "Where are you now?"

"Geneva, Switzerland."

"Give me a number where you can be reached."

Kitra did so. "This is extremely urgent."

"I heard you the first time." The man hesitated, then added, "The mark on his forehead is from a powder burn."

Kitra clicked off and set down the phone. Forced herself to breathe.

Marc expected the call to take some time, at least an hour, perhaps most of the night. So he suggested they continue with their routine and have dinner. Kitra confessed she was tired of the hotel's rich food, and Amin said he would fetch a Middle Eastern-style meal. Bernard offered to help with the errand. Thirty minutes later, the two returned bearing sacks of aromatic dishes with which they covered the suite's oval table.

They dined in elegant splendor, the balcony doors open to the night and the spring rain. Over the simple but delicious meal they went through the details of what they knew and what they needed, then set up a series of watches to stay on alert in case the call was delayed into the night hours.

The waiting and the weather pressed down on Kitra, and Marc noticed. "Anything the matter?" he asked, his voice low.

241

She disliked her inability to conceal her frame of mind from this man. "You mean, other than how we are hiding from gunmen, surrounded by risks, and fighting against a threat that could take thousands of lives?"

He ignored her sardonic tone. "It's fine if you decide to go home, Kitra. I've told you—"

"I'm not leaving, Marc." She forced herself to answer softly, to show a quiet determination in her voice as well as her words. A professional. "I am part of this, Marc. I am staying."

Once they all had cleared the table, Rhana and Kitra retreated to the bedroom balcony. They stood watching the rain fall for a time, the silence comforting. Kitra said, "This morning I received two calls. One was from my brother, the other from the plant manager. I have been involved in setting up a new factory. The manager is desperate for me to return. There are problems."

"There are always problems." One businesswoman to another. "Do you want to discuss them?"

"Thank you, but the problems are not the real problems."

"That too I understand."

"My brother, Serge, urgently wants me to come home. He is strong and intelligent and courageous. People love him. But he is not a leader, not the kind that—"

"He does not see the way forward," Rhana said. "He needs someone to point the way."

It seemed that having this woman understand her would cause her emotions to rise. "All day I have been hearing these two men, my brother and the plant manager, continue to talk in my head. But they were not saying what they spoke on the phone. What they said was, You have a choice."

Rhana wrapped her jacket more tightly about herself. "Was this your heart speaking, or your head?"

Kitra nodded. A very good question. It showed the woman understood not merely what Kitra was saying, but also what lay beneath the words. "The reason the plant manager called, and the problem that most troubles my brother, are one and the same. Our sales director—the plant's main connection to the world buyers for the rare earths we process—has had a serious heart attack. It comes at a crucial moment. We have many new contracts that must be finalized, and our factory is late in coming online."

"So it is true. They do need you. Desperately."

"And yet my father could see to these things. He and my mother arrive back from France tomorrow midday. He is the community's founder and leader. I know he will have answers. He and I work very well together. We argue, and yet there is mutual trust."

She watched Rhana turn away slightly as she lifted her hands and swiftly wiped her cheeks. Kitra thought of the woman's loss of family and knew they were communicating far beyond the words they exchanged. She heard the soft intake of breath and was somehow grateful that the older woman was there to shed tears for them both. *Connected.*

It gave her the strength to continue, "When we arrived at the church this afternoon, I realized what I really was hearing was that I had a choice. Did I want to return to the kibbutz?"

"Yes. You could easily fit into your salesman's position," Rhana said, nodding slowly. "Here is a job you could take, important work in which you would do well. You would be excellent at this. Better than anyone else, in my opinion."

"It would give me the chance to . . ."

"To leave the kibbutz," Rhana finished for her. "To leave and yet to remain in contact."

"I would stay linked to my community." There was no reason speaking these words should leave her breathless.

"And it frightens you to think on this, yes?"

"All my life, all I've ever wanted is to do what I am doing—to lead this community when my father steps down."

With a nod, Rhana said, "Two things. First, being here in this place, isolated from your familiar world, cut off as much as could possibly happen, has given you a chance to see things from a distance. It has liberated you. You are free to ask questions you would otherwise run from. Or simply step over in the busyness of the day-to-day issues."

It was Kitra's turn to wipe her cheeks. "You speak as though you can read my mind's script."

"Second, you have arrived at a juncture. One of the hardest you might ever know. And why is this? Because both directions are correct. There is no right way, and no wrong way. You are free to choose." She smiled. "Of course you are troubled."

Kitra whispered, "What am I going to do?"

"If you are asking, which direction should you take, I cannot say. But I have spent all evening thinking on what you said to me in the church kitchen. And I feel that I can only tell you what you told me. The only way you will know peace is by asking a *different* question, one that you are running from. One that is even more frightening than the power of choice. We are strong and independent. We are daughters of cultures that expect women to be obedient and subservient. And we are neither."

Kitra felt her body caught by tiny vibrations, as though

she were a tuning fork and each of Rhana's words were a small strike. "I was right to speak with you."

"Here is the answer," Rhana said. "I know it is the right answer because I have heard this in the words you shared with me. I can speak these words, though they are both new and alien to me. Like you, my vision is clouded. But I am tired of not seeing clearly, and not doing the right thing."

Kitra could hear the tremors in her words. "Tell me."

"You must ask the one question I have spent my entire life running from." Rhana's gaze was a burning flame. "You must ask which direction will lead you closer to God. Because if you take the other direction, even if you win, even if you gain everything that you use to define success, you lose. And your days will become nothing but ashes. And your memories will be—"

"Stop," Kitra whispered. "Please. Stop."

"Ask for God to make a clear path forward." Rhana laid a hand on Kitra's forearm resting on the balcony railing. "Then you must wait. And he will answer you. How do I know this? Because once more my father's memory is alive in my heart. What I thought was lost forever is with me again. Yet I know it has been there all along. Waiting for me to stop giving in to the wrong voices, taking the wrong paths. And instead heed the one voice that will give me the two things I forgot I even needed. And in the future, when your days are coming to a close, be that tomorrow or fifty years from now, you will know peace."

Chapter Twenty-Nine

Kitra and Rhana remained in the bedroom, seated now by the balcony doors. Marc entered twice, once to bring them cups of mint tea and again to offer refills. Otherwise they were alone. Rhana threaded together the rest of the evening with old memories, tales from her childhood. The way she spoke left Kitra certain that Rhana had not shared these memories with many people and not for many years. The woman's voice became musical, and the shadows lifted from her gaze. Even her visage changed, revealing the beautiful young woman she once had been. Kitra listened and felt the wounds of her own confession gradually beginning to diminish.

The call came through three hours later, just after eleven. Kitra's phone read simply *International*. She carried the phone into the parlor, where she found the men poring over maps that Bernard had brought. The injured detective was stretched out on the sofa.

Marc nodded to her.

She touched the connection. "Kitra Korban."

"It is good to know you have managed to survive," the gruff voice said. "So far."

"A moment, please."

Bernard took the phone from her and put it into a portable speaker system, with a Bluetooth microphone in the middle of the dining table. Amin helped Remy rise to a seated position. Marc said, "Testing, testing."

The gruff man switched to English and demanded, "Who is that?"

"The guy whose life you saved," Marc told him. "Thanks."

"Agent Royce. Yes. Good evening."

"I owe you."

"It is good when debts are acknowledged. Are there others with you?"

"Four. Bernard Behlet, FIS. Inspector Remy Reynard, Geneva Police. And two allies from inside the Iranian diaspora."

"Am I right to assume one of these allies is Rhana Mandana?"

Marc waited for Rhana to nod before replying, "That's an affirmative."

"I assume there is a purpose for this call."

"May we ask your name?"

"You may call me Chaver." The man turned the *ch* into a soft guttural sound.

Kitra said, "'Chaver' is Hebrew for *friend*."

Marc said, "Let me start with a sit-rep." Chaver made a sound indicating his agreement. Marc began with the explosion at the Geneva gallery and finished with his report to the U.S. ambassador. He left little out. He did not mention Amin by name. He did not name the Divonne church. Other than that, it was complete.

When he was finished, Chaver said, "Wait a moment." The phone went dead.

The room remained silent until Rhana murmured, "What is happening?"

"He has others in the room with him," Marc said. "They are reviewing what I told him, to see if there's anything they didn't already know. And if there are any holes."

Bernard asked, "Do you think he already knew about Hesam?"

"I'll ask," Marc replied, "but I doubt he'll say."

Which was precisely what happened. When Marc posed the question, Chaver said it was not time for him to divulge such information, and then, "All right. We have your report. Now give us your assessment."

"If there's a nuclear warhead being readied," Marc said, "I gather you and the Americans will take it out."

The speaker phone crackled softly. Otherwise there was no response.

"Ditto for the risk of something being on the container vessel you're tracking from Pakistan," Marc went on. "I assume U.S. ports are being carefully monitored. *If* a ship bearing missile components is approaching the Strait of Hormuz, we don't serve any further purpose. We can all go home."

The man did not respond.

"The question is, what might we have gotten wrong?" Marc said. "Everything about this Hesam and his actions have been lies. Nothing is as it first appeared. So the risk is he's playing a shell game on the high seas. We need to ask, what if the U.S. port has never been his target?"

The phone connection remained silent.

"What if the target is somewhere else?" Marc continued. "The Iranians' official line is that the U.S. and Israel are so closely intertwined that an attack against one is an attack against both. What if they never intended to attack the U.S. directly? What if they had always intended to go after Israel?"

There was a creaking sound, as the man must have shifted his weight. "That is the specter that has robbed my nights of peace."

"Everything about this guy has been laced with subterfuge and false trails," Marc said. "To make a head-on assault on American soil goes against everything they assume. They know full well the Americans would retaliate by invading Iran. The ayatollahs and the Revolutionary Guard would be wiped off the map. They know this."

"We agree."

"Let's say the U.S. Navy boards the container ship they're tracking. They find nothing. Iran responds with a formal protest to the UN. And while the right hand is waving this red flag in the face of the world, the left hand—"

"Exactly," Chaver confirmed. "Where is the left hand?"

Marc hesitated, then confessed, "I'm unable to reach Ambassador Walton."

"The ambassador, I'm sorry to say, is out of the equation."

The quiet finality was chilling. "Is he . . . ?"

"He's a fighter." The voice carried the soft sibilance of Judean deserts. "He's down but not out."

Marc released a breath of tension. "Admiral Willits has ordered me home."

"So I have been informed." Chaver was silent for a long moment, then added, "Your future is not as bleak as it probably looks from where you're standing."

"Not reading you—"

"Admiral Willits will be required at some point to confirm that their first direct identification of their target, Hesam al-Farouz, came from you. Your work was valid. You flushed

250

him out. You sent him scampering back to Iran by way of the first flight out."

"We don't know that yet."

"It's how you can paint it. And I will back you up. So will your ambassador there in Geneva. What I'm saying is, if you obey their orders and go home, you still have a career. You've earned a ticket back into the intelligence community."

Marc felt the temptation gnaw at him, a grinding in his gut. He knew the man was offering him the perfect out. He had orders. He had a future. He had a *choice*.

But he also had a job that wasn't finished. He knew what it was like back in Washington. The senior officials had massed up behind the party line. They had taken aim. They were waiting for the green light. Anyone who offered an alternative viewpoint at this stage was just so much cannon fodder.

They were probably right. *But what if they weren't?* What if they were missing something vital, something that could kill uncounted innocents, presage something even worse? Marc decided, "I need to stay in the hunt."

This was clearly what the man had been waiting for. "Then you and your team must travel south at first light. My allies and I are facing the same battles here in Israel. All the big guns are lined up behind the number-one fear, that the Iranians are three days from having a working nuclear weapon."

"And when we arrive—"

"We need you to do what we officially have been ordered not to do. Are you willing?"

Marc glanced around the room, then replied, "Absolutely."

"That is good to hear, Agent Royce. Regardless of what happens now, you and your team have earned my nation's gratitude."

"Will you answer one question for me?"

"Perhaps, Agent Royce. Ask and we shall see."

Marc rose from his seat to stand over the map of Israel. "Chaver, can you find out for me what direction the wind blows in Israel at this time of year?"

Marc bade the others good-night and retreated to his room. He stood for a time by the open balcony doors, letting the rain blow against him, wishing it had the power to wash away the conflicting emotions whirling through him. The longer he stayed in Kitra's presence, the harder it became to see any other life than one that included her. It was only then, as he stood and endured the windswept storm, that he realized they had failed to pray together. The people and the tide of events had swept them up, and he had forgotten their agreement. It unsettled him, because there was no telling what else he had failed to do. Or see. Or anticipate.

He pushed away the fears as best he could, pulled out his phone and keyed in the number. When a sleepy British voice answered, he asked, "Is this Sir Geoffrey?"

"Who is asking at this time of night?"

"Marc Royce, sir. I apologize for the hour. We met—"

"Of course I remember you, Mr. Royce." Every vestige of slumber vanished. "You are the extremely capable young gentleman who saved my life."

"Only after I was at least partly responsible for putting you in harm's way."

"Young man, I signed up for that when I first made contact with your agencies. Remember that. I came to them. And you understand why, yes?"

"You are a patriot."

"Well, yes, that and more, Mr. Royce. And I thank you."

"Please, call me Marc."

"Yes, Marc. I am convinced that the only way for the human race to reach its full potential, and possibly even survive at all, is through the implementation of democracy around the globe. People must take responsibility for their lives, for their governments. Leaders must be held accountable to the people they rule. For this principle I would willingly sacrifice my life." He paused, then added, "Of course, it is far easier to hold forth this way when I'm safely ensconced in my London townhouse and don't have bullets raining around my head."

Marc found himself liking the man immensely. "I have a favor to ask."

"Of course, my dear boy. Ask away."

"We need to go off grid, and we need some supplies when we arrive at our destination. Urgent supplies, brought to us in total secrecy."

"Wait, let me find a pen and paper. . . . All right, what precisely do you have in mind?"

Marc sketched out his needs and where he needed the supplies to be delivered.

"I don't see how that should be a problem. When do you need this delivery?"

"Noon today."

"Then I had better get cracking. Can I reach you at this number?"

"You can. I'm sorry to bother—"

"Don't give it another thought. Am I to assume someone is going after the men who attacked us at the spa?"

"Yes, their superiors. We hope."

"I thoroughly dislike being shot at," Sir Geoffrey said wryly.

"I would count it a pleasure to be involved, at least in some indirect fashion. Plus there is the small matter of a Rodin bronze now on display in my library. I understand you had something to do with that."

"It seemed the least we could do."

"My dear young man, being granted the company of a Rodin ballerina for my lifetime was as great a joy as my knighthood. Perhaps more. I'll be in touch when I have something to report."

Chapter Thirty

The Geneva authorities did not permit flights to land or depart between ten at night and five thirty in the morning. Amin met the group at the hotel at a quarter to five and ferried them through silent, predawn streets to the private air terminal. Inspector Reynard led in a police vehicle, his badge clearing them quickly through customs and out onto the empty tarmac. The sky was gradually clearing, the clouds pulling back with reluctant grace. The air still carried the sweetness of the previous day's rainfall, not quite overcome by the strong overlay of diesel fuel from the large jets warming their engines by the main passenger terminal.

Right at five thirty, a sleek white needle dropped from the sky and pulled over to where they waited by the private jet terminal. The stairs descended to reveal a grinning Carter Dawes.

Reynard took the opportunity to shake the hand of each in turn, saving Marc for last. "I must tell you I was wrong about you."

Marc liked the man's grip, solid and sparse. "No, you were following protocol, just what you should have done given the circumstances."

Reynard leaned on his good leg and smiled crookedly. "I was trying to apologize."

"No need."

"You really should come back again, you know. Enjoy our hospitality."

"I'd like that."

"Of course, after all this, you may find Switzerland a little boring."

Marc picked up his bag. "After this, boring will be exactly what I'm after."

As they found their places in the jet, Marc could see that the women were unsettled by the speed of events, maybe even Bernard and Amin. Both men hid their unease with the pretended calm of professionals. But Marc knew what the group was feeling. He felt it himself. Things were not totally under control, had not been since he had arrived in Geneva at the start of this mission. And they were headed now into more uncertainty, with even greater implications—for good or for evil.

When they had reached cruising altitude, he went up front and spoke at length with Carter Dawes and a copilot Carter didn't bother to introduce. Bernard and Amin had come forward also and stood in the doorway to listen. The daylight strengthened, and soon they left the Alps behind, swooping high above the French Riviera and out over the crystalline blue of the Med. Marc returned to the main cabin and told Kitra and Rhana they had three hours and suggested they rest. He folded back the table and joined two seats together, forming a padded leather bed. He lay down, not expecting to sleep, but in less than five minutes he was out.

He awoke to the sound of Rhana Mandana talking on the pilot's phone. She spoke in Arabic, then French, then back to Arabic again. She sounded chipper and brisk to Marc. He walked to the galley at the back of the plane, where the pilots had laid out a large coffee thermos and a tray of sandwiches. He glanced at his watch. He had slept two hours. He ate a sandwich and downed two mugs of coffee. He should have felt more refreshed than he did. But a nap at thirty thousand feet had little effect on the burdens he carried. It did, however, he was glad to note, make his mind sharper. He refilled his mug and stared up the main aisle to where Kitra lay, still asleep. A blanket covered all but her head. She was curled up like a dark-haired kitten, her face a porcelain oval in the light through the side window.

He forced his gaze away when Amin started toward him. "Rhana is making reservations for us at the Ritz-Carlton."

"Okay. Fine."

"This place is extremely expensive. She says she will handle it. I would like to ask . . ."

"If I'm able, I will make sure she is reimbursed."

When Rhana completed her call, Marc accepted her place in the fold-down navigator's seat between the doorway and the pilot's berth. The jet's phone was bulky and connected by a coiled cord to the main radio. He called Walton's cellphone, and when the answering service picked up, he left another detailed message. He then phoned Ambassador Samantha Keller in Geneva on her direct line. When a young man answered, Marc identified himself and asked to have a word.

The man had clearly been prepped, for he responded with "Yes, sir. Hold, please."

Thirty seconds later, the ambassador said, her voice low, "I am in a meeting and cannot talk."

"Can you listen?"

"Go ahead."

"We're about twenty minutes out from landing at Sharm el-Sheikh."

"Do you have anything new?"

"Only that some portions of Israel's intelligence community share our concerns enough to send in several undercover agents. We will liaise with them and start the hunt."

"For the missing research vessel?"

"Affirmative."

"I thought the target was the . . . the other direction."

"We assume you will be covering the American seaboard. We are looking at alternative sites."

"Understood."

"Do you have any update?"

The ambassador lowered her voice to a shred of sound. "Interception of the original vessel is imminent."

"Any change in the timeline?"

"Formal military warning goes up in eighteen hours." She gave that a beat, then went on in a more normal tone, "I have heard this morning that your friend's health is improving. They've moved him from ICU to a regular wing. He still has a pulmonary infection. They were concerned about his heart. This is no longer an issue."

Marc breathed somewhat easier. "This is good news. Very good news."

"Here's something less positive." She lowered her voice again. "The admiral is gunning for you."

"That's to be expected."

"Your only hope of reviving your career is to bring in the goods."

"Madame Ambassador, my career is not the issue here."

She was silent for a moment, then, "Walton is fortunate to have you on his team. As am I. As many others will be. Good hunting."

Chapter Thirty-One

Sharm el-Sheikh was a resort city located on the southern tip of the Sinai Peninsula. They crowded around the cockpit door as Carter Dawes approached from the south, flying up the Red Sea. The tip of the Sinai was known by two names, depending on the side. On the left, the Muhammad Strait opened into the Gulf of Suez. To its right, the Straits of Tiran marked the beginning of the Gulf of Aqaba.

Sharm el-Sheikh was a shimmering jewel in an otherwise ocher vista. The pilot motioned them back to their seats as three connecting highways appeared, stretching like dusty arteries to bind the city to the rest of Egypt. The waters below them were dotted with hundreds of boats, everything from shipping vessels to military destroyers to ocean liners to private yachts to lateen-sailed dhows. The Gulf of Aqaba connected Saudi Arabia, Jordan, Egypt, and Israel. The entire Saudi Peninsula lay between them and the Strait of Hormuz. If Marc was right, the U.S. Navy was nine hundred miles off target. If wrong, and the deadly vessel was indeed steaming for Hormuz, it meant the end of Marc's career, a risk he was prepared to take.

They landed and crossed the airport's baking tarmac, led by a bored customs official, and entered the private customs hall. Not even their varied passport originations raised an eyebrow. Their luggage was given a perfunctory search. When they emerged from the terminal, two dusty, vintage Mercedes were there to greet them.

Sharm el-Sheikh was bleak. Rubble and scrawny dogs and starving palm trees lined the empty stretches. Then came a postage stamp of luxury. The private villas were hidden behind vast concrete walls. The hotels were rimmed by palm trees and lawns and flower beds that looked artificial in their perfection. Guards with uniforms imprinted with hours of sweat strolled the grounds. Then the opulence ended, and there was another stretch of rubble and desert, waiting for the bulldozers and the money.

The Ritz-Carlton was located on the finest of the Red Sea beaches, just beyond the main tourist strip known as Naama Bay. The hotel's main structure was built from bricks, one shade off red and the color of the surrounding desert. Out front a giant fountain mocked the desert dryness, while another sparkled inside the vast lobby. A third played in the waters of the pool area beyond. The hotel beach was rimmed by private villas of the ultra-rich. The air-conditioning was set so low they all shivered.

A male voice called in English, "Dominique? Can that truly be you?"

To her credit, Kitra showed neither surprise nor confusion over hearing her assumed name. She glanced once at Marc, received a nod in response, then turned and smiled, then laughed. "What are you *doing* here?"

A compact young man wearing a white linen shirt and swimming trunks hurried across the lobby from the café, his sandals slapping against the marble tiles. He swept Kitra up in a dancing embrace. She slipped her arms around his neck and played along. The man was handsome in the classical Mediterranean fashion—dark hair and deep tan and strong legs and sharp features. His smile was brilliant, his gaze easy in the manner of a man who had known far too many conquests.

He released her only when a beautiful woman, probably in her late twenties, emerged from the café and demanded, "Should I be jealous?"

"You remember me telling you about Dominique?"

"Of course I remember." She slipped her arm possessively around the young man. "All too well."

Marc stepped forward, hand extended. "Hello. I'm Marc Royce."

As they exchanged handshakes, the young woman asked, "You are with this one?"

"I am. Yes."

"What a relief. I am Sandrine. And this is Henri. You have heard of Henri?"

"Sorry. No."

"This is shocking news." The young man showed Kitra mock dismay. "You did not tell him about me?"

Kitra played the role, stepping over and slipping her hand into Marc's. "I'm sorry. I forgot."

Sandrine smiled. "I feel even better."

"Listen, you must drop your bags and come with us," Henri told them. "We have rented a boat. We are going to snorkel around the outer reefs. There is a protected area off the peninsula, live coral atolls, over a thousand species of fish."

Marc got a whiff of the jet's air still clinging to Kitra's hair. "We're pretty beat, we've just flown in—"

The man made a scoffing noise. "Who cares where you came from? This is happening now! It's a beautiful day, we ride the boat, we swim, we watch the sunset. What could be better?"

Kitra looked at Marc and broke his heart with her smile. "I could think of no finer an invitation."

Marc surrendered with, "Can our friends come too?"

They dropped their luggage in their rooms and changed for the beach. Kitra appeared in a swimsuit covered by an ivory shirt that reached her knees, as delicate as gauze. She had never looked more beautiful. Marc greeted her with a smile he had wanted to show her since forever. But when he started to compliment her, Kitra whispered so softly he did not hear so much as see her shape the words, "Don't. Please."

Their new-old friends, Sandrine and Henri, joined them in the lobby and led them across the rose-colored sand toward their boat, anchored thirty meters off the beach. A young Egyptian rowed them out in a dinghy from another era. He accepted Marc's payment with a musical salaam and sang his way back to the shore.

Their rental turned out to be a beautiful Hatteras yacht, perhaps thirty years old but impeccably maintained. It had the stumpy look of an outdated Buick. The lone crewman helped them onboard, stowed their goods, made a process of offering drinks from the cooler. The boat slipped from its anchorage and began to ply through the sparkling waters.

Rhana had turned the seat across from the skipper into her personal rest area. Bernard and Amin lounged on the starboard berth, exchanging pleasantries with the couple performing the part of hosts. Marc settled in the back, Kitra beside him. They watched the waves and played at having a good time for any curious bystanders with binoculars.

The group ate a meal and chatted among themselves as any wealthy tourists would do, past the main commercial harbor and then the naval base. The water was dotted with a multitude of crafts, all sizes and ages, and they exchanged waves with many other vessels. As they sailed farther from the shore, Marc settled onto the aft swivel chair by the rumbling motors and returned to his silent aloofness. It was the role Kitra found easiest to endure, he told himself, needing to repeat it every time she glanced his way.

They passed through the Straits of Tiran, motoring past the two main islands marking the entry into the Gulf of Aqaba's calmer waters. The tip of the peninsula held the Nabq Preserve, a broad stretch of mangroves and dunes and water birds. As they entered the Red Sea, the shores dropped away and the waters emptied of all save the larger commercial craft. And then these vessels were gone as well. The sea belonged to them alone.

Only then did the Israeli couple drop the smiles and empty chatter. The young man said, "I am Dov. The lady's name truly is Sandrine. She tends to forget her aliases. A pity. Such a lovely lady, but her mind is like a sieve."

The young woman flipped a hand at his shoulder. "We have no need for different names. We carry French passports, we are tourists. But Dov loves his games."

"You have to find pleasure where you can, no?" The man's dark eyes flashed toward Sandrine, and he grinned. It looked like she was used to his teasing. Then he cocked a thumb at the skipper. "Our driver is Shimon."

Their pilot called back, "Please thank whoever is responsible for this vessel and all our little toys."

"First chance I get." Marc made the introductions again, then asked, "You are friends of Chaver?"

"We hold that honor, yes."

Sandrine added, "Chaver's definition of a friend is someone who survives. Let us hope we all hold that honor for a very long time."

Dov pointed beyond the bow, out over the empty sea. "Our friends have located the research vessel. They did a flyover at thirty thousand feet—nothing to raise alarms. The boat is thirty miles out and closing. But there is a mystery. It travels at a tourist's pace. You understand?"

"The ship is in no hurry," Marc replied. "Maybe it wants to enter the Strait after dark."

"The Gulf of Aqaba is tightly patrolled at night," Sandrine said. "Tourist vessels are forbidden out of the harbor after sunset. The Egyptians, the Israeli Navy, the Saudis, and the Jordanians have destroyers operating in these waters. Even the smugglers work in daylight."

"So maybe they're timed for a rendezvous," Marc suggested.

"Yes, indeed. With us." Dov pushed open the cabin doors and motioned them to join him. "Let's get started."

They shifted the threadbare cushions and pulled open the seat tops. Sandrine unlocked hidden bolts to reveal a series of secret lockers. They began dumping items from the central crawl space onto the table—web belts, flippers, goggles, packets of C4 explosive, blast caps and timers, night-vision glasses, waterproof radios, carbon blades, and pistols wrapped in plastic bags. The pile of carefully selected equipment grew by the minute.

Marc said firmly, "The two ladies who travel with us won't need to gear up."

The aft holds contained two rubber dinghies and compact gas canisters for inflating them. Marc unlashed the netting, twisted the release valve, and stepped back. The dinghies unfolded in lightning speed. He and Dov lashed the skiffs to the gunnels and fitted on ultra-quiet motors. The sunset was a ruddy glow on the western reaches, the sky a flamboyant display of fading colors. They pushed hard, for timing was everything now.

Amin hesitated over the selection of personal gear. Marc took that as his cue and ordered him to stay onboard and see the two women safely back to the hotel. Their decoy duties had been completed, and the Hatteras would ferry them to the commercial port. There wasn't time to make it back to the hotel. The nighttime curfew through the Aqaba waters was strictly enforced. Amin did his best to hide his relief, quickly agreeing.

Marc nodded toward Sandrine, silently acknowledging her training and skills as part of the team. He asked Bernard if he had ever trained for a waterborne night attack. Bernard showed him a soldier's grin and replied, "The waters of the Swiss lakes are far colder. Does that matter?"

Dov, a true professional, took over the operation, repeating the instructions several times as they prepped. Their target was the Pakistani research vessel. Dov passed around containers of black face paint and stated the facts with the calm ferocity of a tiger ready to be unleashed. First, they had to confirm that the vessel contained both the blowers and the chemicals. They then were to set the charges and flee.

Afterward, Dov explained, they would hide in the mangrove swamp by Ras Muhammad. Then at dawn they would rendezvous with the Hatteras, and all would return to the hotel. They were to radio the Israeli Navy only in an extreme emergency. All Israeli vessels were shadowed by either the Egyptian Navy or the Saudi Navy, or both. Radioing the Israelis would mean igniting an international incident.

Dov eyed them intently, then finished with, "There will be no emergency."

"Roger that," Marc said. "Let's move."

They boarded the two skiffs and set out. Dov ran one motor, Marc the other. Bernard traveled with Dov, Sandrine with Marc. One skiff could have carried them all and their gear, but it would have ridden low and cost them the flexibility to split up and patrol. Plus they were hoping to return with both evidence and prisoners—anything to shame the Iranians into a public admission.

His face blackened, Marc peered out across the waters as they pulled away. Kitra stood by the aft gunnel, her dark hair blowing away from her face in the evening wind. She called something, words he wished she had spoken while he was still close enough to hear. He lifted his hand in heartfelt farewell.

The dinghies were black, as was all the gear and apparel. The little boats were fitted with tentlike tops that could be folded back and stowed away. When they were up, they looked like crinkled black aluminum foil held in place by collapsible rods. The tops were radar deflectors, and the rods were carbon fiber. With the tops up, the boats were lost to the tossing waves. Enemy radar would read them as porpoises or some other sea mammal.

Each crew member was fitted with black knit vests that

could be cinched tight. Dov showed how they included tiny gas canisters that would inflate automatically upon severe impact, flipping the body on its back in the process. Marc had heard of these but never seen one, as he had not been involved in a seaborne action in years. The canisters were the size of his little finger and filled with an ultralight gas, so even when the vests were fully inflated they were less than a third of an inch thick.

The water, warm as a bath, splashed over the gunnels. They pushed through the gathering dusk and the rising wind. The Red Sea stretched out around them in utter isolation. Marc didn't see a single vessel, not a sail, not even a seabird. The stars came out one by one, and a silver thread of moon peeked over the horizon. Soon it was night, one filled with the engine's whisper and the splashing waves. They pushed on.

Sandrine handed him a pair of night-vision glasses. The other dinghy leaped into ghostly view. The waves showed a sparkling froth. Otherwise the sea remained spectral and empty. Sandrine operated a miniature radar, held like an iPad. She aimed the radar over the bow and directed Marc with hand signals.

Then the vessel appeared up ahead. It was no less ugly for the night or the goggles. Marc steered over to where Bernard could reach out and draw the two dinghies close. Motors cut, they sat studying the vessel ahead, which was about three hundred yards away. It was massive and turned into an ungainly lump by the various tarps covering her decks. The wheelhouse was a metal thumb rising from the vessel's middle. The motor throbbed steadily across the water.

"I don't see anyone," Dov said.

Marc felt the creepy-crawly tendrils spread through his gut. "Check out the wheelhouse."

A moment, then, "So?"

"It's empty."

"You don't know that. The glass is small and cracked. You see only half the chamber. Less, perhaps."

"The decks are empty too."

"They are eating. They are using the head. They have the ship on autopilot. At this speed, why not? The sea is theirs."

But Sandrine must have heard the concern in his voice, for she demanded, "What is it, Marc?"

"I was sent to investigate a gallery in Geneva suspected of money laundering. I entered and discovered the owner dead. It was set up with infrared triggers connected to shaped explosives. I barely escaped."

Dov's only response was to remove his goggles and pick up a pair of binoculars. Sandrine asked, "You think this is a trap?"

"All I know is, there's no sign of life anywhere."

Dov said, "Their lab is onboard. The gear too."

"Correction. All we see are tarps. There could be anything beneath them. Or nothing at all."

"You say we should not move?"

"I'm saying we need to be extremely careful."

Dov grunted. "We circle the boat, taking opposite directions. We meet back here."

They took their time, trolling in close enough to be shrouded in diesel fumes. Marc found light glowing from every portal, but no movement of shadows, no people. Nothing.

When they circled back, Dov shook his head. Sandrine said, "I have a bad feeling about this."

"We have our assignment," Dov shot back. "It hasn't changed."

"And if this is a trap?"

Dov bounced one fist off the air-padded gunnel, thinking hard. Then he asked Marc, "How are you with a rifle and night scope?"

"Unknown rifle, ditto on the scope, in an inflatable dinghy being tossed by waves." Marc pretended to give it serious thought. "Call it twenty feet."

"That's still fifteen feet further accuracy than Sandrine."

"Give me the gun," Sandrine countered. "I will show you how accurate I can be."

"Bernard and I will go in," Dov decided. "You stay back, keep watch. Sandrine, you take his position by the engine. Marc, arm yourself."

Marc didn't like it, but he could not think of a better alternative. But Dov was in charge at this point, and this was combat. "Roger that."

"Bernard, you will take me to the stern landing deck. I will go up alone and check, then flash you with my light. Only then does the second boat approach."

"It's a solid plan," Marc confirmed, wishing his creepy-crawlies would subside.

Bernard said, "Enough chatter. I came to dance."

Dov liked that enough to show his engaging grin. "For a Swiss, you are not a bad sort. All right. Let's move."

The engine was so quiet they could hear nothing after the vessel had moved two lengths away. Even the splash of waves was silenced by the padded hull. Marc settled in the bow and cradled the .40-40 on his knees. The night scope was battery-operated and amplified all light to alien brilliance. He tracked the other boat's forward progress, working at maintaining a steady aim despite the dinghy's rocking motion. He kept both eyes open so as to see the other skiff's shadow as it approached the stern and through the scope watch Dov tumble onto the stern platform, then scale the narrow ladder.

Dov emerged above the stern gunnel one inch at a time. He scouted the vessel for what seemed like an hour. Finally he turned and waved at Marc, a swift up-and-down motion. Marc took a long breath, released the rifle's safety, and fitted the weapon more tightly to his shoulder.

Dov slipped over the railing onto the deck. He took one step.

The entire night blasted with a light so brilliant Marc was blinded in both eyes.

Chapter Thirty-Two

They recovered Bernard first. He was floating faceup, which meant the inflatable vest had worked as intended. Blood leaked from his nose and one ear, turning his face pink in the flashlight's gleam. His eyelids fluttered, and his limbs moved feebly, which Marc took as a very good sign.

Dov's body floated amidst the vessel's wreckage. Marc pulled him from the water and wrapped him in the dinghy's anti-radar cover. Sandrine tried to help, but she was sobbing too hard to be much use. Marc started the motor and headed north, back toward Sharm el-Sheikh. Sandrine wrapped her arms around the shrouded body, her own body shaking as she wept.

By the time they approached landfall, Sandrine had recovered sufficiently to hand Marc her computer pad. She showed him how to read the built-in radar and GPS. He watched her unclasp a ceramic star from around her neck and break it open. She unfurled a bit of waterproof paper and typed the numbers into the pad. Instantly the screen lit up with a map of the waters and a fragment of land up to their north. She explained in sorrowful tension that they could not safely return to the Aqaba waters until daylight. Marc took the pad and told her to check on Bernard.

Three minutes later, Marc watched the screen as what could only be a trio of military vessels powered toward the blast site. He steered well east of them. A pair of high-powered lights flashed overhead, and the air was filled with the throbbing of marine diesels. He did not resume his northern course until the lights and the engines had vanished beyond the horizon.

Their destination was the Nabq Protected Area, a vast wildlife preserve that stretched inland from the point of land known as Ras Muhammad. The promontory separated the waters of the two gulfs, Suez and Aqaba, from the Red Sea proper. The first sign Marc had of their approaching destination was the smell, swampy and fetid. He powered down and entered the mangrove swamp at a crawl. Twenty minutes after wending his way through tight curves and clouds of mosquitoes, they pulled into a protected pool whose northern curve was a beach turned silver by the rising moon. Land crabs clattered a warning as Marc stepped into the tepid water and secured the dinghy. Somewhere in the distance a bird chirped its worry, then went still.

He checked on Bernard and was vastly relieved to see the man able to focus his eyes on Marc's light. Marc set up a small butane stove and made tea, then soup. He spooned the liquid into the Swiss agent and pretended not to hear as Sandrine gave herself over to grief.

Bernard was the only one who slept. At dawn, Marc woke him with another cup of tea laced with honey. This time, Bernard was able to sit up and hold the mug himself. His nose still dripped a little blood, and his voice was muffled, like he was recovering from an overdose of Novocain. But Bernard was able to answer Marc's questions, even chide him when Marc asked where they were. "How am I supposed to know that? Off the map, I suppose." He swiped at a mosquito that had managed to burrow through the covering of repellent they all had smeared on every part of their bodies not covered. "It will be nice to breathe without bugs."

"You'll live," Marc decided.

"Of course I will live. I am Swiss. We are very hard to . . ." Bernard glanced at the body in the metal shroud and the woman who sat with her back on a stunted palm, and did not finish. "How long do we stay here?"

"Until we get the rendezvous alert."

Bernard watched Marc mix another packet of soup and bottled water and set it on to boil. "Our situation reminds me of a lesson I heard in training. 'If the enemy is in range, so are you.'"

"I might have had the same instructor," Marc recalled grimly. "A lesson I heard a lot was, 'When the pin is pulled, Mr. Grenade is not your friend.'"

"Tracers work both ways," Bernard recalled.

"Only trust a five-second fuse for three seconds."

Sandrine spoke for the first time since daybreak. "If your attack is going extremely well, you are probably walking into an ambush." She wiped her face. "Dov should have listened more carefully." Her voice broke on the last word.

Marc took that as a signal and carried the first mug over to her. "Drink."

"I'm not—"

"Drink." He stood over her and waited until she had finished the soup. "More?"

"All right. But you first."

He went back and poured another mug, drank it, then handed a third to Bernard.

The Swiss agent took it, drank half, then said to the mug, "Never tell a sergeant you don't have anything to do."

Marc refilled the mug. "If you see a bomb technician running away, follow him."

Sandrine said, "Don't draw enemy fire. It irritates the soldiers around you."

Marc carried over another mug and pretended not to notice her tears. "My favorite is, 'Bravery is being the only person who knows you're afraid.'"

She wiped her face with the hand not holding the mug and said, "Our pad has started pinging. For real, not a soldier's quote."

Marc walked back to his gear and saw she was correct. "What does it mean?"

She set down the mug. "They have come to take Dov home."

The computer pad's mapping system was military grade, accurate down to inches. Which was important because the stream they were on meandered and cut back upon itself and narrowed down to where they could touch both banks. Even in the daylight Marc would have never made it out alone.

They emerged into open waters to discover an ancient dhow anchored in the shadows. The wooden vessel was perhaps sixty feet long and fitted with a single lateen sail, colored like toffee by age and hard use. A pair of young men in turbans and cutoffs cast circular nets in graceful motions as Marc powered toward them. The fishermen were joined by another man, this one wearing a sweat-stained skipper's cap and a threadbare shirt over his sun-blasted chest. They reeled in the nets and were ready to grip the dinghy and heft Dov's body onboard. They stowed the gear, deflated the dinghy, and quickly drew them all into the shelter of the dirty wheelhouse. The boat smelled of fish and bait and diesel and years of sweat. The sail was stowed as an ancient two-stroke engine chugged to life.

Once they were under way, the skipper pulled out a bulky satellite phone and pressed the speed dial. He spoke a single word, then handed Marc the phone.

The Mossad agent he knew as Chaver said, "Tell me what you think happened."

"They off-loaded far out," Marc replied, ready for the question, and liking the man's terseness. "They probably used boats just like this one."

"This is my thinking as well."

"You need to get agents into Sinai."

"We can't. The new Egyptian government is run by the Muslim Brotherhood. They have not declared that Israel is now an enemy, but they also have not called us their friend. Which means there is great friction within the new regime. We cannot trust them with this knowledge. There is too much risk they would alert our enemy. We have warned our allies within the Egyptian military. For the moment, that is all we can do."

Marc had been expecting this. "I may have an idea."

"I am listening."

Marc described what he had spent the night working on. When he was done, Chaver was silent for a long moment, then decided, "It is a good plan."

"There are a lot of rough edges."

"Of course there are. But some friends of mine can help smooth them out. You understand what I am saying?"

"We are allies," Marc said. "I trust you."

"Correct. Now let me speak with Sandrine."

She sat in the skipper's padded chair, watching the day with leaden eyes. She listened for a moment, spoke harshly, listened some more, then argued with the dark insistence of a subordinate trying to convince a superior to change his mind. Marc knew the sound all too well. And so he was ready when she handed him back the phone and said one word in English. "Please."

Chaver said, "She wants to stay. I cannot assess her state. She and Dov were more than agents, you understand?"

"She was an enormous help, before and after the incident," Marc said, holding her gaze.

"You can truly count on her?"

"Absolutely. What's more, I need her."

"Revenge can cost the lives of more good agents."

"She is not after revenge," Marc said. "She's a professional who knows the lives of thousands depend on her keeping it together."

Her features went through a rugged change as she wrenched herself free of the fog. Sandrine nodded.

Marc heard the man sigh. "Give her back the phone," he said.

Chapter Thirty-Three

They pulled up in front of the Ritz-Carlton's beach, and one of the dhow's crew jumped out to hold it steady. Sandrine, ever the professional despite her loss, had her laugh and chatter ready. Her face paint long wiped away, she was dressed once more in a flowery beach shirt over a one-piece swimsuit, and carried a beach basket and flippers and goggles. She flirted with the young man as he helped her down. She waded to the shore, calling back to Marc.

Bernard caught him as he started over the gunnel and pleaded, "Let me come."

"We've been through—"

"I'm recovered. Feeling fine."

The man did not look fine. Fresh blood had clotted his ear. His gaze still floated slightly. His features were pasty. Marc said as gently as he could, "We're heading into Indian country. You know what that means?"

"I am not afraid of enemy fire."

"This isn't about fear. This is about operating at a hundred and ten percent." He clasped the man's shoulder. "Go and report in. Your best effort is making sure our new Israeli friends do their job."

He jumped into the water before Bernard could protest

further. The sea was too warm to be refreshing. At the first glimpse of the hotel, Marc's body released the floodgates and allowed the exhaustion to take hold. The bruises to his chest had not ached until that moment. Or the weariness in his legs. Or the sore back. Or the scratchy eyes. And the headache. He was assaulted by fatigue.

A dark-haired figure came racing down the beach, out into the water, her face filled with emotions she did not bother to hide. She waded out to him, impatient that she could not get there any faster. "Oh, Marc."

And suddenly his weariness meant nothing.

Marc showered and ate a meal on the room's balcony, talking with Kitra as he dined. They spared only a few moments for the personal. They both heard the silent clock ticking. The complete conversation would have to wait. But just the few things they shared was enough. That she had worried about him. That she hadn't slept. That she had feared he was gone, and she had lost the chance to tell him . . .

Marc was sorry when she didn't finish the sentence. But at the same time, he knew he needed to be sharp and tightly alert. If she had completed the thought, he would have been unable to stow his emotions away. And just then he had to set all those things aside.

He finished his meal, saw Kitra off, and lay down. His last thought before drifting away was an electric determination to finish this assignment and move on to tomorrow. It had been a long time since that word had held any meaning beyond the usual marking of time. He carried the smile with him into sleep.

Following his instructions, Kitra and Rhana with Amin and Sandrine put the plans in motion while Marc slept. When Kitra awoke him at two the next morning, everything was ready. His body ached with a need for more rest. But a stretching routine and another meal and shower had him as ready as he could possibly be.

Two late-model Mercedes were pulled up at the hotel entrance when he arrived in the lobby before daybreak. Their drivers smiled effusive greetings as the five filed through the hotel entrance. The aim was to once again establish tourist bona fides by traveling to central Sinai's premier destination, joining the hordes that rose early to watch the sunrise over the desert mountains. Rhana and Kitra and Sandrine all conversed with the easy gaiety of old friends as they stowed the picnic hampers and backpacks. The sleepy doorman and the two bellhops on all-night duty smiled and waved them off on the familiar trek of many who stayed at the hotel.

The roads were not empty. The Middle Eastern world did not run on the same clock as the West. Traffic was light, yet they weren't the only nice cars headed north in the predawn dark.

Beyond the airport, the road was black and the night swallowed them. Occasionally they passed Bedouins leading camels or donkeys along the relatively smooth verge. Trucks rumbled past, flashing their lights and honking their horns, almost as if the drivers were using both to stay awake.

Amin and Sandrine rode in the first vehicle. Kitra and Marc occupied the second car's rear seat while Rhana traveled up front on the passenger side. Marc waited until the older woman dozed off to lean over and say, "You can't know what it meant to have you meet me like you did."

She slipped her hand into his. "We have only now, this moment, for me to offer you my apology." Her gaze sparked in the car's dim lights as she glanced forward. Rhana still slept. "These words of mine must be spoken. Will you not interrupt, please?"

"All right, Kitra."

"I was wrong to ask you to join me on the kibbutz. If I loved you as fully as I claimed, I should have known it was not something you could ever do and survive as the person you are. No, wait, Marc. I asked you not to speak. Hear me out, please." She paused until she was certain he would not interrupt, then said, "I did love you. I do now. With all my heart. But the night before last I faced myself with the honesty of thinking I might have lost you forever and so lost the chance to speak the truth. The *real* truth.

"Part of why I asked you to join me in Israel was because I knew you couldn't. I feared your love. I feared losing myself to you. Someone I could not control. I have fought all my life to be independent. I was fighting against you. No, not you. Against my own love."

He reached over and covered her hand with his other one. She looked into his face and continued, "Our prayer times in Geneva became a mirror for me. I see now that my life has reached a juncture. I have a choice. I can give myself to love, and know the sacrifice, and accept it. Or I can remain where I am and live for the kibbutz. Will I ever love again? Perhaps. Most likely. But it will not be our love.

"What has been most important for me to realize is that *both* of these decisions are right, *both* are good in God's eyes. Each one would keep me within his divine will. The question is, what do I want? It is hard to think of giving up life on the kibbutz. But I have also learned that it's possible I need not give up the kibbutz entirely. They need a new sales director, someone to handle the contacts with the mines in Kenya and the end users in America and—"

"What are you saying, Kitra?"

"Yes. I have not told you because I feared even thinking about this. The timing is God's, no? The invitation to make this decision came at this precise juncture. And its arrival has done two things for me. It has helped pry away my frantic hold on the myths I have told myself, and revealed that it was I who should have chosen between you and the kibbutz, not forced *you* to choose. And second, it has shown me that God is with me in both choices."

Marc gave that the time it deserved, then asked, "What will you do?"

"Pray," she replied, after a time. "Pray for the strength to do what my heart has already decided."

Chapter Thirty-Four

The road wound through some very steep climbs and steadily worsened as they progressed. An hour and a half after leaving Sharm el-Sheikh, they turned west and entered the area known as the Roof of Egypt.

The central Sinai Mountains contained Egypt's highest summits. The ridgeline cut razor edges from the still-starlit sky. The car's powerful engine rushed them through one cutback after another. Headlights of cars ahead of them shone over great yawning drops, with no guardrails, into utter blackness. They met two cars coming toward them and had to creep into the hillside to maneuver past.

The two vehicles arrived at the outskirts of the city of Saint Catherine just before dawn. They off-loaded their gear, paid the drivers, and set off. It was good they had come prepared, for the air was bitingly cold, not more than a few degrees above freezing. Saint Catherine sat at an elevation of five thousand feet. Even so, the city was alive with tourists pouring from cheap hotels and guesthouses. Their breath drifted like silver fog in the city's few lights.

The group bundled into sweatshirts and knit caps Kitra had purchased in the hotel gift shop, hefted the picnic hampers, and joined the people making for the cliffside paths.

They were greeted by a mystical illumination, a glow that took hold of the ancient cliffs and turned them into something not quite earthbound. The benches and surrounding paths were filled with people gazing at the ancient phenomenon. And yet the entire gathering held to a monastic silence. The rocks grew orange, then gold, and the surrounding peaks became a sea of sharp edges. Far down below them, the shadows gradually rolled back, and the monastery was revealed.

They ate the sandwiches and drank the coffee in silence. Only when they had started their descent did Rhana say, "Whatever else comes, whatever happens now, I thank you for the sunrise."

Sandrine had not uttered a word since their arrival, nor did she speak now. She simply wiped her face and moved more swiftly down the path.

The buses began rumbling into the parking lots surrounding Saint Catherine, coming from Cairo and Tel Aviv and Amman and Eilat and Petra and a dozen other places, drawn to a monastery that had been active for more than twelve centuries.

It was named the Sacred Monastery of the Mountain Where God Walked, but was known as simply Saint Catherine's. From the year 800 until the present day, thousands of pilgrims made the difficult trip every year. Built as a medieval fortress, the monastery was situated at the mouth of the gorge, Amin explained. Two guest wings stood to either side of the main western gate, great halls open to all who wished to share the monastery's simple fare. There were three chapels, private living quarters for the monks and official visitors, the original church, and a much larger basilica that was called modern, though it was itself over seven hundred years old.

Sandrine opted to stay outside and tour the grounds as the others joined the crowds entering the basilica for the morning service. The prayers echoed through the vast stone chamber, rolling cadences in a dozen different tongues, melding with the incense and forming a liturgy that was without beginning or end.

As they met again at the doors after the service, Sandrine's phone rang. She answered, spoke briefly, then told them, "Our ride is here."

Marc met Rhana's gaze. "Return to Sharm el-Sheikh. Please."

She had clearly been expecting this, for she responded without hesitation. "All my life I have worked toward this moment. Even when my motives were wrong. Even when my actions were false. Even when my thoughts were all lies. I must do this, Marc. For my father."

Marc did not understand, but he accepted that further argument was futile. He looked at Kitra and said the words, knowing they were pointless, but needing to try.

"It is my country under threat, Marc," Kitra said before he could begin. "My people. I must do what I can to help them."

He turned to Amin, who had his response ready. "I too have spent a lifetime waiting for this moment. This is the beginning. I know you fear it will also be my end. But for this, I am ready. I have been ready all my life."

"We are all coming," Kitra said. "We are a team." She slipped her arm through Rhana's, caught Sandrine's in the other, and the three started toward whatever awaited them.

Chapter Thirty-Five

They hiked the gorge leading away from the monastery and found the truck precisely where it had been described to Sandrine, parked in a defile so narrow the doors could not open without scraping the rock on either side.

The driver was a grizzled Egyptian with a lazy eye. His teenage son was slender and handsome and very sullen. Both smoked rancid cigarettes and watched as a bearded man walked over and swept Sandrine up in a fierce embrace. She accepted it for a moment only, then pushed the man away. Marc saw the man wipe his eyes as he spoke. Sandrine clenched her entire body and nodded a response. The man stepped over. "You are Royce?"

"Yes." Marc introduced the others.

"I am Schlomo. Dov's uncle. Your friend in the boat with Dov, he lives?"

"Bernard is going to be all right."

"Is good." Schlomo gave each word a guttural twist. "Sandrine says you tried to warn Dov."

"I wasn't sure of anything. I could have said more."

"Dov was a good man. But he disliked the thinking and the planning. He was like bullet. You point, you shoot—how you say?"

"Impetuous." Marc shrugged. "If I had been team leader, I would have climbed into the vessel just like he did."

Schlomo liked that enough to clap Marc on the shoulder. "We go, yes?"

Schlomo had come with a backpack of supplies and another of clothes. He handed Marc and Amin outfits similar to what he and the driver wore, shapeless and ancient and moderately clean. They walked around a boulder and changed. The shoes were a problem, leather-soled and slick with wear. Marc kept on his hiking boots and told Amin to do the same. Keeping traction in a moment like this was crucial.

When they returned, the women had slipped voluminous black robes over their clothing and tied up their hair with brightly colored polyester scarves. Rhana traded her designer sunglasses for a pair of knockoffs. Marc climbed into the back of the truck and seated himself on the hard wooden bench next to Kitra. She gave him a tentative smile. As the truck climbed away from the monastery, Marc asked Schlomo, sitting across from them, "You trust the driver?"

"His other son, his eldest, is in a Tel Aviv jail on smuggling charges. He does this, we live, his son comes home." Schlomo nodded and gave a warrior's grin that split his beard. "I trust him."

Sandrine sat on the other side of Marc. Across from them were Rhana, then Amin, along with Schlomo. They climbed slowly through the Sinai hills. The canvas top blocked most of the wind and captured the heat. The truck's shocks were long gone, and the springs jounced and squeaked. The rear hold stank of rancid lettuce and animals. Marc watched the world through the truck's rear opening, occasionally catching a glimpse of Kitra's face, wishing he could somehow accept her confidence and calm as his own. *Tomorrow.* He could still hear her say the word.

He felt Schlomo's eyes on him and confessed, "My mind is like this road—full of twists and turns."

Sandrine called over, "That is a general's challenge."

Schlomo raised his voice to be heard over the engine's grinding roar. "Is true, this. A general must be constantly searching out the unseen, asking the difficult questions. There are never enough answers. Never enough evidence. Never."

As they started up another rise, Marc started to tell them both that he was not a general. But something in Kitra's calm presence beside him kept him silent.

Schlomo went on, "Me, I am the good sergeant. I keep it simple. I focus on the next step only. I protect my men. I trust my generals to look beyond the bend, study the terrain, ask the questions for which there are no answers."

They descended into the central plains, connected with the Taba Highway, and turned north. The main road ran within sight of the Egyptian-Israeli border fence. The heat and humidity rose steadily. Marc knew the women must have been sweltering beneath their double layers of clothing. But no one complained, not even Rhana.

They halted at midday. The air was still and stiflingly hot. The fence ran to their right, horizon to horizon. They had passed several watchtowers and seen a number of military vehicles driving a similar road on the Israeli side of the fence. The region was flat and featureless, a truly timeless desert. They stood in the shade of the truck and drank lukewarm water. None of them was hungry, but Schlomo made them down two energy bars each. The driver and his son squatted as far from them as they could get and still stay within the truck's shade. The two Egyptians talked softly, ate dates and cashews, then lit up more of their vile cigarettes.

Rhana asked, "Why are we here?"

"This is the only road running from the southern Sinai to Gaza," Marc told her. "The people we're tracking won't risk taking this route, not with nine container loads of gear."

"The Israeli vehicles you see," Schlomo confirmed, "they are all hunting these trucks."

Marc went on, "So the Iranians have just one option. They transship to dhows and travel up the Suez Canal to Abu Zenima. The road from there heading north is awful. They join the highway at Ismailia and head east."

"Which means we could be ahead of them," Amin noted.

"That's our hope," Marc said. "That's why we're pushing so hard."

"Even if they traveled all day and all night, they won't reach Rafah before nightfall," Schlomo said.

"You are watching that road as well?"

"We can't. The Muslim Brotherhood rules Egypt now. The new ambassador, he has told us that an overflight of Egyptian airspace would create an international incident."

Rhana said, "But how can you be certain they are going to Gaza at all?"

Kitra looked at Marc. "You asked Chaver about the direction of the wind."

"That's right. I did."

"This time of year, it blows from the south and east for days on end," Kitra said.

Schlomo asked, "How are you knowing this?"

"I was born and raised in a Galilee kibbutz," she replied. "So they will blast holes in the Gaza wall. They will attach the blowers. And they pour poison gas into Israel." Her voice trembled. "All the cities between Ashdod and Tel Aviv—"

"No, Kitra. Look at me. We are *not* going to let this happen."

Sandrine spoke for the first time since boarding the truck. "Dov gave his life to stop them. Dov did not die in vain."

Schlomo brought out a small butane stove and made tepid tea, which he sweetened heavily. He offered the first to the driver, who hesitated a long moment before accepting it. The rest of them passed the other two mugs from hand to hand. Schlomo heated pan after pan, urging them to drink all they could. Marc disliked the flavor, but drank nonetheless.

The driver watched all this, rose and climbed into the rear hold. He unlatched a metal trunk welded to the back of the cab, lifted out a tray of tools, and withdrew two bundles tied with hemp cord. He unfurled a pair of blankets, spread them on the truck's floor, then laid a threadbare Turkish carpet on top. The other bundle contained a half-dozen cushions. He climbed down without a word, accepted Schlomo's thanks with a single nod, then returned to the cab.

Rhana asked Amin, "Why are you smiling?"

Staring at the carpet, he replied, "I was thinking of another journey. In another truck. On a carpet just like this one. It is one of my earliest memories. News had just arrived in Isfahan. The shah had fallen. We fled with everything we could carry. The owner of the truck was my father's distant relative. Still he demanded the ownership of our apartment as payment for this journey. My parents and my older sisters were terrified. I thought it was a lark. I played on the carpet and wished the journey would never end."

"I also traveled in just such a truck," Rhana said. "Though I find no reason to smile."

"We have survived," Amin said. "We are here. Seeking to cast out those who robbed us of our homeland. If we are successful, perhaps those who have persecuted us will be the ones in the back of 'just such a truck.' What better reason is there to smile?"

Schlomo's grin defied the day and the heat. "I carry a message to you from my superiors. They wish you to know that they acknowledge their debt. My government seeks allies inside the Persian community. They seek friends they can trust. They hope to forge such ties with you and those you represent."

The truck started with a rumbling cough. The driver ground the gears. Amin climbed into the hold and reached down to offer Rhana his hand. "You see? Already the miracles have started to arrive."

Chapter Thirty-Six

Rafah, a miserable excuse of a town, reminded Marc of the shantytowns sprawling around Mexican border cities like Juarez or Tijuana. Rafah had a fishing port of sorts. The boats were heavily monitored by the Israeli Coast Guard. Petrol stations lined the east-west highway. Otherwise the place was simply a web of dirt tracks and rutted lanes, makeshift dwellings and rusting warehouses. The settlement existed for one purpose only: to smuggle into Gaza.

The truck halted in front of a diner, its outdoor grill formed from an oil barrel split lengthwise. The kitchen consisted of a vintage mobile home missing one entire side wall. A mildewed canvas shade flapped noisily in the hot wind. The driver and his son were loudly salaamed as they descended from the truck.

Marc and Kitra and Sandrine were taking their turns on the cushioned carpet. Kitra had fallen asleep, then struggled up through the heat to wakefulness. "What is happening?"

"Looks like a smuggler's rendezvous," Marc replied, peering out the back.

Schlomo passed around bottles of water and more energy

bars and asked, "Do I need to urge you not to eat in the diner?"

They stationed Amin and Rhana by the rear opening, for they both spoke fluent Arabic and could pass for Palestinians. Schlomo instructed them, "If anyone asks, we are the driver's relatives from Taba."

Kitra asked, "What are we waiting for?"

Schlomo said, "Our driver is negotiating. He seeks a deal for 'us and our animals.'" He grinned meaningfully. "We hope to sell our mules in Gaza for a sizable profit."

Kitra rubbed the sleep from her eyes. "But we don't have any mules."

"We also are not entering Gaza," Sandrine put in.

Schlomo shrugged. "They would come in a second truck."

Marc said to Kitra, eyebrows raised, "You really need to wake up."

Schlomo went on, "Smuggling animals means we can use only one of the largest tunnels that operate hoists at both ends."

"Just like the blowers," Amin said. "Very smart."

"It was Marc's idea," Sandrine said. "A good one."

Schlomo addressed Sandrine in Hebrew. Sandrine replied in English, "I am fine. We will succeed and we will stop the attack. That will make me better still."

Schlomo opened his pack and drew out a black computer pad similar to the one Sandrine had given Marc to navigate the Red Sea. "If we separate, we rendezvous at the BP station we passed on the highway into town. Everyone knows the station, yes? Just follow the main road south."

Schlomo turned the pad so all of them could see. "Our people, we monitor all the smugglers' tunnels from Sinai into Gaza."

Sandrine corrected, "All that we know of."

"We learn of them very fast. It is how we survive." Schlomo tapped the pad, revealing a drone's-eye view of the border region. "There are rumors of a new tunnel. Very deep. Run by Hamas. It operates from a business four hundred meters from here. This place, it is supposed to repair cars." He flicked the photographs forward. "But see in the garage bay's open doors when they take delivery. No cars. Surprise, surprise."

"They have been very smart," Sandrine said. "They have another deep tunnel forty meters away."

"Yes, is so. The second is older and is located here," Schlomo said, pointing.

Marc studied the pad but could make out nothing more than another concrete-block structure beneath the man's finger. It did not matter. He liked the way they tag-teamed the discussion. They had studied the terrain and the enemy's movements. They knew what they were doing. That was all that mattered.

Sandrine went on, "We used to think two deep tunnels so close would be too risky. The earth could become unstable. But our information suggests this new one is the deepest ever. Almost two hundred feet. Built by miners they brought in from Morocco. Brick walls and steel I-beam supports. With a guide-rail system to transport heavy loads. Pneumatic hoists at both ends, like generator-powered elevators. Very sophisticated."

"So they use the proximity of the first tunnel to hide the other," Marc said. "Where does it come out?"

"We think here. Two hundred meters inside Gaza. Farther than any other tunnel we know of. This building to the south is a Hamas political office. This other structure is supposed to be a residence. Four families." He tabbed the controls. "How do I shift to infrared?"

"Give it to me." Sandrine reached for the pad.

"I can do it."

"If we had days, perhaps." She took it from him. "Just like a man. Considers it an insult to let anyone else drive. Even when the woman knows where we're going."

"I asked for help—not a critique of my life."

"Good, because I do not have the weeks for that."

Schlomo flashed a grin at Marc. "Such a pleasure, being in the field with this one."

"All right." Sandrine shifted the pad so they could all see. "This image is from last week. And these from every night the week before. Twelve to twenty people. Everyone stands. No one sleeps. You see? Very interesting for a residence of families."

"You do drone flyovers of Gaza every day?"

"Every day and every night," Schlomo replied. "It is how we survive."

Sandrine switched to a new image. "Now look carefully. Can everyone see? This is from last night."

Marc felt the breath clog his throat. "How many are in there?"

"So many they make one heat image. Two hundred? Three hundred?"

"A wedding?" Rhana asked. "Or funeral?"

"On all three floors of this building?" Sandrine flipped back to another daylight image. "This from today. See how they spill out into the area by the Hamas office?"

"Not a funeral," Marc said. "An invasion force. Enough to blow two dozen holes and attach blowers and fend off the Israelis who try to stop them. This is our place."

Kitra asked softly, "What do we do now?"

"What I told you," Marc said. "We don't let this happen."

Chapter Thirty-Seven

The driver and his son completed their discussions and returned to the truck, dissatisfied expressions telling the world that the negotiations had not been successful. Which of course was a lie. They had not been after making a deal. They had been after explaining why these people riding in their truck were here. Their street creds were established now, the negotiations done.

There followed a quick conversation through the window connecting the cab to the rear hold. The driver nodded understanding and ground the starter a few times before the engine rumbled to life. Schlomo told the others, "He knows a place where we can rest, close to the site. We will go to ground. It buys us time."

Their temporary accommodation was basic in the extreme. Their need for a line-of-sight on the suspect garage reduced their choices to one. The two rooms had formerly served as stables and still smelled of their former occupants. The floors were covered in threadbare carpets. The drywall separating the rooms was so flimsy it ballooned each time a door opened. A small barred window overlooked the rear alley. Beyond that was a slightly larger lane, and on the other side stood the garage.

Schlomo, now calling the shots, broke them into teams. He paired with Kitra, Amin with Sandrine, Marc with Rhana. An Arabic speaker and an operative in each group. His second holdall contained pistols for them all, the Israeli-made Jericho 941. Marc considered it a poor weapon for high-intensity situations. The power-weight ratio meant it rode up with each shot, spoiling the shooter's aim. His reaction to the choice of weapon must have shown, because Schlomo smiled and said, "You think the gun is too lightweight, perhaps? A pistol for scholars and women?"

Marc started pulling 9mm bullets from the open box between them and fed them into the clip. "Six in the clip isn't enough for field conditions."

"You Americans need so many bullets because you can't aim," Sandrine scoffed, resisting a grin.

"You like your Colts," Schlomo agreed, "because when you run out of ammo you can use it for a club. Here, give it back, you don't like it so much."

Marc started feeding another clip. He was mildly surprised to find everyone seemed comfortable with the guns, including Kitra and Rhana. "I think I'll hold on to this for a little while."

Schlomo dumped the rest of his supplies on the carpet. "We have radios, one for each team. Flash-bang grenades in case we go in loud. A satellite phone with scrambler and signal suppressor so no one can ride the call to our location. And these are stun guns, one for each team, to use instead of the pistols if you can. Less noise." Schlomo picked up the final item, a pair of binoculars with an odd third eye set on top. "You know what this is?"

"I do," Marc said. "Laser range finder and target identifier."

"Perhaps you Americans not so bad with the training, huh?" Schlomo then ordered one team to go for supplies. Another was to shower and rest. The third monitored the garage through the rear window.

They sat and sweltered through the remaining afternoon. Twice Sandrine took calls on the satellite phone, which was bulked up from a scrambler and required two hands to hold. Both times she simply looked over and shook her head. Marc used the phone to call Walton, but the ambassador's voice mail was full. He then called Ambassador Samantha Keller in Geneva on her private line. When her voice mail clicked on, Marc left a brief summary of what was happening, obscure enough that only she would know the details if someone else should happen upon the message. Then he moved to where Schlomo and Sandrine could hear clearly, and placed the third call.

Carter Dawes answered with, "E. T. phones home!"

Marc liked having a reason to grin. "Tell me you've had a talk with Samantha Keller."

"Now, that is one tough lady. Wouldn't want to meet her in a dark alley, not even with a Special Forces platoon as backup."

"We're definitely talking about the same woman."

Carter asked, "Where are you calling from?"

"The beautiful resort city of Rafah. Five-star accommodations, world-class cuisine. You should join us."

"Thanks, but I think I'll pass. I assume you're phoning because you need help?"

Marc sketched out what he had in mind. Schlomo and Sandrine listened intently, but found no reason to correct him.

Carter said, "This is pretty much what I already heard. Things are moving ahead at this end."

"How much more time do you need?"

"Couple of hours max. You phone, we deliver. Meals on wheels. Hot and now."

Marc cut the connection and said, "We're good to go."

Schlomo asked, "You can trust this man?"

"He's served as backup in the past. And saved my life."

"I am asking only because the lives of a million Israelis hang in the balance."

"He will do his job," Marc assured the man.

They prepared a meal from tins cooked over a single electric burner and Schlomo's butane stove. They first boiled the utensils, plates, and mugs that came with the place. The meal wasn't bad—beans and canned mashed potatoes and tuna fish and crackers, and fruit cocktail for dessert. Even Rhana ate with a good appetite.

Amin smiled knowingly as Rhana scraped her spoon about the metal plate. "So I am hungry," she said crossly. "So arrest me."

"I mean no disrespect, madame," Amin said.

"Famished, actually." Rhana reached for more saltines. "I am promising myself a weekend at the Ritz when this is done."

Kitra asked, "Can I come?"

"My dear, I would have it no other way. The question is, do we allow your young man to join us?"

Kitra looked across the circle to where Marc leaned against the side wall. "Only if he is very good."

Rhana sniffed. "Is that even possible?"

The room's furnishings were limited to a linoleum-topped table, two folding chairs, and a variety of musty-smelling cushions. Everyone but Rhana sat cross-legged on the floor. The second chair was stationed by the window, where Sandrine was on duty. She kept the satellite phone on the chair and ate standing up, the binoculars dangling from her neck.

Marc said to Rhana, "Tell me about the man we're up against."

"I have told you everything I know about Hesam al-Farouz—which is very little indeed."

Schlomo said, "Tell us again how you met."

She set her plate on the narrow table and replied, "Through Sylvan Gollet."

Marc explained for Sandrine, "The Geneva dealer they murdered."

"The poor man actually bragged about it." Rhana held out her mug for more tea. "How one of my countrymen had become his best client. Sylvan described how he was being paid to wash money, and was I interested. I knew I had finally found the enemy. Or rather, that the enemy had found me."

"Sylvan Gollet might have been a counterfeiter and a gambler," Marc said. "But he wouldn't have told you unless Hesam had first checked you out."

"We danced around for almost a year," Rhana went on. "I pretended I was not especially interested. All this was by throwaway phones. I used dozens. I insisted upon the secrecy and the slowness. It drew him in. Finally we reached an agreement."

"Doing what, exactly?" Schlomo asked.

"Trading high-end art from dealer to dealer," Marc said. "Skimming millions from each transaction."

"No one knows how much a particular item is worth," Rhana said. "It was a good plan."

"But these are small sums," Sandrine protested. "A few million means nothing to Iran."

"Not the country," Amin corrected. "This was never about overcoming the embargo. They wanted a slush fund. Out of the country, hidden from almost everyone. Only a very select few would ever know it existed."

Marc said, "Tell me something new about Hesam. Something I don't already know. Some characteristic you recognize from other people like him."

Rhana's eyes flashed, and she nodded. "Hesam and his kind, they love to lie. He absolutely lives for it. Cheating and lying, these are traits to take pride in."

"Hesam is the dark face of Persia," Amin agreed. "He and his kind have always been there. They thrive in the shadows of my country. And these days, there are very many shadows."

"You in the West listen to the Iranian negotiators make promises about their nuclear program," Rhana said. "Then you are shocked when everything they say turns out to be lies. What you don't know is how people like Hesam, they think less of you because you trusted them in the first place."

"Even desiring the truth is a sign of weakness for such as these," Amin put in.

"Honesty is some disease that thrives in the slums, among the peasants," Rhana said, shaking her head. "This trust you value, to them it is a tool to use against their enemies."

Amin and Rhana wore the same expression now, a taut mask of holding back their turmoil and rage. Amin went on, "Over the past three decades, more than six million of my countrymen have fled their homeland. Six million tragic tales. Christian believers in Iran have either left or perished. All of them. And millions more have been arrested and beaten and made to vanish. This is the price we pay for our shadow princes. This is why they must be brought down."

As Marc listened and nodded with the others, his mind was caught by a different thought. The scene before him underwent a remarkable shift, as though he had been abruptly granted the ability to see it through a different lens. What he saw was a disparate group from supposedly warring communities. Messianic Jew and Israeli commando and two Persian refugees and an American intelligence agent. Sitting in harmony. Aimed at the same goal. And strengthened as a result.

Kitra asked, "What does Hesam personally mean to gain from this?"

"That is simple enough," Rhana said. "Empire. He and his kind want to rule the Middle East."

The lowering sun abruptly turned their lone window frosted and opaque. Marc was on duty and found himself blinded trying to see through the glare. "We can't see the target until the sun goes down. I'm going to make a recce," he told them.

He expected a dozen arguments, but all Schlomo said was, "Once around the perimeter. Then return and another will go."

Rhana was already on her feet and moving. "I'm coming with you. Less noticeable if your woman is trailing a few steps behind."

The stables fronted a central courtyard. Two children played by a dry water trough, watched over by a black-robed woman who ignored them entirely. They passed the main office, where a bearded manager eyed them through his cigarette smoke and grunted in response to Rhana's salaam.

They joined the pedestrians crowding the edges of a busy road and turned right. The air was thick with odors, some of them even pleasant. At Rhana's insistence, they moved with the flow, holding to the main road, until they reached a juncture and could swing back toward the garage.

She asked from behind him, "Why do you seem so upset?"

He waved at the sun that bladed its rays over the rooftops. "I should have thought of this."

"What, the sunset?" She was genuinely astonished. "It is nothing."

"We've lost sight of our target. That's hardly nothing."

"You are exhausted. You carry burdens. The wisest man in the world overlooks things."

"It's a mistake. If I missed this, what else have I over-looked?" Marc rubbed his eyes. He had been able to ignore his fatigue until that moment. "Those people in there rely on me to keep them safe. In the field, mistakes cost lives."

"It is *not* a mistake. A mistake is a wrong move. This is . . ."

She was close enough that Marc was able to hear the swift intake of breath. He looked over his shoulder and saw the tightening of her features. "What do you see?"

She turned slightly, staring down at a child who drew with a stick in the dust. "He is here."

Marc's fatigue vanished in an adrenaline rush. "Hesam?"

"Do not look. Stay as you are." She smiled at something the child said. "Give this little one a coin. There." She spoke to the child in musical Arabic, then led Marc farther down the rutted lane. "Now lift your hand to my kerchief. Do not drape your arm upon my shoulders. Arabs do not show the opposite sex such affection in public. You are adjusting my headscarf. Yes. Now look over my shoulder."

"You would make an excellent spy."

"Impossible. This terrifies me. You see him?"

Marc stared into the sun's blazing orb. "All I see is a silhouette. One of many."

"But it is him. Come, we must walk."

Marc tugged on her kerchief a final time. The sharp shadow of a tall man strode down a side lane toward the garage's entrance. "You're certain?"

"One hundred percent." Her racing heart gave a faint drumbeat to her words. "The walk. The height. The arrogance. It is him."

"Go get Schlomo." Then he heard it, a faint trace of noise that rose above the surrounding din. "Wait."

She started to speak, then heard it also. Large trucks rumbled and halted, their brakes squealing, then rumbled again. Maneuvering down tight lanes.

"Alert the others," Marc ordered. He glanced back again, just in time to see Hesam enter the garage. "The containers have arrived."

"What will you do?"

"I'm staying on watch," Marc replied. "The target's made."

Chapter Thirty-Eight

Hesam al-Farouz did not stay in the garage very long. He emerged and started back down the same road Marc and Rhana had taken. Marc followed at a distance, slipping from shadow to lengthening shadow.

Hesam did not fit the town. Even in silhouette he cut an alien form. He strode too confidently. He ignored everyone with a lifetime's ease. The only people he noticed were his guards. Two in front, three behind. The five bodyguards strutted like junkyard dogs. Their size did not matter. Their guns and their menace stretched them into giants.

This smugglers' town knew when to go blind. The six aliens walked the rutted streets alone. Everyone else melted into the shadows.

Marc tracked them at a cautious angle. He kept his head low and his face averted. He moved one street over, cut back, angled off in the other direction. He raced ahead, then waited for them to catch up. They were not hard to monitor. They made no attempt to use cover. Here in this dusty realm they considered themselves princes.

The trucks rumbled in, four or five minutes apart. Marc scaled a wall and raced across a rooftop, creeping to the edge, studying the quarry until he understood. Hesam was a fidgeter. The man hated inaction. The wait worked on his nerves like acid. Marc recognized the type. He had known several otherwise good agents wash out because the empty hours ate at them. Just like Hesam.

Marc watched him talk on his cellphone. Hesam waved his arm in a grandiose gesture. Marc knew he was just struggling to fill the minutes. Hesam was addicted to the action.

The sun dipped below the horizon. The next truck's headlights caught him like a spotlight. Marc drew back from the edge, crawled across the roof, and returned to the ground. He slipped down an alley, timing it so he would emerge just as the rear trio of trucks passed by. The five guards were a problem. He had to find some way to improve the odds.

Marc was still watching twenty minutes later when Hesam returned to the garage. The bodyguards were not identical in the sense of body mass, but Marc thought of them as the alien quintuplet. Two were solid six-footers with catlike grace. Another was very small, maybe five-foot-three, and carried himself like a snake with legs. Marc assumed his weapon of choice would be the narrow blade. The other two were fireplugs, low to the ground and stone-solid. He was trying to figure out how to take one when Schlomo slipped up beside him. "Where is our shadow prince?"

"He just went back inside."

They were positioned a block away, hidden by the dusk and the absence of streetlights. The surrounding businesses were shutting down. The streets emptied at a rapid pace, as though the daytime dwellers were racing the night. The traffic diminished. Car windows rolled down as the day cooled. The vehicles were slowed by the street traders, who wearily pushed their handcarts home, and by the massive truck that blocked the T-junction at the end of the road. Marc sat on an empty fruit crate, hiding in plain sight. His face was partly masked by sunglasses and a shapeless hat. Schlomo slouched by a rubbish dump that stank of rotten vegetables. "Who are the ones that do not off-load?"

"Hesam's bodyguards. Five in all. Two are inside with the man himself."

"We should take one."

"I've been watching for that. I haven't seen an opening. They're pros."

Schlomo huffed his unconcern. "Here comes another truck."

The trucks were timed so only one at a time was stationed in front of the garage. The narrow lanes held no room for the others. "They must be holding the others outside the city." Another thing Marc had failed to consider. "We could have taken them out there."

"And find them how, precisely? We cannot do regular fly-overs, remember?"

Marc watched the stationary truck leave and the next roll in. "I should have thought of this."

"Now you are being a general." Schlomo did not mean it as a compliment. "We would have no guarantee of hitting the right trucks. We could miss part of the shipment entirely. Our plan is a good one. So long as your friend does his job."

"Carter Dawes will deliver." Marc rose from his studied nonchalance and scanned the streets. The building between them contained an electronics shop and a café. Through the café's front window Marc saw a wall-mounted television blaring some Arabic news channel. A wizened man exited the business next door, locked the entry, and drew metal security blinds down with a loud clatter. The café was now the only business open on the street.

Schlomo saw his expression in the passing headlights. "What is it now?"

"I am worried about collateral damage."

"It should be minimum. That is the beauty of your plan."

Marc knew there was no good in fretting. Nor anything to be gained by arguing with Schlomo.

The idea hit him just as lights came on around the garage's perimeter. Both loading bays were open, and the street around the parked truck was a hive of activity. Two men operated forklifts. Another half dozen scurried back and forth with hand dollies. Four others used rusted wheelbarrows, carting one canister inside at a time.

"So many canisters," Schlomo growled.

Marc didn't respond. He watched the truck off-load while wrestling with his idea. Each truck held a pair of blowers the size of three washing machines, with an ugly snout at one end and a wide, fan-driven aperture at the other. The canisters were lashed to the truck's walls with canvas belts. Each was about four feet tall and eighteen inches wide, capped with expandable nozzles.

Marc decided he had taken the plan as far as he could. He turned to Schlomo and outlined what he had in mind. The Israeli soldier was so worried over the sight of the canisters glinting in the garage's security lights that it took a few moments for Marc's words to register. Finally it dawned on him what he was hearing. He turned to Marc and said, "Go through this again."

Marc did so, not minding in the least the need to repeat things. It helped solidify the plan in his own head.

Schlomo pursed his lips. "You come up with this when?"

"Right here, right now. What do you think?"

The soldier allowed his grin to surface. "I am thinking you will make a very good general. A general to command the generals." He clapped Marc on the shoulder. "Come. It is time to make the world go bang."

Chapter Thirty-Nine

Back in the stables, Marc repeated to the team his idea, refining the plan as he did so, with Schlomo inserting details of his own as appropriate. Then they waited while Sandrine called their headquarters and described it. He liked how her voice remained calm and flat, keeping her emotions and any possible distractions hidden down deep, even a broken heart. He felt Kitra's gaze on him, and knew she was thinking the same thing. It was good to feel this connection, operating far below the level of thought.

But all that was going to have to wait, because Sandrine shut the phone and said, "We are in the green."

Schlomo asked, "They are prepped at the other end?"

"They are ready to move on our say."

He passed out energy bars and bottles of water, then nodded to Marc. Now it was his play. Marc asked, "Everybody clear on their roles?"

They spent the next thirty minutes going over each detail and fitting out their gear. Marc liked how they met his gaze. That they were all afraid was to be expected, but they managed their fear well. They understood the risks. They had lived with risk all their lives.

Sandrine remained on station by the rear window, observing

now through infrared glasses. "The ninth truck is leaving," she said.

"It's time to move," Schlomo said.

Kitra asked, "Do you think . . . ?" She stopped and dropped her head.

Marc urged, "Say it."

"Could we take a moment to pray?"

Schlomo's eyes rounded. He said something to Kitra in Hebrew. She looked at him blankly and responded in English, "That is correct. I and my family are followers of Jesus."

He exchanged a second look with Sandrine, then said simply, "Understood."

The four of them gathered and held hands, Marc and Rhana and Amin and Kitra. Marc then reached out toward where Sandrine and Schlomo stood, watching. He did not speak. It was their choice. After a moment's hesitation, Sandrine walked over and took his hand. She then turned to Schlomo and said, "Come."

The six of them stood in a circle. Kitra said, "Speak for us, Marc."

Daylight was fully extinguished. The few vehicles that passed were night crawlers, blaring gangsta rap from open windows. Men hung elbows on the doorjambs and observed them with vulture eyes. A trio of women passed, their kerchiefed heads aiming downward, seeing nothing and moving fast. Marc moved with Kitra back to the block with the café. He entered the narrow path between that building and the next, so tight he could touch both walls without fully extending his arms. He stood on a garbage can to check the barred windows, and as before saw only silent darkness inside the shuttered businesses. He pointed out hand- and footholds to Kitra, then used them himself and scaled the wall, reached for her as she came near the top.

The roof was flat and dotted with satellite dishes and stray tables and a clothesline that held chef aprons and stained washcloths. They crouched behind a large trash can as a café worker came through the door on the roof's other side. The man carried a plastic hamper and gathered up the dry laundry, humming a tune as he worked. When he left, Marc signaled Kitra to remain where she was and moved in a crouch across the roof. He scanned the other side, watched the workers by the last truck, then gestured Kitra forward. "Radio Schlomo, tell him they're off-loading the last blower."

As she spoke into the radio, Marc activated the sat phone and dialed the number.

Carter Dawes answered on the first buzz. Not even the scrambler's static could erase the man's adrenaline cheer. "Dialing for dollars."

"We're in position."

"I'm two hundred and ten klicks out, thirty thousand feet above the Suez Canal. Green across the board."

"Back to you in one."

"Roger that."

He handed the phone to Kitra. "Make the call."

She coded in the number from the paper Schlomo had given her. She spoke briefly in Hebrew, listened, then cut off and said, "They move in five."

"Radio the others an update." He took back the phone, called Carter, and said, "Ready to light the target."

"Well, what are we waiting for, sport?"

"Hold one." Marc pointed Kitra to the other side. "Tell the others to go."

She spoke the one word into the radio, then shocked him nearly out of his socks. She dropped the radio, gripped his face with both hands, and kissed him hard.

Then she turned and scurried back to the other side of the roof as he'd instructed.

Marc was so stunned it took a few seconds to realize the phone was squawking. "Say again," he rasped into the receiver.

"Finger's on the trigger, sport. Clock is ticking. Where's my target?"

Marc nestled the phone between his shoulder and his ear. He lifted the bulky binoculars, switched on the laser, and fastened them on the garage's second story. "Target is lit."

"I have you five by five. I am weapons hot. Repeat, weapons hot."

"Fire away."

"Missile is away. Inbound in one hundred and ninety seconds."

Marc was about to cut and run himself when a shout rose from the street below. One of the tall bodyguards pointed up at the laser pinpointed on the garage wall. He followed the glow back and saw Marc. Their yells brought out the other guards, who raised weapons and took aim just as Hesam stepped out of the open garage bay.

Which was when the night was split by thunder.

Chapter Forty

It was not a single explosion. It sounded like a hundred freight trains all colliding milliseconds apart. Even though Marc was expecting it, the noise was appalling. For the men down below, it must have scrambled their brains. They fired off their weapons in every direction, as though trying to shoot the noise out of the night. And that was exactly what Marc had hoped would happen.

Led by Schlomo, the team ran down parallel streets, tossing flash-bang grenades onto roofs, down alleys. Firing off rounds at windows and dropping in more stun grenades. Creating a rolling havoc.

Marc's idea.

The Israeli-Gaza-Egyptian border was a potential free-fire zone. The locals would all have a bolt-hole of some kind, with reinforced walls and armored doors. If possible, they would have put it underground. Many of the apartment buildings had a collective basement with steel-and-concrete walls. It was time to find safety. And fast. Marc watched the locals vanish, prayed again that the human toll would be kept to a minimum.

Marc slipped down the rear wall and checked the main road. The street was utterly vacant. Even the workers off-loading the last truck were gone. The final blower was poised in midair, the forklift engine chugging softly, the door open and flapping. From inside the garage came a high-pitched caterwauling. A pair of diesel generators drummed a faint line of tension from behind the garage. Outside, the two remaining bodyguards crouched behind the truck and fired at the sky. They shouted something, which Marc assumed was their calling for the others to take position.

Then Marc saw him.

Their prey was fleeing out a side door Marc hadn't noticed until that moment. Marc knew it was his target, though all he saw was a shadow, and only for a few seconds' time. He started forward, then stopped as if a hand reached down from heaven and steered him back. The sight of the quarry had momentarily pushed out the thought of what was incoming.

He turned around and ran back, skirted down the narrow alley, flitted across the next street, and was just about to turn toward the garage when the night lit up a second time.

The Joint Air to Surface Standoff Missile, or JASSM, had only recently been brought into full service. The pilots who had fired them in combat all used the same words to describe the effect, describing the JASSM as the "ultimate wow factor." It wasn't long before the new cruise missile had gained the nickname *The Penetrator*.

The Penetrator carried a half-ton payload, the largest of any jet-fired missile currently employed by any armed forces in the world. The missile itself was made from lightweight composite materials, and the fuel it burned was actually lighter than air. The result was a massive amount of force delivered to target.

The missile was designed to launch well away from border defenses, and built to kill deeply buried targets. As a result, the warhead was broken into three components, called multimodes. First there was what in munitions terms was classed a long rod penetrator, which basically meant the missile could grind through thirty feet of solid concrete like it was cutting through butter. Then there came the aerostable slug, which released fragments as the missile dug home. Finally there was the high-heat submunition that burned at a temperature only slightly lower than the surface of the sun.

Though Marc was shielded by two blocks of buildings, the force was such that he was propelled a full forty feet, out of the alley and across the street and into the door of the building opposite.

When he had finally managed to right himself, he started running before he could shape the reason behind it. His brain told his legs to run. Marc assumed the purpose would come clear momentarily.

Of the garage, there was nothing left. The hole did not even smolder. The surrounding structures all bowed away, as though aghast at the force they had just witnessed. Two had collapsed entirely.

Marc spotted Hesam struggling futilely to draw his legs back under him. He knew it was Hesam because he was the only other person on the street. Marc raced over and slammed the man back to the ground, ground his face in the dirt, too angry to strike him with his fist, knowing if he did he might kill the man. And he needed Hesam alive. Marc had forgotten exactly why, but he knew it was important.

He rose and dragged the man upright with him. He frisked

him, only to discover that the man's fine clothes had been turned to rags by the blast. Hesam wore only one shoe. His hair was gummed tight with dust and debris. Marc rammed his pistol into the groaning man's ear, leaned in close, and growled in a voice he did not recognize, "You're under arrest."

Chapter Forty-One

During the initial seventy-two hours following their successful assault on the Gaza tunnel system, the fallout just kept on growing. Marc did his best to ignore it all. He stayed on the kibbutz and worked at whatever task was assigned. He refused to enter a room where the television was on. He ignored all discussions of politics or external events. His only contacts with the outside world were two lengthy conversations with Samantha Keller, which he endured because he wanted updates on Walton's health.

Mostly he rested. He rose for meals and worship and showers. He saw Kitra for fleeting moments, as she was doing precisely the same. The second evening he dined with her, Serge, and their parents.

Three days after his arrival, two intelligence agents assigned to the U.S. Embassy in Tel Aviv came to the kibbutz, commandeered an office in the admin center, and grilled him for five hours.

The fourth morning, Kitra was asked to deal with an urgent crisis at the factory. Marc volunteered for work detail. For the next five days the farm managers tossed him the absolute worst possible jobs and waited for him to fold.

Marc drained and repaired a sewage pump. He helped

rebuild a decrepit farm truck's engine. He picked a crop of late-blooming lemons. He dug fence-post holes in the rocky earth. He toiled from dawn to sundown. He relished the tasks with a simple pleasure that both delighted and worried him. He came to understand the lure of this place. How he was joining to a world dominated by cycles and seasons. If he chose, he could reside here the rest of his days, removed from the trials that dominated global politics. He could work until his days were done, then be laid to rest in the soil he had helped to farm.

He could be content. Almost.

He saw Kitra every day. Their talk was of small things. A new calf, a new child, the next crop. She described her slow progress in bringing the factory up to speed. She talked of how rested her parents looked after their holiday. She related how many of the managers had described Serge's gradual rising up to the responsibilities, growing into the man who truly resembled his father. Marc listened more than he spoke. They would talk of the world beyond the kibbutz another time. And their future. Someday.

Eleven days after the strikes, Ambassador Walton felt well enough to return to his office in the White House basement. His first conversation with Marc started with, "Don't come home."

"Don't worry."

Walton sounded as though the effort of speaking drained him. "Admiral Darren Willits is being reassigned to a base in Okinawa. I'm told it's the military's way of telling him to retire gracefully."

"He won't be missed over here," Marc said.

"No, I suppose not." Walton paused to cough. After he

caught his breath, he said, "His briefing consisted mainly of criticizing you."

"He's angry because it turned out I—"

"No, son. He's mad as a boil because you publicly proved him wrong."

"I haven't said a thing."

"You don't need to. The Israelis are doing it for you. Not to mention the Iranian chemist they have kindly allowed us to debrief."

The next day, Samantha Keller phoned to say Walton was back in the hospital, basically because it was the only way to make the man give his body time to heal. Marc thanked her and did not press for details. It was enough to know the old man would be forced to take time to mend.

Marc had never thought he would ever find such peace in a foreign desert. The isolation was, in fact, a true pleasure. Despite the blistering heat, the arid landscape held a singular beauty. Marc found himself energized by the place, the people, and the work. Seeing Kitra's world from the inside proved a delight.

Kitra was housed with the other unmarried women, in a dorm on the synagogue's south side. They met at meals, at chapel, and twice each week they joined her parents for a fine dinner.

He and Kitra discovered a bench at the kibbutz's western border, beneath a carefully tended strand of desert pines, and made it their sunset meeting point. They walked through the grove of Valencia oranges, the leaves impossibly green against the pale desert sky. A few blossoms still clung to the branches, perfuming the sunset with a glorious scent.

Claiming a special bench was part of the kibbutz's court-ship process. It announced the seriousness of the couple in a silent and solemn manner. By then, everyone knew his name. Everyone greeted him.

Marc kept waiting for the enjoyment to fade. But it didn't happen. Instead he felt a faint sense of mounting pressure—not quite an impatience, but more like a siren that rang in the distance. One he knew he should respond to. But it was easy to ignore the alarm and the tension. All he had to do was throw himself into the next task. Join with the others for prayer. Walk with Kitra through the orange grove. Sit and watch the sun go down.

The news of the foiled attack was everywhere. During the fourth week, despite his best efforts, Marc found he could no longer escape the clamor. At first the Egyptians had been vicious in their condemnation. The Muslim Brotherhood government accused the Israelis of invasion by proxy. The words became a rallying cry throughout the Arab nations. Invasion by proxy.

Only the Iranians remained strangely silent.

The Israelis cordoned off the blocks surrounding the Gaza bomb site. The Palestinians rioted, so the Israelis brought in tanks and extended their cordoned area even farther. To all the criticisms and international furor, they replied simply, "Wait." Wait and we will show.

And show they did.

It took three weeks of meticulous excavation, but they finally brought up an intact industrial blower and several canisters. The equipment in both the Sinai and Gaza houses had been completely destroyed, lost to fires that burned over sixteen hundred degrees, hot enough to erase every vestige of the deadly chemicals. But those items caught inside the tunnel remained intact.

The furor went silent overnight. Not even Israel's worst enemy could condemn a country for stopping a biochemical attack of this magnitude. The thought of a million innocents dying from such a chemical cocktail sent shock waves around the world.

Still Iran said nothing.

Only then was Hesam al-Farouz drawn into the public spotlight. He was subdued and cowed and would not stop talking. Three weeks in an Israeli prison, with the prospect of a lifetime of the same, erased any hesitation the shadow prince might have held. He named names. He gave details. He described the approval process, all the way up to the ayatollahs in Qom. He held nothing back. The world press had a field day.

The week after Hesam appeared on the world stage, Walton started calling. Marc had expected the calls, and refused to answer. He kept the phone off and skipped over a week's worth of messages. He pretended it didn't matter. Yet gradually the distant claxon rose in his brain. Especially at night, when he lay in his little room and wished he could stay. Forget the world. Ignore the call. Claim this as his home.

The next day, the kibbutz discovered that he and Kitra had played a vital role in stopping the attack.

One moment it was their carefully kept secret—Kitra hadn't even mentioned it to Serge—the next, and the news was everywhere. Their photographs were splashed across the news, the television, everywhere. The entire kibbutz was transformed. Marc was turned into a hero. He knew then that his time here was drawing to a close, and there was nothing he could do about it.

The following evening, the bullish man was there when they emerged from chapel. Marc knew it was Chaver even before he greeted Kitra and her father, even before he turned and shook Marc's hand and said, "Come, let us walk."

Marc put two and two together. "You told the news about us."

"Don't look so outraged. Our people should not know that two national heroes live among them?"

Chaver was an aging bull, scarred by a lifetime's battles and careless of his afflictions. The man leaned heavily on a cane. Even so, he moved with impatient grace, down the sidewalk and across the fields and away from watching eyes. "It is a good place, this kibbutz. A man of worth needs a place to stop and breathe the good air. Pray with people who live simple lives. Feel the earth in his hands." He stopped and surveyed the hills going dusky gold in the sunset. "A good place."

"Did Ambassador Walton call you?"

"He had no choice. You were not responding."

Marc liked Chaver's blunt honesty. He had the sudden impression that it would be hard to say no to this man. "You're saying this life is not for me."

"I like you, Marc Royce. If anyone has earned the title, Friend of Israel, it is you. I would like you to join us. But your home is elsewhere. Your loyalties, your oaths, your future—they are across the waters."

"I thought, maybe . . ."

"You are in love. The truth shines from your face. You love her so much you would give anything, do anything, to make it happen. Don't deny it, my friend."

"I wasn't going to deny anything."

"No? Not even deny the truth to yourself?" He turned and

glanced behind him. Marc's gaze tracked back as well, and discovered Kitra standing a few paces away. He motioned her forward with his cane. "This is a good place. Filled with good people. I hope your actions will ease their entry into Israeli society and free others of the sorrow your people have known."

Kitra said quietly, "If that happens, everything we endured will have been worth it."

Chaver said to Marc, "Friend of Israel, I invite you to return here often. You are always welcome. My country owes you a lifetime debt." He poked Marc in the chest with his free hand. "But know your place and your calling."

He shook hands with them both, then started back, waving for them to remain where they were. His movements were as abrupt and solid as his speech. At the grove's far end, he turned and said, "And if you ever need anything, you will call, yes? Good. For you, I and my friends are always available."

Marc took her hand and walked with her out to the kib-butz's perimeter, then seated himself beside her on their sunset bench. He didn't speak. His heart and mind were too filled with tumult to shape simple words. He felt as though the outside world had invaded his private space. He could not put together anything that made sense. Or perhaps it all made too much sense, and he was afraid.

So Kitra said it for him. "It's time for us to leave, Marc."

"Us . . ." He breathed the word again.

"I have accepted the position as sales director for our new factory. Most of my clients are in the United States."

"When did this happen?"

"Last week. No, the week before."

"When were you going to tell me?"

"When you were ready."

He understood. "Not ready to hear. Ready to move on."

Her gaze was solemn and flecked with gold from the day's final light. "I am glad you came here, Marc. Glad you have come to know my world."

"I love it here, Kitra. So much."

She nodded. "Very glad."

He knew it was time then. And felt the flaming words rise up, burning away all the pressures and uncertainties and mysteries to come. They were the only thing that mattered. "Marry me, Kitra."

She smiled, both solemn and joyful, and replied, "It's time."

**Davis Bunn** is an award-winning novelist and a lecturer in creative writing at the University of Oxford. His books, translated into sixteen languages, have sold nearly seven million copies worldwide. Formerly a business executive working in Europe, Africa, and the Middle East, Davis draws on this international experience in crafting his stories. *Strait of Hormuz* follows on the success of *Lion of Babylon*, which was named one of the Best Books of 2011 by *Library Journal*, and of *Rare Earth*, which earned a 2013 Christy Award for excellence in suspense fiction. He and his wife, Isabella, divide their time between the English countryside and the coast of Florida. To learn more, visit DavisBunn.com.

More Marc Royce Adventures

To learn more about Davis Bunn and his books, visit davisbunn.com.

Undercover agent Marc Royce is back on assignment. As war breaks out in Kenya over valuable land, how far will he go to bring peace?

Rare Earth

As a new coalition rises in Iraq, an ancient threat is silently amassing power. When Royce's off-grid mission unearths a trail of explosive secrets, his actions could change the destiny of millions.

Lion of Babylon

 BETHANYHOUSE

 Stay up-to-date on your favorite books and authors with our *free* e-newsletters. Sign up today at bethanyhouse.com.

f Find us on Facebook. facebook.com/bethanyhousepublishers

an open book

Free exclusive resources for your book group! bethanyhouse.com/anopenbook